Even
Willows
Weep

Even Willows Weep

CINDY LYNCH

 My Three Sons Publishing

Book 2 in the *Bye For Now* Trilogy

Pheonix

Published in the United States by
My Three Sons Publishing, LLC

mythreesonspublishing.com

ISBN: 978-0-9864476-1-7

Book cover design by: Ivan Terzic

Interior design by: Katie Mullaly, Faceted Press

Author's photo by: Sharisse Coulter

To my fellas,

Believe anything is possible.

Listen to that voice within.

Just believe.

PROLOGUE
Callie

May 1988

"These are so beautiful," I utter under my breath to no one as I walk past another painting on the table. Wide-eyed fascination. Hands trembling as I fumble with the pen to write down a bid of $100. *This is the one.* The dragonfly painting has a placard resting next to it that reads: "Fly above your dreams. Nothing can ever bring you down. Just keep flying."

Floating around the room, looking at each of the children's paintings and sketches, the words from each description come at me in three dimensions.

"I got my inspiration from my journey with cancer, because in my fight, I know all I have to do is have faith. When the world says, 'Give up,' HOPE whispers, 'Try it one more time.' I live each day to the fullest. None of us have the promise of tomorrow."

I swipe at my eye as the moisture pools. My feet have a mind of their own, carrying me back to that simplistically beautiful dragonfly. My heart is being tugged and stretched to its breaking point as I stand there, staring into the kaleidoscope eyes of that dragonfly. My own eyes burn. Slowly, I close them in a series of deliberate blinks. I have been staring so long that I don't realize I have reached out to touch the rough, weathered paper. To my surprise, it appears to be moving, and without warning, the dragonfly buzzes off the canvas and flutters to my outstretched hand, causing a tickling sensation that puts a smile on my face.

Heat radiates from its tiny legs. Everything moves in slow motion. The bulbs in the room dim and the crackling neon from the store frontage casts flickering light over the already shimmering silver wings. I'm mesmerized by the spectacle. One after the other the dragonflies splinter, each one regenerating new legs from its thorax. Long, fragile, silver wings unfold from the newly formed legs; each dragonfly divides into two. I tilt my head, furrowing my brow. I watch in amazement as they multiply. A thin bead of nervous perspiration emerges from my upper lip as I stand entranced. I turn my head with a twitch, *doesn't anyone see this?* I feel like someone has a magnifying glass over the skin of my arms in the dead of summer. With each radiating flit of the tiny appendage, it feels as though the heat from the sun's rays bore holes into my forearm in the hope of catching fire, as if trying to burn a leaf. This burning sensation intensifies with each step of the hundreds of legs that crawl along my skin. I nervously begin swatting them off, crushing their beautiful wings, leaving greasy trails of slime on my arm. I brush them off slowly at first, then beat at them in frantic succession. "Pheonix!!" I shout.

"Callie. Cal. Callista, wake up. We're here," Jimmy says, jostling and poking my arm until my eyes pop open, staring blankly back.

"We're here?" I ask, slowly coming out of my haze.

"Home again home again…" Mom says enthusiastically as she closes the passenger side door and walks to the front of our home in Missouri. It feels so strange to be back here again, albeit temporarily. If all goes well, Maddie will be moving, after she graduates next year, into an apartment with me. Fingers crossed, her parents and doctors will give her the okay.

"Yeah, duuude, that must have been some dream," Jimmy says, laughing, as he carries the first of many of my college boxes to the storage space in the basement. He is home briefly to help with the move.

"Yeah." I say cautiously, not quite fully awake, rubbing my arm silently taking inventory. I'm unable to shake the tingling remnants of burning flesh.

"Who's Pheonix?" Jimmy asks quizzically, grabbing the second box. I think for a moment before responding, "I have no idea."

CHAPTER 1
Callie

"Hey, Mad, would you hand me that box over there," I ask, impatiently pointing to the box marked 'momentos.'

"Just for the record, I hate moving," Maddie complains as she hands me the heavy box filled with my childhood things.

"I'm not thrilled to be moving again, so soon."

"What are you saving all this shit for anyway?" she asks while rooting through the box. Pulling out a shoebox and lifting the lid, she recognizes the address on letters received long ago.

"You kept all these letters from Wyatt?" Maddie asks bewildered.

"What was I going to do with them? Just throw them away?"

"Not for nothin' but…yeah."

Recognizing that the feeling in the room has shifted, I decide we need a break from our move.

"How about a lunch break?" I suggest.

"Yeah, I could stand to put some grub in this pie hole," she agrees, smiling and pointing at her mouth.

I'm thrilled to have Maddie back in my life again. It was a long road to recovery for her, but she made it through and I'm so proud of her. After I graduated in 1988, I found myself without a job, without a friend, and without family. My parents moved to Missouri my senior year for a teaching job my dad was offered at a charter school. After discovering that living on my own, and getting my masters in art therapy was not going to be cheap, I decided to move in with my folks for a while. As much as I have enjoyed being with Charlie these past few years, I figure if this relationship is meant to be, he would wait for me. I know it's time for me to find my path and determine what I'm going to do with my life. I had been living with my parents for a year, working on my masters, when Maddie and I had a conversation on the phone about the possibility of her moving out here. When Maddie received the green light from her doctors, and eventually her parents, she was quick to make the move before anyone could change their minds. Upon her graduation, she packed her bags and reached Missouri by the following week.

"So what's the plan tonight?" Maddie asks between bites of sandwich.

"I'm in the middle of this internship at Cardinal Glennon Hospital right now, so it'll be an early night for me. What did you have in mind?"

"Doesn't that bum you out? Working with sick kids all day long?"

"Sometimes it does, but I feel like this is a pretty special place to be. These kids have so much to say and such little time to say it that I'm happy to help out any way I can."

These children that I've been working with have terminal forms of cancer, and since grad school, I've been looking for employment. The internship came through a few months after my move to Missouri, and I jumped at the chance. Most days I work at Cardinal Glennon Hospital in St. Louis in a cheery building with a yellow submarine painted on the wall. Everywhere you look, there is something pleasant to see; a hallway painted as though you are underwater, fish with patients' names on them, a chandelier with ascending bubbles floating above your head.

Everyone at the hospital is friendly, but each smile holds some unspoken sadness, like looking at your reflection on the lake surface as waves roll in. The image is yours yet broken into fragments, rippling and wrinkling, slowly becoming your own again.

"I just don't think I could do that day in and day out. You're a better person than I am."

"Well, that's true," I tease, with an elbow to her rib cage. "Have you called the warden yet to tell her how the move went?"

"I think I'm gonna make her sweat this out a little bit," Maddie snorts.

"That might not be such a good idea. She may send the cops out looking for you."

"Hey, if they're young and good looking, I'm all for it. It's been awhile since I've seen any action. If he wants to slap on the handcuffs, I won't complain!" With a laugh we leave the sandwich shop and drive back to the apartment to unpack what's left of our boxes.

"Good morning, Natasha. Who are we working with today?" I ask my mentor, who sits at a small round table with one little girl in a room that gives the illusion of a pirate ship.

"Callie, this is Allie." A small smile peeks out behind wisps of thinning brunette hair. "Allie, Callie is going to sit and paint with you today." Allie moves her IV of platelets aside to allow me to sit beside her. A quiet giggle erupts from her lips, "That rhymes."

Smiling back at Allie, I ask, "What color should we start with today?" As we choose colors, in walks a little boy pulling his own IV beside him. "I'm cold," he complains, sitting beside Natasha.

"Dion, sometimes the fluids make you cold, right Allie?" Allie nods in agreement. Natasha pushes back from the table and walks out of the room. In a moment, she is back with a warm blanket she drapes around Dion's shoulders. As Allie finishes painting a large orange circle on her paper, I ask, "Do you want me to get some yarn out to glue onto the paint? Maybe put some googly eyes on there to make a scary pumpkin?"

Gathering more supplies from the cabinet, Natasha strikes up a conversation with Allie, "What are you doing at school today?"

"Five tests." She lists the tests she has to take and Natasha asks if she's ready. It's obvious that she has missed a lot of school due to her illness and is having a hard time keeping up with the material.

"It's Munchie Monday!" a nurse sings as he rounds the corner with food in his hands. Unfortunately, it's from a local fast food restaurant, Lion's Choice. Due to her many dietary restrictions, Allie will be unable to eat, however, Dion is up and moving his IV down the hall swiftly.

A man with a bushy beard, grey hair, and friendly eyes dressed in jeans and a denim shirt cautiously enters the art room. He sits in a cushioned chair behind Allie.

"Natasha, my cat Snowball ate some ribbon the other day. I don't know why he likes to eat that so much, but he does. Every time he eats it, he gets sick. I found a ball of gooey orange ribbon all balled up in the middle of the kitchen floor. It's disgusting." Now comfortable and engaged in conversation, Allie continues,

"Sometimes it gets caught as he's pooping, and you have to help him by pulling it out."

"Allie, sweetie, that's enough about Snowball," Allie's dad gently suggests from the chair behind her. Allie's IV pole begins beeping, causing the nurse who was singing a moment ago about Munchie Monday to return. His nametag reveals his name is Trevor. Trevor has come into the room to replace the empty platelet bag with an IV of clear liquid for Allie. In the meantime, Natasha and Allie's dad have decided that she can eat the veggies packet provided by Lion's Choice.

A little boy wanders over to the table next to Natasha, and she goes through the list of supplies asking which he would like to start with.

"How old are you?"

"Four years old."

"Do you have any pets?"

"I have a dog named Rocky."

He has a camp rainbow t-shirt on. "Chunkie and Marcus are my brothers. I ain't got no sisters."

"Allie, honey, they're ready for you," Allie's dad says and gives a nod to Natasha. She in turns says, "Thanks for painting with me today, Allie."

Turning her attention back to the little four-year-old boy, she says, "Do you have a favorite color?"

"Green."

This little boy's mom and his nurse round the corner, conversing.

"Walgreens can deliver to your house. We can set that up for you."

"Thank you. How often will Dion have his infusions?"

"Two months of infusions three times a week."

A nicely dressed woman walks into the room carrying a plump baby boy around one year old, with a triple chin. He has the cutest dimples and plume of black curl atop his head. Trailing behind is another boy around the age of seven, and pulling up the rear is the grandmother.

"Chunk, leave that alone!" Grandma barks.

"Chunk, get that out of your mouth!" Chunkie is a handful: a very lively one year old. It's obvious that Mom and Grandma are having difficulty controlling his behavior.

"Chunk, get over here!" Grandma says as she pulls on his arm and he goes limp. She pretends to kick him and stomp on his leg and Chunk begins to laugh. It's evident that Grandma loves this little chubby toddler and they have a rapport that I don't quite understand, but it works.

On our break, Natasha explains that the kids come and go as they have time waiting for one infusion to finish before the next infusion begins. During that time, Natasha and I get to work with the kids to help them any way we can. Some come in quietly and some come in ready to talk about everything under the sun. There is one little girl that she hopes I will meet in a few weeks. They have a special bond, and she looks forward to introducing us.

Our day continues with many children filtering through our workspace. Several months before I came aboard, volunteers worked on creating a pirate ship inside the hospital. The exterior of the ship is made of real wood hammered into the wall with the bow extending into the hallway and the stern touching the back wall. The interior walls of our ship are the two interior room walls painted to match the wood. Letting out a deep sigh, I peek at the clock and think to myself, *finally*.

CHAPTER 2
Callie

The phone continues to ring as I try unsuccessfully to unlock my apartment door. *Why can't I get the damn key to work?* The phone rings behind the door, as if mocking me. The lock finally dislodges, allowing me in.

"Hey, Cal! I'm so glad I caught you. After the 15th ring, I thought you weren't going to answer."

A glow spreads instantly across my face. "Hi Charlie," I say with a sigh as I flop onto the couch next to the phone.

"You okay? You sound exhausted."

"It was a rough day, but hearing your voice makes it all worth it," I confess with a smile.

"I wish I could be there to give you a big bear hug. Here, wrap your arms around yourself."

"Come on Charlie…"

"Indulge me."

"Okay," I venture, wrapping my arms around myself, holding the phone between my ear and shoulder, "Done."

"Now squeeze real hard." He waits a beat before asking, "Better?"

"Oddly enough, yes, I do feel better. I miss you."

"Me too."

"When can I see you again?"

"Well, someone has a birthday coming up. Perhaps I can make a visit happen some weekend soon?"

"Ah, that would be awesome! I have to warn you, our place is a disaster. Mad isn't exactly the tidiest person," I say giggling.

Walking through the door, Maddie stops and says, "If you're talking about me again, I'm going to refuse to take out the garbage for a month."

Removing the phone from my mouth, I say to Maddie, "How is that any different than what you do now?" I replace the phone and quickly dodge a flying pillow.

"Call me back when you know for sure when you'll be in. Can't wait to see you!"

"Are you hanging up on me?"

"Charlie, I'm exhausted. As much as I love talking to you I can hardly manage a conversation right now. I gotta eat something and just relax for a while. We'll talk soon."

Sounding dejected, he concedes, "All right. I'll call you when I know for sure. Get some rest. I want you to show me the sights and sounds of the Show Me State! See you later alligator."

Walking into the kitchen, Maddie opens the fridge, pulls out a beer, and cracks open the top. "Want one?" she offers, holding the Budweiser up in the air.

"Yeah, sure, why not." Grabbing a second one from the fridge, she twists the top off and brings it over to me on the couch.

"How did job hunting go for you today?"

"Well, if the douche-bags would get their heads outta their asses and realize I'm a gem and more than these girls right here," she says with an aggressive shimmy, "and give me a job, we wouldn't have a problem. But seeing as most of the men that interviewed me today couldn't lift their eyes above my shoulders, I'd say the day kinda sucked."

"I'm sorry, Mad," raising my beer to hers, I try, "here's to tomorrow being a better day."

Even with the greenery around me fading to a rusty shade of red and the wind having a slight edge to it, this place can still be humid during these late September days. With the amount of sweat seeping from my pores as I run the last mile home, I look as though I've been caught in a summer shower. *All this sweat and it isn't even 8:00 in the morning.*

Walking through the apartment door, I notice it is unusually quiet. Most mornings, Maddie is up and making coffee before I leave for my run. Today, surprisingly, she's still in bed.

Knocking gently on her bedroom door, I whisper, "Mad, you getting up? Don't you have an interview at 9?"

"Yeah." She rolls out of bed with her PJ bottoms on inside out and backwards, and a pink tank top slipping off her shoulder. Her hair is in a messy ponytail looking like a squirrel has squatter's rights for her head.

"Want me to start the shower for you?"

"Thanks." She walks to the kitchen and starts the coffee machine.

"You okay?"

"I'm a little queasy today. Not sure what's going on. Maybe the beer we had last night didn't agree with me. I'll be fine once I get in the shower and you make my coffee the way I like it," she says, walking past me with a wink and closes the bathroom door.

My Maddie. How boring my life would be without you in it.

After my shower and two cups of coffee, I dress in a long white skirt, brown strappy sandals and a bright pink top, and walk out the door.

"Hi, Tasha. Busy this morning?"

"Nah, it's a little slow right now. It'll pick up after music class. Want some coffee?"

"I better not, or I'll float out of here. If you're headed down to the coffee cart, though, I'll walk with you."

As we walk, she says, "I think the girl I want you to meet may stop in today. Her name is Pheonix."

I stop walking, causing Natasha to stop abruptly. "Wha? What's her name?" I ask, almost inaudibly.

"Pheonix," she says, looking at me with knitted brow. "She's a real sweet girl. She's young, but has a very old soul. You'll see when she comes in. Do you know her or something?"

"No," I stammer, "it's just an odd name that I've heard before." I resume walking, thinking about the dream I had a year ago. Carrying her coffee to a chair in the lobby of the hospital, we continue our conversation.

"Her artwork, along with many others, will be on display and for sale at Art from the Heart, the art fair fundraiser we have every year. You should try to make it to that event."

"I think I will. Do you have many fundraisers throughout the year?"

"We do, but the big ones are Art from the Heart and the one held at the Ritz-Carlton; Friends of Kids with Cancer Fashion Show luncheon or dinner. That one is coming up soon."

"I'll see if I can make it."

I marvel at Natasha's passion as I listen to her speak to a child's parent in the art therapy room.

"I loved psychology and I loved art, so I majored in both," she says with a smile. The mother nods as Natasha continues, "I work here, and I also work at Mercy other days of the week."

Arianna comes into the room riding her infusion pole with a fuzzy purple vest. She's mostly bald with a little tuft of hair just above her forehead. "Arrrgh!" she says, rolling her eyes, exasperated with her beeping line. "Tasha, I'm out of fluid again."

Trevor comes over to check the line, turns off the beeping alarm and brings her a replacement bag.

"Tasha, look!" a wide-eyed Arianna says proudly as she holds up her craft made of felt.

"It's beautiful!" Natasha says with the needle felting in her hand. "How about making a few more? We could use them for the Wreath and Menorah Show." Natasha had told me about the design competition and auction held in December. People can bid on the beautiful works of art created by professional artists and architectural designers. All proceeds benefit *Friends*, and our young patients make the awards, felt menorahs and wreaths, presented to best of show.

As Arianna works on another menorah, I notice her lips losing color. She looks very pale. Arianna's mom and Natasha are talking about the treatments they are going through. "We're six weeks off-six weeks on treatment. We have three options. Option one- status quo; Option two-doing better, improving; Option three- We aren't going to think about that. That's when it's bad news."

"I want Zofran. Mama, I'm not feeling well."

"Do you want to eat or lie down?" Arianna's mom asks as she places a hand on Arianna's fuzzy head and rubs gently.

"I want the Zofran." Arianna begs.

"It's not time yet, love, I'm so sorry."

Natasha asks her quietly, "How often can she have it?"

"Every six hours."

Turning to Arianna, Natasha asks, "Do you need a bucket? Is it a throw-up kind of pain?"

Arianna's mom answers, "I think she just gets frustrated. She seems to get frustrated more quickly lately."

As Arianna sits at the art table, the color continues to drain from her face and she leans back with a sigh.

"Sweetheart, you don't have to finish this today, you know."

"But Mama, I want to."

"She's getting tired," Natasha observes as Arianna begins to close her eyes.

"Why don't we go lay down and close your eyes. We'll finish the wreath a little later. Mama will help finish it."

"I'll walk back with you and help get you settled," Natasha suggests.

They all walk back to a bed and place the wreath on the nightstand.

Together, Natasha and Arianna's mother manipulate Arianna's body like a rag doll to get her into bed. I'm finding the scene difficult to watch. Trying to swallow around the knot that has formed in my throat is proving difficult.

CHAPTER 3
Callie

After entering my apartment, I close the door, immediately crinkling my nose at the pungent odor of vomit.

"Maddie, are you all right?" I ask with concern at the bathroom door.

"No," Maddie squeaks out between retching.

"Do you have a bug or something? Can I get you anything?"

"I'll be out in a sec."

I busy myself with changing out of my clothes into my comfy sweats. Within a few minutes, Maddie has flushed the toilet and is sitting on the oversized couch, knees curled up under her as she clutches a pillow, looking as though she may start crying. Or worse, start throwing up again.

"Here, see if this helps," I say as I pour her a 7Up and stir the bubbles out so as to not upset her stomach any more than it is.

"Thanks, Cal."

"So you think maybe it was something you ate?" I say, sitting next to her.

Maddie's eyes well up as she shakes her head slowly. Taking a swallow of her 7Up, she slowly places the cup on the stand next to her. "Only if that 'something' is a small human being."

"Wait...What?" I ask, confused.

"I'm a week late."

I feel as though my wet finger has plunged into a wall socket, sending shock waves through my system. "Do you want to talk about it?"

"Not much to talk about."

"Have you taken a test?"

"No. I'm afraid to."

"Well, we can't be sure until you test. I'll run down to the store and get a box for you. You stay here and keep this bucket close just in case you need it," I say, as I hand her the red bucket we use for washing the floor.

After running quickly to the store and back, my head is spinning with the possibility that Maddie may be pregnant.

"I can't look. You look and tell me," Maddie says with a slight panic in her voice. "The box says to set the timer for two minutes and look for one line or two."

She hands me the used test, and I take it to the kitchen. I set the kitchen timer for three minutes hoping that extra minute will reward us. I sit on the kitchen counter staring nervously as the seconds tick by. When the buzzer finally goes off, I look down at the plastic stick that holds Maddie's future; two blue lines indicate that Maddie is, in fact, pregnant.

Maddie is still sitting on the bathroom floor, and as I walk through the door I offer, "You want to talk about it now?"

She takes the stick from me and begins to weep openly.

"Mad," I coo, sitting on the floor next to her, my arms around her.

"Is it Frankie's?"

Between sobs she manages, "Yeah, we had one wild night the last night I was home. I knew it would be the last time. I just wanted one last night with him, you know? Like a memory that just he and I would have. I'm so stupid! Why didn't I have him wear protection? I just wasn't thinking," she says as she starts to wail.

"You should call him. He should know," I say gently, producing more tears.

"Cal, you have no idea what he'll be like when he finds out. He never wanted kids."

"I'll help you through this. Whatever you choose to do."

"Shit. The warden will say 'I told you so,' can't wait to hear that," Maddie says between sniffles.

"Let's not worry about the warden yet. After a good night's sleep, things will seem clearer."

Hugging me a little tighter she says, "Thanks." In her next breath Maddie says, "Now enough of this sappy bullshit," and gently pats my back as she eases out of our embrace.

"Frankie, we need to talk. Yeah, I'm okay. No, nothing is wrong. Well, yes, something is wrong and that's why we need to talk. No, I'm not sick. Well, I am sick but not sick like *dying* sick. Frankie, will you shut up for a second! I have something serious to talk to you about. I'm late. No, not late for work, geez, Frank, will you listen to me for sec! I'm late as in a week late. I've been puking for two days. What do you mean *what do you mean?* I mean I'm pregnant, you idiot. No, it's not someone else's, it's yours. Yes, I'm positive. Because you were the last person I slept with, or have you forgotten already? I don't know what I plan to do yet. What would you do if you were me? Seriously? Are you joking? I can't do that no matter how messed up my life is. Yeah but ... No. I am serious. If I have to, I'll do this by myself. Why did I even call you? Right. Well, same to you, ass-wipe." With that, Maddie slams down the phone.

"Well, that went well," she says, walking into my bedroom.

"I'm sorry, Mad. I wish he had been more sympathetic. What did he say?"

"He swears it's not his."

"Oh man. Do you plan on seeing him again?"

"That's doubtful."

"Let's celebrate!"

"Have you lost your mind?"

"Let's get you a gallon of ice cream and two spoons."

"What do *you* have to celebrate?"

"I get to watch you get fat, which, in turn, makes me look super thin."

"You know, I really hate you right now," Maddie jokes.

"But I still love *you!*"

Maddie and I manage to finish off a container of ice cream, lending itself to a sugar coma. I waddle to bed with a full belly. Maddie's predicament is weighing on me. There's so much uncertainty in her life right now. I'm not sure if it's the sugar overload quickly followed by the plunge in blood sugar that has me feeling melancholy, but whichever it is, I feel the need to phone Charlie.

"Hey, what's up?" I say, unable to sound normal.

"Oh boy, what's wrong? What'd I do?"

Smiling at his playful banter, making me miss him even more, I say, "I don't think you did anything, but it's still early, you're bound to do something wrong."

"Very funny. Now spill it." So I do. I tell him about Maddie and Frankie and what a dilemma she has gotten herself into. "Can you imagine? She's too young to have a baby."

"Cal, I hate to break it to you, but she's not that young. Sure, younger than she had planned, but still fully capable of having a healthy baby and becoming a terrific mom with or without Frankie."

"I just can't imagine."

"Sometimes life deals you cards you have to play, and sometimes those cards are the winning hand. She's a bright girl. She'll figure it out. So, enough about Maddie, let's talk about how much you miss me."

I'm thoughtful for a moment. "I miss you more than I'd miss drinking coffee...if I ever gave up coffee...which will never happen."

Charlie laughs, "Whoa, more than not drinking coffee? You must really miss me. Go on." So I continue, laughing myself.

"I got one. I miss you more than an old man misses the toilet." His laugh is as soothing as warm soup on a frigid wintery day. Feeling much better now, we say goodnight and make plans to talk over the weekend. In three weeks, he will be coming to town to celebrate my birthday, and I can't wait. My Charlie. What a good guy. I wonder how that conversation would have gone if I were the one who was pregnant. He certainly would make a great daddy someday. I slip into slumber, dreaming of Charlie chasing around two little kids in our yard with our dog. Everything seems so perfect. Things have a way of distorting in dreams. If only life could be so simple.

CHAPTER 4
Callie

"Sure, I'd love to have lunch with you. How about tomorrow around noon? I can take my lunch break then. Okay, sounds good. See you tomorrow." Hanging up, I find myself looking forward to seeing her more than I had anticipated. *It'll be good to catch up.*

"Who was that?" Maddie asks as she walks by in her uniform. She's decided that comfort trumps style, therefore, her uniform for the past few days has been her pink zebra striped PJs.

"My mom. She wants to have lunch with me tomorrow. Probably to catch me up on *The World According to Jimmy*. I swear he's like watching a soap opera. Ever since he and Riley moved in together when I moved to Missouri, things have been kinda nuts. I think he's going a little stir crazy living in Vermont. Country life takes some getting used to. Thank goodness he has a good job with the Eveready. Maybe they'll move here, who knows."

"I don't think I'd wish for that. With her comes her family. It's a package deal, and I'm pretty sure you don't want that to happen."

"Eesh. You're probably right."

Maddie walks past, pats me on the shoulder and heads straight back to bed with her bottle of water and dry toast.

"I'm going to work, Mad. Maybe we can get some dinner tonight? Maybe some big juicy burgers and fries with lots of mayo and ketchup. Mmmmm."

"Stop it! I think I threw up in mouth a little bit," she calls from her room.

With a stifled laugh, I say, "Bye for now, Mad," and close the door. *Bye for now?*

"Hi there, Arianna. You're looking pretty today," I say with a smile to the young cancer patient.

"Yeah, I had a lot of time to rest last night." She twirls in her purple sequined tutu. "You like my new tutu, Callie?"

"Oh, very much so. Do they make one in my size?"

Arianna giggles, "I don't think so. You're too old."

Pulling up my elastic waist skirt just below my bra, I say, "You're probably right. I better stick to my old-people clothes." Arianna howls with laughter. It's so nice to hear her laugh after the afternoon she had yesterday. It seems like her laughs are getting fewer and farther between. Pulling my skirt down to its normal position, I adjust my turquoise blouse and suggest, "let's get some artwork done." And that's just what we do for the next several hours.

Natasha is working with Dion as Chunk waddles in to say hello. Some new faces arrive along with some old. All in all, it has been a good day. As I am leaving on my lunch break, Trevor is walking out of the building.

"The kids holding up okay today?" Trevor asks as he holds the door open for me.

"Thank you. Yep. Today's been a really good day so far."

"Where are you headed?"

"Gotta meet my mom. We have some catching up to do. I should only be gone an hour or so. Where are you going?"

"I'm going to grab a quick lunch and then stop in to see Alex. I'm not sure if you know him."

"I don't think so. Is he a patient here?"

"He was. He's at home now on hospice. His mom said that he only has a few days left at best," he says, his face twisting in grief as his eyes moisten.

"Oh, my gosh. That's so sad. How old is he?"

"Just shy of twenty-one." The pain he feels for this young man is evident. "I told his mom that I would watch the football game with him tonight, but just in case he doesn't make it that far, I thought I'd pop in with a surprise visit after lunch," he says with a sniff. His reaction causes me to instinctively reach for his hand and squeeze it once.

"He's lucky to have a friend like you." Departing the hospital, I wonder what kind of young man this Alex is and how hard this job must be, knowing you'll lose most of your patients. *I don't know if I'm up for this.*

"So tell me all about Jimmy. How are he and Riley doing? Is he still blissfully happy? Is their place just as cute as Miss Cori's Cave?" This is a reference to a childhood favorite story of mine, eliciting a chuckle from my mom. Over and over, she would read me this story about a lioness that made a home inside a cave. The home was immaculately clean, sparkling from wall to wall. At night, she would be rocked to sleep, lying on her hammock made of tree branches, listening to the whirling wind sweeping past the opening of the cave, echoing off the walls. She would look out into the sparkling night sky and fall mellifluously asleep. Until one night some rebel lions came and ate all the stored food for winter and ruined the interior of her cave. She had to leave and find refuge elsewhere. She climbed out of her cave and found a new home among the trees, but it never truly felt like home. She no longer had the comfort of the walls surrounding her to keep her warm and dry. She missed her home terribly. With the help of some unlikely friends, a surfeit of skunks, she reclaimed her home inside her cave. Thinking of this story brought on an overwhelming feeling of nostalgia.

"Well, you know your brother isn't the neatest person in the world, but Riley is doing a nice job decorating. They seem to be very happy. I even think, dare I say, they may get married." Well, this is news to me.

"I hope he's happy. To think there might be a Jimmy Jr. running around here some day."

"I certainly hope he chooses another name," Mom says with a smile.

"How's Dad like his new teaching job?"

"It's a bit of an adjustment, but I think he'll find his groove."

"Does he have a large class?"

"He has a pretty small group this year, but then again, they just opened, so I'm sure their numbers will grow."

"Have you heard from the Wilsons lately? I'm just wondering how the family is getting along. Now with little Tyler running around, I bet Grandma and Grandpa are, super, busy."

"Ha, yes, they are busy. They babysit Tyler quite a bit as Samantha takes on more hours at the bank. He's a sweet little boy, by the sound of it."

"Oh, geez. Look at the time. I promised I'd be back in an hour. Sorry to eat and run."

"Look how grown up and responsible you've become. I'm so proud of you, Callista. Really I am."

Queue the tears.

"Awe, Mom. You really did miss your calling in life. You'd *so* get paid big bucks for those tears." smiling I stand, leaving money on the table, which she quickly places back in my hand.

As I hug my mother goodbye, I swear that I'll stop by the house and say hello more often. Possibly even call for a lunch date. I haven't been the best daughter in that department. I've had a lot on my plate lately.

Driving home my thoughts turn to Riley. *Is she really happy? If Tyler had survived the attack in Lebanon, would she have changed her mind and gone back to him when he returned?* Surely not. I mean, Jimmy is my brother and all, but he's still a good guy. An image of Wyatt's flushed face crosses my mind momentarily. It's the moment of our first kiss. *I wonder what he's doing with his life. Heck, he may even be married and have a kid by now.* This last thought brings Maddie to the forefront. *Schmaddie, what have you gotten yourself into?* I don't have the heart to tell my mom about that situation. She would be reduced to a puddle of tears... again. Maddie was talking with Frankie on the phone yesterday, and it wasn't going well. It sounded as if she wanted to meet with him to talk in person, but he really didn't want anything to do with her anymore. It's so sad.

Parking my car in my designated spot, I walk back in to finish my day.

CHAPTER 5
Jimmy

Jimmy walks through the door and sits on the couch with a deep sigh.

"Dinner will be ready in a minute," Riley exclaims from the tiny kitchen. "You wanna beer or something?"

"Yeah, that'd be great." Riley walks in and hands him a beer with a kiss on the cheek.

"Tough day?"

Letting out a sigh, he says, "Yeah, but no worse than usual. I have to train a new guy, and his idea of working and my idea of working are totally opposite. He'd rather sit around and wait for things to happen instead of getting them done himself. I'm beginning to feel like he's not going to make it in this department."

"Will you have to fire him?" Riley asks while rubbing his shoulders.

Exhaling deeply, he says, "I hope not."

Something in the kitchen begins to boil over, and the room fills with the aroma of burned plastic.

"Shit!" Riley scrambles back to the kitchen, "Shit, shit, shit!" Taking the pot off the stove, she assesses the damage. "You've heard of brown rice before, right? How does black rice sound?" She throws the dishtowel she is holding in the sink.

"You know what sounds good? Take out." Jimmy gets up off the couch and riffles through the drawer until he finds the takeout menus. "What sounds good to you? Pizza, Chinese, or burgers?"

"Let's just order a pizza and call it a night."

"Sounds good to me." Jimmy picks up the phone to make the call for a delivery in 30 minutes. Once he sets the phone down, he pulls her into his lap. "This is perfect. A nice cold beer, a nice comfy couch and a nice warm body to play around with while we wait for the pizza to arrive." With a laugh, she begins to unbutton his shirt.

With minutes to spare, the pizza arrives. Jimmy pays the pizza delivery guy and brings the piping hot pizza to the couch where Riley is wrapped up in a blanket. They sit and eat in silence.

"Hey Rye, are you happy?"

"What kind of question is that?"

"Are you happy with your choices?"

Wiping the grease off her chin, she says, "I'm very happy. I know that you're the man for me," and gives him a slippery kiss.

"I have a hypothetical question for you. What if I were to say we should get married, hypothetically. Would you say yes?"

"For real?" Riley squeals.

"Why not make this all official. I don't need any fanfare, just a small wedding. Heck, we could elope if you want." He regrets his words the moment they leave his mouth.

"Yes! Yes, yes, yes!" Riley screams, dropping her half eaten slice of pizza, wrapping her arms around Jimmy's neck. The rest of the pizza remains in the box uneaten, cheese congealing, grease seeping through the cardboard leaving dark blotches on the lid.

Before Jimmy can drink his first cup of coffee, Riley starts in about getting married. She's barely lifted her eyelids when she exclaims, "Let's just do it. Let's just go somewhere and get hitched. Why not? We don't need anyone but each other, right?" Riley is on a roll. "We could just go to Vegas and get married."

"Whoa, slow down. Let's think this through. I should have thought it through before I mentioned eloping. We could elope, but I'm telling you my family would be really upset if we didn't at least invite them to a ceremony," Jimmy says, throwing the covers off as he walks into the kitchen to clean up the pizza from the night before.

Following close behind, she says, "I don't really have a family. I don't have anyone to walk me down the aisle and give me away. I have to do this myself, so why not do it the way I want to do it."

Jimmy is feeling uncomfortable with this conversation now. He loves her, he knows that. He'd loved her the first time their eyes met at Stewart's, but something doesn't feel right. This isn't going as planned. None of it is going as planned.

There was no plan.

"Let's slow down and think about this. How would your sister and Grandmother feel if you didn't invite them to see you get married? I know they would be hurt."

"They'd get over it in time. Just think about it, okay?"

"This isn't something we have to rush into right this second. We need a plan." *Jesus, we need a plan. Why didn't I think this through a little bit before spouting off about getting married?*

"I'm gonna shower and get to the office early. What's your shift at Stewart's today, early or late?"

"Late. I'm going back to sleep. Have a great day," she says, as she kisses him on the lips and climbs back in bed. Her lips feel foreign to him suddenly.

Jimmy takes his time showering. Running his fingers over his lips, he contemplates the feel of her lips once more. The kiss seemed so ordinary. Grabbing the soap, he runs the bar between his hands and places it back on the ledge. There he eyes a large crack in the tile that he hadn't noticed before. It seems ominous. *How do I fix this?*

Drying off, getting dressed, the room appears to have lost its light. Everything seems gray, devoid of any sparkle. Something has shifted in their home overnight. The uneasy feeling he felt lingered; unable to wash it off in the shower. *I love her.* He repeats to himself as he's dressing. The statement begins to change into a question. *I love her?* He can't pinpoint what is causing this uneasiness.

By the time he arrives at work, he has talked himself into thinking that maybe this eloping idea isn't such a bad one. They could deem it a destination wedding. What's not to love about Vegas? The bright lights, the nightlife, the little white chapel. If they really wanted to go all out, they could even hire Elvis to officiate the wedding. *Can you imagine Mom's eyes watching Elvis sashay up to the bride and groom?* This brings a smile to his face. *Everything is going to work out just fine. Go with it.* Riley's bubbling enthusiasm is hard not to get wrapped up in. *We could make this work. Call Mom and Dad and tell them that I've asked Riley to marry me and explain about her lack of family and how important it is for her to have a small wedding with just the two of us. I could invite them to our destination wedding, but explain that I understand if they can't make it. Yes, this will work. I'll smooth things over with my parents and make it work.*

CHAPTER 6
Callie

Driving home, I think about Alex and how Trevor has to say goodbye. My mind is preoccupied as I park the car and walk into the apartment. Opening the door, I walk in on a sobbing Maddie sitting on the floor, holding a pillow to her stomach, and Frankie standing over her, veins in his neck bulging, looking much older than his 37 years. I enter the apartment as Frankie continues with his condemnation, our eyes meet briefly as he continues to spew his ugly words.

"Where do you think you're gonna live, you dumb bitch? Here with Callie? You think this is the place to raise a kid? Stop saying it's mine. Who knows how many guys you've been screwing around here. I bet you got nervous when you found out that you were knocked up and decided that none of these guys would help out. *'I'll call Frankie. He'll pay for the kid.'* Well guess what. No. I won't do it. I'm sure as shit it's not mine. We hadn't even been bangin'. If I recall, you're the one that broke it off with me. Remember that night? *You called me.* Said something about how our relationship was a mess and that you needed to get away from all your "demons." Then you came crawling back to me the night before you left. Why would you move halfway across the country and *then* tell me. Bullshit. I'm not getting sucked into this. I don't want any kid! You know that. You knew that from the beginning. You know what? I feel sorry for you. You think by dangling some kid in front of me I'm going to take you back and we're gonna live in a nice house with a white picket fence and live happily ever after? Not gonna happen, baby. You were fun for a while, but I'm done with you."

I am shocked that Frankie is in our apartment and being so cruel to Maddie. I'm standing here, just standing—with the door wide open, and my hand still on the doorknob—listening to his tirade. I look at Maddie cowering on the floor. Her eyes are cast down as if intensely interested in the fabric of the pillow she's holding. Her skin has grown pale throughout the confrontation. She looks like a shell of the strong Maddie I know. As I am about to jump in and try to diffuse the situation, Maddie's cheeks begin to pink, lending her the look of a cornered wild animal. Her face slowly rises up to Frankie with her eyes darkening, brows lowered and mouth set; I can tell she's about to strike. Like a feral cat, she's on him; pillow thrown to the ground, a guttural, throaty growl emanating from her mouth. Before I realize what she's doing, there's blood on Frankie's face. She lunges for his eyes with her outstretched claws, but in the process, nicks his chin. Frankie tries grabbing both hands, but she is wildly beating his chest, making it difficult to grab the moving target.

"You son-of-a-bitch! Get out of my goddamn apartment! Get out of my life! My mom was right. You are a complete fucking loser! Worse than that, you aren't worthy of this child. YOUR child. Get out! Get out!" She continues shoving him with all her might, but he finally catches her wrist. Frankie wipes his chin and sees blood on his hand, then says in a menacing voice, "Bitch, you're gonna pay for that. You and your bastard kid." He throws her hands down with such force he nearly knocks her over. Marching out of the apartment, he yells one last threat, "You'll get what's coming to you," and slams the door. A sketch of a willow tree I made while working on my art degree comes crashing to the floor, sending shards of glass everywhere.

As I walk to the closet to get the dustpan and broom, I'm not sure what is more broken, the picture frame or Maddie. Sweeping up the mess, I say, "those were idle threats. Don't let him into your head. He's long gone by now, and I say good riddance. We need another gallon of ice cream to celebrate." Said nervously, hoping to lighten the mood, but from the silence in response, I can tell it didn't help.

I dump bits of glass and debris from the dustpan and turn to see Maddie standing there, visibly shaking. She looks like someone has just told her that her beloved golden retriever has been run over in front of her house.

"Maddie? Mad, you all right?" I put the broom and dustpan down, walk to her, and bring her into a bear hug. Slowly the shaking subsides and she begins to weep. Struggling to get free of my arms, she walks past me and closes her bedroom door.

I walk to the navy blue velvet sectional and lay down hoping to pass the time watching some trivial sit-com. An old rerun is on, showing back-to-back episodes. I sit and stare at three in a row not really watching. The TV is just white noise surrounding my thoughts as I wait for Maddie to return.

The creak of Maddie's bedroom door catches my attention as she walks over with red, swollen eyes to the couch and says, "I need food." With a smile, I click off the remote and jump up to grab my car keys.

"Right. Food makes everything better," I say with a smile.

⚘ ⚘ ⚘

After dinner, I take Maddie to Babies R Us to look at all the adorable baby items they have to offer. It is a bit overwhelming for her. The list of items she needs is never ending. "What about this one?" I ask, standing next to a crib made of cherry wood. It sways side to side when pushed.

"I have no idea. It's pretty but *oh marone*, did you see the price tag on this? I don't even have a job. How am I supposed to bring a baby into this world without any money?"

"I'll help you until you get a job. Don't worry. We'll figure it all out." Lifting up an adorable pair of denim overalls, I coo, "Aw, Mad, look at these!"

"For the love, Cal, I'm not gonna be living down on the farm. Slopping pig slop. Bathing this here kid in a trough," she drawls in her best southern accent.

Ignoring her comment, I continue, "what if you have an adorable baby boy? I bet he'll have freckles and dark black hair like his mama. Have you thought about names?"

"He or she is barely the size of a grain of rice and you're talking names already?"

"You gotta be prepared! I'm gonna make a fantastic aunt. I'm gonna spoil him rotten. Let him eat all the sugar he wants, stay up late, watch R rated movies before he's 17... and if she's a girl I'm going to put her in cute little dresses and braid her hair. I'm an excellent braider. Don't put her in pink, though, okay? It has to be purple. Purple is a strong color, and you want a strong little girl to stand up to any smelly boy. Right?" Turning my attention from the turnstile of cute baby clothes, I notice Maddie has gone quiet. "Mad, what is it?"

"I'm just feeling kinda crampy. Too much excitement for one day. 'Sprout' needs to get home and rest," she says, while holding up a children's book that boasts the word "Sprout" with a picture of bean sprouts on one of the pages.

"Sprout, I like it. We needed something other than 'it' or 'baby.' Okay then. Let's get Sprout home." A little uncomfortably I ask, "Do you think you need to call the doctor?" pointing to her hand over her abdomen.

"Nah, not yet. I have to call and make an appointment tomorrow anyway."

"Well, if you want someone to go with you, I'm your girl."

"Thanks, Cal."

The conversation on the way back to the apartment is animated, dwelling on the sex of the baby, when Maddie is going to call home and tell her parents about her little surprise, and what her future plans are.

"I am *not* looking forward to that conversation. It'll go something like this:

'Ma, I got something to talk to you about.'

'You're on drugs again.'

'No, Ma, I told you, I'm never doing that again.'

'Let me guess, you're pregnant.'

'Geez, Ma, you have a lot of faith in me.' pause. 'Yeah, I'm pregnant.'

'Jesus, Mary, and Joseph. That no good loser got you pregnant, didn't he?'

'Yep, you were right about him all along.' Doesn't that sound like a fun conversation to have with your mother? It'll take her weeks to say the rosary enough times to absolve my sins."

I feel for Maddie as we drive into the apartment complex. Her life is certainly messed up right now. After parking, we walk down the sidewalk to the front door, and I notice there is something on the front porch.

"What's that?" I ask curiously.

"It looks like a Raggedy Ann doll. I used to have one of those when I was a little girl."

Getting closer, I say, "I hope you didn't have a Raggedy Ann doll like this one." The doll's decapitated head sits on the porch next to the body, and its dress has been burned. The one button eye that remains hangs tenuously by a single thread.

"What the hell is that doing on our porch?"

"No idea, but I have a pretty good idea who put it there," Maddie says with a slight hitch in her voice.

CHAPTER 7
Callie

Weeks pass without incident, and we have forced the image of the tortured doll into the recesses of our minds. I finally hear from Charlie about his impending arrival.

"So what are your birthday plans, Cal?"

"Hopefully plans with you," I say wistfully.

"Consider it done. I wouldn't want you to celebrate your twenty-second birthday all alone."

"Well, I won't be alone. Maddie is here. I'd love for the three of us to do something together."

"Sounds like a plan as long as part of the plan is Callie/Charlie alone time."

With a laugh, I respond, "Of course we'll have some alone time, you goof ball."

"Then I'll be there before you know it!"

"When are you flying in?"

"I'm going to make some calls and I'll have a date dialed in before you can say birth control."

We continue our conversation about him moving up the ranks within the Park's and Recreation Center in Bethel, Connecticut.

"Congratulations on the promotion! Program director, huh? That sounds so official. So grown up."

"Cal, I'm twenty-five. Don't you think that it's time to grow up?"

"You? Grow up? Isn't that an oxymoron?"

"You're the moron."

"Oh, nice. See, it's not possible."

"Touché. I gotta go now."

"What's the rush?"

"My Easy-Bake oven is preheated and it's time to put the brownie mix in."

"Funny."

"And after that, I plan on going out back and playing in my sandbox before I run through the sprinkler. With my clothes on. Man, Mom's gonna be so mad."

"All right, all right. Stop. My cheeks hurt."

"Maybe, if you're lucky, I'll slip you a note that asks if you like me, and you'll have to check a box. Yes or no. Choose wisely." Hearing the playful tone makes my heart ache to see him.

"I like you. I'll check yes."

"Phew, that's a relief. See you in a while crocodile."

After a week and a half with no word on when Charlie is coming to visit, I begin to think something is up. I have a feeling Maddie knows exactly what the plan is. She keeps dropping hints.

"Hey, Mad, look at this band coming to town. Wanna check them out?"

"When is it? You might have plans that night. Just sayin'."

"It's on my birthday. It'd be fun to go to the 7:00 show and have the rest of the night free."

"You might be busy at seven. I wouldn't make any plans."

Thankfully, work has kept me busy for the past month, therefore not leaving me a lot of time to dwell on the fact that I am left in the dark.

At work, Trevor has been in a foul mood. Most of the week a dark cloud has followed him everywhere. Natasha would later tell me that his patient, Alex, had passed away. I don't look forward to having that happen with one of my kids.

On my way home one Thursday night, knowing that my birthday is Friday, I start to feel the excitement build. The great part about Charlie is that I can always expect the unexpected from him. True to form, he is in my apartment at 12:01 A.M.

Rolling over in bed, I bump into something, or rather someone, nearly causing me to scream. "Happy birthday, Callista."

Smiling, I sleepily say, "Hi, Charlie."

"I wanted to be the first person to wish you a happy birthday."

I reach over to my alarm clock and plop it on my bed as it turns to 12:02. "Mission accomplished."

"*And* I want to be the first person you *see* in the morning."

"You are," I yawn, "definitely the first person to wish me happy birthday and the first person I see on my birthday. I don't suppose Maddie left the door open for you tonight, did she?"

"I'll never tell." he says, pulling me into his arms as I rest my head on his chest and quickly fall into a deep sleep.

The annoying beep of my alarm wakes me the next morning, followed by the aroma of coffee wafting into my room. Pulling on my robe, excited to get my birthday weekend started, I walk into the kitchen to witness Maddie arranging donuts on a birthday paper plate. "Make a wish," she demands, lighting a candle in the center of the top donut.

"You guys! Thank you!" I wish for everyone to stay happy and healthy. I don't want anything to change. As I blow out the candle, a shiver runs down my spine.

"What is it?" Maddie asks.

"Who me? Nothing. Everything's great!" I say, tackling them both with a hug. "You guys are the best!"

"We haven't even done anything yet," Charlie chides.

"I bet you made these donuts in your Easy-Bake oven."

"Guilty as charged," he teases, feeding me a bite of donut sealing it with a kiss.

When the phone rings, I know by the time on the clock who it is.

"Hello?"

"Happy birthday to you, happy birthday to you, happy birthday dear Callista, happy birthday to you."

"Thanks, Mom."

"Twenty two years ago today my life changed for the better when we welcomed you into the world," she says wistfully.

"Mom, don't start crying. It's only 7:30 in the morning.

"You know me too well, Callista. Have a great day, sweetheart."

"I will, and thanks for calling." She is always the first one to sing happy birthday to me on each and every birthday since I can remember. It's an endearing gesture.

It's time to get a move on. "Can't wait to see what else you guys have up your sleeves, but I have to get to work. I'll be home around 5:30. Do we have dinner plans?"

"Do we have dinner plans, pfft, please. Who do you think you're dealing with? Amateurs? This ain't our first rodeo," Charlie scoffs.

After a quick shower, I'm off to the hospital where Natasha greets me with yet another cup of coffee. Around the art table many patients are making colorful cards to wish me happy birthday. This is a great beginning to my day. Arianna is first to bring me her card.

"It's beautiful. Thank you." she leans in for a hug.

After all the kids have presented their birthday cards, I stand next to Natasha, who is leaning against the wall to observe. "Tash, what do you think will happen to these kiddos?"

"Well, that one over there has stage 4 neuroblastoma, which means the abnormal cancer cells have spread to bone marrow, skin, lymph nodes and other organs. Her blood work came back this morning with high levels of ferritin, which is important for metabolizing iron in your system and is known to be a tumor marker. Her cancer right now is recurring. The doctors are using chemo and radiation right now but are thinking about trying stem cell therapy. Her parents are hopeful but realistic."

"Hopeful but *realistic*?"

"Hopeful that the treatment will shrink or eradicate the tumors, but they've been down this road before. Realistically, she has about six to eight months."

"How do you stay so positive every day? Do you ever stop thinking about them?"

"Never. I think about them every waking moment. Being positive is the easy part. I do what I would want someone to do for me. Provide me with positive energy and let me shine while I still have time on this earth."

Placing a warm hand on my shoulder, she says, "Excuse me, Callie, it looks like Pheonix just walked in." At the mention of the child's name, I feel an electric current run through my body, causing a prickly sensation at the base of my neck; immediately my hands begin to shake. A waif of a child enters the room. Her skeletal frame protrudes at points through her blue jeans and plaid red shirt. On her head, she wears a soft black pageboy cap. She has a radiant smile for Natasha when she offers a hello and gives her a gentle squeeze.

"Pheonix, I have someone I'd like you to meet. This is Callie."

"Hi, Pheonix, it's a pleasure to meet you."

Her smile evaporates with the shy hello. I fumble with the art supplies, dropping the construction paper on the floor. *Pull yourself together. She's just a little girl.*

We sit at the art table to start working on a painting. She helps pick out the colored construction paper in pale blue.

"What are you thinking of working on today, Pheonix?" I ask with a shaky voice.

"I'm not sure yet."

With the silver, black and red paint, she begins to work.

"How old are you?"

"I'm twelve," she says matter-of-factly. I had assumed by looking at her that she was eight or nine years old.

"How old are you?" Pheonix asks me unapologetically.

"I'm twenty-two. Today, actually."

Pheonix gently sets aside her paintbrush. She looks up at me and holds my gaze with her cloudy auburn eyes and offers a sincere, "Happy birthday." *Those eyes*, like I am looking into an eighty-year-old woman's eyes. She's felt things in her short life that many people decades older than her have not experienced.

"Thank you," I say, distracted. "I really don't know what I'm going to do today. After therapy, I'll probably go home and go out to dinner with some friends. My boyfriend came into town to surprise me. Well, not to surprise me really, I knew he was coming. I just didn't know the exact time." I am rambling and I know it. Something about this child unnerves me.

"I'm finished now, Tasha. Where should I put it to dry?" As she hands the paper over, Natasha says, "Pheonix, you need to sign it so that everyone knows who the amazing artist is." Pheonix dips her brush into black paint and scrawls her name across the corner of the pale blue construction paper. I hadn't paid attention to what she was painting as I was rambling. Noticing it now, I audibly gasp. The sound draws Pheonix's attention, and she slowly turns toward me.

"That's a dragonfly. That's a painted dragonfly," I stammer, as the goose bumps rise on my skin. My hands, which had ceased shaking before, begin again. I think to myself, *that's the very painting that I dreamt about.*

Natasha, searching my eyes to explain my behavior says, "Yes, isn't it lovely? Pheonix is going to enter this in the auction at Art from the Heart."

Trevor enters the room rolling an IV pole beside him. "Pheonix, it's time for your treatment, honey."

What just happened here?

"All right. It was nice to meet you, Callie."

Lost in thought, her voice doesn't even register until she is nearly out the door. "Yes, it was nice to meet you, too," I reply, but she's left the room. I can see her frail body walking slowly down the hall, holding on to the IV post for stability as the door closes behind her.

"What's wrong with you?" Natasha asks abruptly.

"I...uh. I'm sorry. This painting. I've seen it before. This exact painting was in a dream I had," I confess, holding the painting in my quaking hands. I describe the dream to Natasha in detail, wondering what she thinks it all means.

"Interesting. You know they say everything happens for a reason. I'm sure you'll figure out the meaning eventually. Souls have a way of connecting in the most unexpected ways."

"Tash, didn't she spell her name wrong? Isn't it supposed to be P-h-o-e-n-i-x?"

Laughing, Natasha says, "Yes, it's supposed to be spelled that way, but someone filled out the birth certificate spelling it P-h-e-o-n-i-x and her parents never changed it. She was unique from the start."

The rest of the day was a flurry of activity. So many different kids, different faces, joining us at the table. Some were new and some had been there for weeks. After our lunch break, Natasha and I check inventory and make sure we have enough supplies for the remainder of the day. That image of that dragonfly keeps creeping into my consciousness.

As the day comes to a close, Natasha hands me one last handmade card. Opening the card reveals a small dragonfly with the word *believe* written beneath. The nervousness I felt when Pheonix walked into the room has fallen away. My eyes burn as they blur with newly formed tears. For whatever reason, I feel a kinship, a connection to this child. I have just met Pheonix, and already, she has a hold of my heart.

CHAPTER 8
Callie

As I drive home from work, my mind wanders to the lovely cards the children had given me, and the surprise flowers delivered by a dancing bear. The kids loved that. It really elevated the mood in our crafty little pirate ship. I decided to leave them at work so that the kids in the hospital could enjoy them.

I open the door to a boisterous, "Happy Birthday!" yelled in unison by Maddie and Charlie.

The kitchen is decked out with balloons, and there are presents on the table. Charlie brings out a bottle of wine and uncorks it while Maddie brings out two wine glasses and a can of 7Up. While pouring the wine, Charlie says, "Here's to the birthday girl. Cheers!" It makes me think of my relatives in Vermont and how much happy hour was a part of their day. *I wonder how Aunt Marilyn is doing.*

"Here, open the cards first," Maddie suggests.

There is a beautiful card from my mom and dad, a slightly funny card from my brother and Riley, and then one on the bottom from Aunt Marilyn.

Dear Callie,

I hope this card finds you well. It's been so quiet through the years as you have moved on. Your visits are so few and far between. I hope you get a chance to come visit us up North sometime soon.

I have some new friends that have appeared in the past few weeks. They are the most delightful little fellas. Usually around three or four come to visit. They play among the branches of the pine trees, and dance on the petals of my favorite Snapdragon flowers out front of the camp. In the past day or so, they've become increasingly friendly to the point of crawling on my arms. They like moving along the needles with their beautiful silvery, opalescent wings. Such friendly little guys; I only wish I knew their names.

All my best to your family. I hope you're doing something fun to celebrate. Have a drink on me!

Love,

Aunt Marilyn

Typical Aunt Marilyn with her obscure comments. Inside the card I find a fifty-dollar bill, "I'm buying the first round tonight!" I declare, raising the fifty over my head.

The other two cards are from Maddie and Charlie. Both are equally funny, and each holds a sweet message inside.

"Thanks guys."

"Here, open mine." Maddie hands me a gift wrapped in baby shower paper with blue and pink baby bottles on it. I give her a quizzical look. "I thought I was being funny." Smiling I open it up. Unwrapping the paper reveals a picture frame with my weeping willow tree drawing in it. The once-broken frame has been restored to brand new. Welling up, I utter, "Mad." I clear my throat, "you're the best," and we embrace. We separate. Mad runs her hands down my arms until she reaches my hands and asks, "I wonder why they call those trees 'weeping' willows? That makes me want to jump off the nearest bridge."

Smiling, I say, "I had read some folktales on the topic when I was getting my degree. The story is actually why I sketched the tree. It's essentially about two young lovers that used to sit under the willow tree and plan their lives together. They were killed just before their wedding, and the tree was so upset about their death that it no longer stood tall. From then on, the branches drooped in sorrow. Isn't that the saddest?"

"Yeah, way to keep the mood light," Maddie teases and releases my hands.

Smirking, I ask, "So where are we going for dinner tonight?"

Charlie speaks up, "There's an amazing Thai restaurant down in Clayton I think you're going to love. Our reservations are at 7:30, so if you need to change or anything, hop to it."

A feeling of contentment washes over me when I walk into my room with my glass of wine in hand. I check the closet. Nothing seems to be jumping out at me. Everything seems "tired," as my mom would say. *When did my wardrobe become so bland?* I stare into a sea of greys and blacks. In the far corner of the closet, there hangs a short, deep burgundy dress with a racer back that would look great, showing off my shoulders. I pull out a white wrap just in case it gets cool this evening, and a pair of low-heeled black sandals. As I assess myself in the floor-length mirror behind my bedroom door, my reflection smiles back at me. With just a touch of burgundy lip-gloss and the diamond stud earrings I got from Mom and Dad at graduation, I am ready to go.

"Whoa," Charlie utters. Just the reaction I am looking for.

"Cal, you look smokin' hot. Dang, if I were a dude, I'd do you," Maddie compliments.

"Wait in line," Charlie chastises Maddie.

Dinner is delicious, and the company is even better. How did I get so lucky to have my two best friends with me out here in Missouri or misery, as Maddie and I had been calling it as of late. Without Charlie around, I have been pretty lonely, and Maddie still hasn't gotten into a groove of forming friendships. Especially since finding out she is pregnant. As she puts it, "Who's gonna want a fat pregnant new friend? My moods aren't exactly friend making material. I'm like happier than a pig in shit one minute then a psycho zombie bitch that wants to rip your head off the next. Sounds like the perfect friend, doesn't it?"

Charlie laughs at Maddie's description.

"Cal, is this how you wanted to spend your birthday?" he muses as we walk back inside the apartment.

"Absolutely. It's been a great birthday."

"Next year you're going to be celebrating with me, Maddie *and* her baby."

I glance over at Maddie who is now leaning over the kitchen table with her arms, bent at the elbows, hands under her chin propping up her head, eyes closed mumbling "Mmmhmm" in response to everything we say.

"Mad. Maddie. Hey, Mad, go to bed," Charlie coaxes.

Stumbling from the table, she mumbles goodnight and closes her bedroom door.

"Thanks for a great day," I call out to her. Looking at Charlie, I motion with my head, "Man, and this is just her first trimester. She's gonna be a barrel of fun in a few months."

"Have you thought about this? I mean, long term?" He speaks gently, "I know you're a good friend to her, but I mean, what's going to happen when she has this baby? It's not your responsibility. Don't you think she should call her parents and let them know?"

"I do, but I'm waiting for it to be Maddie's idea. I don't want to push her to do something she's not ready to do."

"I get it." Yawning now, I look at Charlie and ask, "You ready for bed?"

"Not if sleeping is involved," he says with a glimmer in his eye.

Standing, I take his hand and bring him to my room. The lights are off, but the window is open, letting in a nice cool fall breeze; my favorite time of year.

Standing in the moonlight, I wrap my arms around Charlie and hug him tight.

"I hope you're having a great birthday, Cal. I've missed you. This long distance stuff really stinks. I wish you were closer to Connecticut."

"I know. Me too. Once I get enough in the bank, I can see about moving back, but for right now, this is where I need to be. I'm near family. I'm near my friend, who definitely needs to be as far away from Connecticut as she can. Did I tell you about Frankie's visit?"

"No. I thought they broke up a while ago."

"They did, but when Maddie found out she was pregnant, she called and told him. You can imagine how well that conversation went."

"Probably about just as well as it will go when she calls home."

"Right, except he was even worse than I thought. Somehow he managed to get out here and confront her. I walked in on them arguing. It got ugly." I continue to tell him what happened.

With concern, Charlie says, "Cal, I don't like the sound of that. He sounds like a loose cannon. Maybe you should contact the police."

"For a torn and tattered Raggedy Ann doll? I think they would laugh me right out of the precinct."

"Still." with worry in his eyes, he pulls me in.

"We'll be fine." Slowly, I lift his shirt up and over his head. Kissing his chest lightly, I watch as his pulse quickens with each touch of my lips.

CHAPTER 9
Callie

"How was your birthday weekend?" Natasha asks with a friendly smile.

"It was really great. Charlie came to town and took both Maddie and me out for dinner," I say, with a lack of enthusiasm.

With a frown, Natasha asks, "What's wrong? That sounds wonderful."

"I hate when he has to leave. It's really a bummer being so far away."

"I bet. How's Maddie feeling these days?"

"Like a cow," I laugh. "This morning she sat at the kitchen table and literally mooed."

"She sounds like a piece of work, that one."

"She's definitely one of a kind."

"Have you thought about going to the Friends of Kids with Cancer fashion show next week?"

"Yep, I think I'm free that afternoon. Are you going to the luncheon or the evening fashion show? And can I buy a ticket at the door?"

"Luncheon, and yes, you sure can. I think you'll really enjoy it. It's really touching to watch the models on the runway. All have been affected by cancer at some point in their lives."

After our lunch break, we continue our day with the kids. Many of the regulars come through. I keep waiting to see

Pheonix, but she never shows. Packing up the supplies in the supply cabinet, I say, "Tash, have you heard from Pheonix? Do you know why she didn't come in today?"

"Her mom called and said she wasn't feeling up to it. She had her treatment at the other location and went home to bed."

Feeling disappointed that I won't see her, I lock the cabinet and hand Natasha the keys.

The day of the Friends fashion show I ask, Maddie to join me, but she turns me down.

"Thanks, but I'm not feeling up to it. Must be I was on my feet too long today. I've been trying to get my resume together so that I can actually use my degree working with kids. Isn't that a kick in the pants? Working with kids, shit, I didn't know that I would be growing one before I got a job. Eww. Ow," she says, grabbing her stomach.

"Maybe I should stay home with you."

"No, you go. I think I read somewhere that this pain is from my ligaments stretching to make room for Sprout. Stop worrying about me, besides I wouldn't be much fun to hang with today. I'm going to bed with a bowl of ice cream. Now go."

"You sure?"

"Yes, geez, you're worse than the warden. Go. Get outta here."

Walking into the Ritz-Carlton, I can't help but feel the love in the room. After buying myself a ticket, I meander slowly around the lobby, looking at the wares that people are selling. There are many tables set up with anything from jewelry to clothing to sell to anyone willing to buy before walking into the function. I spot Natasha dressed in a beautiful black and silver satin, knee length sheath dress. A band of black satin falls over her right shoulder with the silver and black fabric crisscrossing over her body. Around her neck, she wears beads of crystal and black with matching drop earrings. She looks radiant.

"Having fun, Callie?"

"I am. I'm just not sure which table I'm to sit."

"I have room at my table. Follow me." As we walk into the main hall where the fashion show will take place, Natasha asks, "Have you seen Pheonix yet? She's around here somewhere." The mention of her name causes my heart to race. Natasha turns to look around the room. "Ah, there she is." Pheonix is wearing a pretty light pink sundress with a purple cardigan unbuttoned. On top of her head, she wears a matching sequined pink headband.

"Will she be walking the runway today?" Natasha nods. "I think I'll go say hi," and off I go. "You look very pretty today, Pheonix." Blushing, she replies just above a whisper, "Thank you."

"I'm excited about watching you strut your stuff up there. Who's your escort?"

"I think his name is Scott. He's really tall. I'm going to look so small walking next to him," she says, disappointed. I watch as her face changes from disappointment to surprise as the giant of a man, Scott, comes into view.

"Pheonix, are you ready? I have a little something for you I want you to wear as we walk the stage. Come find me when you're done talking. I'll be back stage," he says with a wink, causing her cheeks to turn pink. She smiles and says, "Guess it won't be so bad."

"Great! Have fun."

Sitting at the table with Natasha, I browse the booklet describing each model and their affliction. One after the other is written about strength and love. My vision is clouded as the MC taps the microphone to begin.

The luncheon is beautiful. The models are happy. This is such a nice distraction from their pain. Ready to leave, I walk toward the door when I hear a tiny voice behind me call my name.

"Callie. Callie, wait!" Turning around, I watch as the pink sequined headband begins to slide off Pheonix's head. She is quickly walking towards me, placing a hand on her headband.

"What is it? Is everything all right?" Panic flutters in my chest.

Taking a minute to catch her breath, she says, "I'm okay. I just wanted to tell you something before I forget. When I was walking on the stage, I looked out to the audience and I saw you sitting at the table with Natasha. There was a shadow behind you. I thought my eyes were playing tricks on me, but when I came out a second time, the shadow was still there. It was like someone standing behind you, but I couldn't tell who it was. It gave me the willies. I don't know. It's just weird. It felt like something important."

Turning around in a slow circle, I take in my surroundings. "Really? That's so weird. Could you see anything? Any details at all? What color hair? Man or woman?"

"No. Just like one of those police outlines that you see on TV, you know? All black, no detail. I just thought it's something you would want to know." With her next breath, she was saying goodbye. "Thanks for coming."

"See you soon, Pheonix," I say, leaving with the feeling I am being watched.

As I drive home, my mind dwells on how much time I have left to get to know Pheonix. She seems to have a deep understanding of her surroundings, and I really want to know more. *Could it have been Tyler?* Thinking of him now as I make a stop at the store, I wonder if he's hanging around to warn me of something? I drive home watching the sunset below the horizon as an uneasy feeling begins to dawn.

When I pull into the parking space in front of my apartment it seems all the lights are on. Feeling a sense of urgency, I throw the car into park and swiftly walk inside. On the couch is Maddie curled up in a ball with the blanket covering her body, sound asleep.

"Maddie?" I say, while gently rousing her. "You should really get to bed."

"Callie … something's wrong. I just feel it. Something is really wrong."

Panicked now, I ask carefully, "With the baby?"

"I think so."

"Should we go to the emergency room?"

"I don't think so, but I do want to go to the doctor's office tomorrow. I'm going to call first thing. I'm so tired right now."

"Let's get you to bed. I'll call in to tell Natasha what's going on and I'll take you to the doctor."

"You don't have to do that."

"I know I don't have to. I want to." Maddie walks back to her room looking like the Hunchback of Notre Dame.

"Try to get some rest. It'll all be better in the morning," I console while pulling up the bed sheets to her chin and tucking her in.

I can't sleep. I can't stop thinking about Maddie's baby growing in her belly. What if we should have gone to the hospital tonight? What if we're too late tomorrow? Too many "what ifs." *Maddie made her decision so just shut it down and get to sleep.*

In the morning, I make my phone calls and get everything situated. I make Maddie's doctor's appointment. I tell Natasha that I'll be working a half-day; we are all set until I walk out the door to get to the car. I feel like I am walking into a war zone. Plastic doll parts protrude from the grass, arms looking as though they are clawing out of the earth, trying to escape their untimely deaths. Doll heads line the sidewalk. Their glassy eyes watch me; daring me to touch them—Frankie is clearly still in town working his magic.

I have to keep Maddie inside while I clean up the yard.

I step back inside, "Hey Mad, why don't you take a seat and we'll wait a minute until the car is warmed up."

Maddie looks at me suspiciously, "Cal, what are you doing? It's not that cold outside. We don't need to wait for it to…," she pushes past me into the apocalypse, rendering her momentarily speechless.

"For fuck sake…" she exclaims as her hand rises to her throat. "What the hell did he do this for?"

"I'm not sure, but let me clean this up before we go," I ramble as I bend over and collect the doll heads and body parts. Bringing out a trash bag, Maddie says, "This feels like an omen."

"Everything is going to be fine. Let's just finish up here, put the trash out and lock the door." I don't want to tell her I feel the same way.

CHAPTER 10
Jimmy

Driving down that serpentine road and taking a right at the water pump reminds Jimmy of all the summers he spent up at camp with his family. He feels contentment, getting a glimpse of the turquoise camp to his left as he makes the turn. The rope swing sweeps past his periphery, and the feeling of falling in love washes over him. That was the very place he truly knew he loved Riley.

Jimmy and Riley's cabin is past Aunt Doris and Uncle Oscar's at the end of the gravelly camp road. Gravel crunches under his tires sounding like the rock tumbler he used to use as a child to grind and polish his rock collection. He makes a left turn into his driveway, slowly rolling over pine needles, which soften the sound of gravel. He sits in the car looking up at the little dilapidated cabin. The dark stained cedar shingle siding needs some work as some of it has fallen off over the years. The tin roof, though he loves the melodic sound of the roof when it rains, leaks in the family room. The screened-in porch along the back will make a great place for family cookouts, if only the screen wasn't full of holes. Yes, the house has its charm but is in dire need of some TLC. Since moving into the cabin in 1987, he has been trying to make it a home for Riley and himself. The previous occupants were friends of Aunt Doris and Uncle Oscar named Ed and Linda Davis, an elderly couple that passed away. Since they never had children of their own, there was no one to take over the place after their passing. They had written in their will that Aunt Doris and Uncle Oscar could have the cabin to give to a family member of their choosing. Mr. and Mrs. Davis had become fond of Aunt Doris and Uncle Oscar's extended family over the years—watching Jimmy and Callie grow and seeing the love for the lake in each of them, they knew just how much this lake meant to the Lamply's children. But never in Jimmy's wildest dreams did he think he would end up with their place. He was touched that his aunt and uncle had chosen him to have it. Economically speaking, Jimmy thought it would make a good investment, and in the future, he thought he could make a sizeable profit. They just need to spruce it up.

If he thinks real hard about it, he can picture having children running around here like Callie and he used to do. This would be a great place to start a family, just not yet. Yes, he is going to elope with Riley. He is going to march into the cabin and tell her right now…only he notices the empty spot next to the trash can where her car usually is and realizes she has left for her shift at Stewart's. Feeling slightly disappointed, he closes the car door and pads across the pine-needle-covered gravel driveway to open the squeaky screen door that leads to the heavy wooden one to get inside.

The musty smell that used to assault his sinuses has grown on him over the years. Entering the sparsely furnished family room, he decides he will get on bended knee and propose to Riley properly tonight. He will go to the jewelry store and buy a ring, knowing it will be a modest ring on his salary. Turning around and getting back in the car, he's happy with his decision. He is going to get married. *In Vegas? Perhaps the justice of the peace. Yeah, I'll see if Riley will go for that. After buying her a ring funds will be tight.*

Three hours later, the stage is set: roses on the table, candles lit, Austi Spumanti chilling in the fridge, soft love ballads playing on the radio, and the simple ¼ carat diamond solitaire ring burning a hole in his pocket. *Why am I so nervous?* he wonders anxiously. As he paces the floor, the sound of churning gravel signals an approaching car. *Oh shit. It's now or never.*

Footsteps on wood stairs. The squeak of the screen door. He had left the heavy wooden one open to allow a breeze to flow through the place.

Riley stands at the entrance of the cabin like a deer in the headlights, not uttering a word.

On bended knee, he says, "Riley, I would be honored to spend the rest of my life with you. Will you marry me?" When he removes the ring box from his trousers, she begins to cry.

"Jimmy..." with outstretched hand, she says the word he's been waiting for, "Yes!"

He places the ring on her finger, and she admires it with a smile on her face as he stands and holds her in a lover's embrace. She leans up to him, and they share a passionate kiss.

"It's the tiniest most beautiful ring I've ever seen."

"Well..." he stammers, "we can upgrade in a few years."

"It's perfect. Thank you."

They enjoy the rest of the evening making promises about the future. It all seems so surreal to Jimmy.

"I was thinking about the whole eloping idea. What if we just go to the justice of the peace here instead? Save some money so that we can take a small honeymoon somewhere."

"Sure we can. That seems practical."

Practical? Pushing the thought aside, he forges on. "We could go this weekend if you'd like?"

"Sounds great! Let's do it!"

"Let me see if my folks can make it up that quickly."

"I thought the idea was to just have it be you and me?" she pouts.

He speaks hesitantly, "You're right. Just you and me."

"Perfect! I'll look for something to wear tomorrow, and then Saturday will be our wedding day! I'm going to have a husband! Husband. My husband. Mr. and Mrs. James Lamply. This is crazy!" she says, hands flung in the air.

Caught up in the excitement, he swoops her up in his arms, cradling her like a child. She reaches for the bottle of champagne as he carries her to the bedroom. *This is crazy!* He feels a fleeting wave of nausea. With her sultry eyes boring into him, his thoughts of panic quickly evaporate.

"Let me show you what you have in store as a married man, Mr. Lamply," she offers in a husky voice.

CHAPTER 11
Callie

"Let's start with your weight," the attending nurse says.

"Oh, for the love," Maddie says, rolling her eyes, "this oughtta be good."

"Okay, ladies, please follow me to exam room three. We're just waiting on the doctor. She has one more ultrasound to do before yours."

"Thank you," Maddie says as she closes the door.

"Thanks for coming with me, Cal. I appreciate it."

"No biggie. I want to see that little Sprout," I say, noticing how honest this answer is, my excitement building.

"Let's hope it doesn't have a huge noggin, or I'm in trouble."

"Right. Ouch."

"Can I tell you something? Something I haven't told anyone?"

"Of course you can, Mad. You can tell me anything, you know that."

I'm finding it difficult to see Maddie in this position; quiet and shy are two adjectives I would never use to describe her.

"I'm excited to be a mom. I've been dreaming about it these past few weeks. I kinda went through a roller coaster of emotions at first, but now that I'm eight, almost nine weeks along, I like the idea more and more. It's like everywhere I look I see little kids. The one thing I do hope this kid has is Frankie's eyes. Wouldn't that be somethin' if she had my dark hair and Frankie's eyes?"

Smiling, I say, "So it's a girl now?"

"Yeah, and even though he's being a twisted MOFO, I think the name Frankie for a girl would be so cool. Don't you?"

"It's unique, but Mad, that MOFO is a psycho. Do you really want to be reminded of him every time you say the baby's name?" We are interrupted by three gentle knocks on the door. Maddie doesn't answer.

"Everybody ready?" the doctor asks as she rolls the ultrasound machine in.

"Hi, Doc. This is my best friend, Callie. I asked her to come with me today. I'm a little nervous."

Shaking my hand, the doctor turns to Maddie and assures, "Nothing to worry about. This procedure doesn't hurt at all. How are you feeling today?"

"Better than the last few days. I've been having a lot of cramping that I just kinda chalked up to what I was eating. Stuff like that."

"I see. Well, lie back and get comfortable," she instructs as she gently rolls up Maddie's top and tucks a table liner into the waistband of her pants. "This is going to feel a little cold. It's just jelly that we use to help conduct the ultrasound waves."

Maddie inhales sharply as the doctor squirts what looks like petroleum jelly onto her belly. "You weren't kiddin."

The doctor turns on the ultrasound machine and types Maddie's name, age, and about how far along she is into the monitor.

The doctor massages Maddie's belly with the wand.

"See that there? That round spot about the size of saucer? That's the amniotic sac. And that little lima bean looking creature is your baby."

Maddie beams, and we smile at each other.

"That little round sac beside the baby is the umbilical cord," the doctor explains as she continues moving the wand and points at the screen. "The baby at this stage of the game has eyelids, earlobes, hands; it's really growing every day. Let's see if we can find a heartbeat."

"Well, darn. I was hopeful that we could see the chambers of the heart beating…oh, oh, oh, look at that. There it is. I just had to find the right spot." Amazement in all our faces. "Did you see that movement?"

Disappointment registers on Maddie's face. "What? Are you shitting me? I didn't see anything."

"Your baby just moved."

Astonished, we witness Sprout wiggle inside its little home.

Tears of joy creep from the corner of my eye, and I try to hide the fact that I am so moved. Crying and laughing at the same time, Maddie looks over at me and grabs my hand, "Did you see that, Cal? That is a freakin' miracle."

"Let's make an appointment for four weeks from now. By then we should see a lot more movement," the doctor says while wiping the jelly from Maddie's abdomen and the ultrasound wand. "Congratulations, Maddie. I'm sure that little nugget's daddy will certainly be happy to hear the news," the doctor proclaims as she walks out the door.

"Can you believe that shit?" Maddie says, annoyed. "How does she know there's a daddy?"

"Um, Mad, do I have to explain this to you…really?" Maddie seems to reflect for a moment, then turns to me and laughs.

"Funny. No, Cal. I mean, it's pretty presumptuous of her to think I still have a man in my life."

All humor ceases. "Yeah, that's true," I pause. "But you have a best friend to help you. That counts for something, doesn't it?" I drape my arm around her shoulder, "Let's go home and celebrate. Your little nugget is sprouting!!"

"No more ice cream. I think I've eaten my weight in that deliciousness these past few months."

"What about a shake? It's not like eating ice cream from a bowl. It's more like a beverage."

Pulling out of the doctor's building her voice is wistful, "Mmmmm, shakes."

CHAPTER 12
Callie

Weeks go by with many phone calls from Charlie. Maddie and I are living in our happy little bubble with Sprout growing rapidly in Maddie's belly. The baby bump is just starting to form, and her next visit to the doctor is quickly approaching. Standing in front of the mirror in the bathroom in her underwear, she asks, "Do my boobs look big to you?"

"That's a loaded question."

"Come on. Tell me the truth."

"You had big boobs before."

"You're not answering the question," she says, viewing her body from all angles.

"Honestly? You won't be offended?"

"Just tell me."

"Hey, boobs are like soda. Nobody likes them flat." Chuckling, I continue, "Yeah, your boobs are big. I have a slight case of boob envy. I'm not gonna lie. Besides, they're supposed to be big."

"Yeah, but I'm not growing an army. There's only one in there."

"Well, it'll be a very well fed kid. Hey, I have something I've wanted to do for a long time. Are you up for an adventure?"

"As long as it's not anything physical, then yes."

"Cool. I was hoping you would say that. I've made an appointment for us at one o'clock today to see a psychic."

"What? Are you outta your freakin' mind? You believe in that shit?"

"There's been a lot of weird stuff going on in my world the past few years that I'd like to know more about. I'd like to see if this woman has any insight. Besides, it's a dreary Saturday afternoon. What else are we going to do?"

"Taking a nap is at the top of my list."

"Come on. If nothing more, it'll be entertaining."

I have no idea how entertaining it's going to be; I just feel the need to have some questions answered. The closer we get to our destination, the more agitated Maddie becomes. In turn, this makes me nervous.

"Would you stop fidgeting? You're making me nervous."

"You have to admit, this isn't the most normal thing to do. I mean, who does this? I think you've lost your mind."

"That can be the first question you ask her," I point out, trying to relieve the tension in the car.

"She's just gonna be some quack ready to make an easy buck like those people on psychic hotline. 'I see a male coming forward. His name begins with an M or a W or a T. Could be an older male. Could be a younger male.'" She changes her voice to sound elderly, "My dog Sammy died six years ago." "Yes, that's it, Sammy," she says, laughing.

"That may be, but I've been curious to check one out, and she comes highly recommended."

"By who? Seriously, who recommends shit like this?"

"My friend, Natasha, at work."

"Hmm. Okay, I'll keep an open mind. I just can't promise to keep it open forever."

We parallel park on the cobblestones of South Main Street in St. Charles and walk a block to Lora's door. I press the buzzer, the latch releases, and we enter. The smell of incense hits my senses, immediately reminding me of Aunt Marilyn.

The second door on the right is ajar. We knock, announcing our arrival. As we walk into the alcove, the light dims and the buzz of the fluorescent bulb crackles. The tinkling sound of wind chimes creates a melodic tune. "Welcome, ladies. Please come in," Lora greets us. "Please take a seat and make yourselves comfortable. Would you like a glass of water before we begin?"

"Do you have anything stronger?" Maddie replies, causing Lora to glance down at Maddie's belly.

"She's kidding. Water would be great, thanks."

Placing a glass by her side, she asks, "Who would like to go first?"

"Seeing as it was her idea," Maddie points at me, "let her go first. I'll wait here sipping on my water, psyching myself up."

"There are some magazines on the stand to your left if you'd like some reading material. We'll be about forty-five minutes."

"I knew you were going to say that," Maddie says sarcastically.

I follow Lora through a doorway, draped with hanging beads, to the back of her building. Parting the beads sounds like scattering a handful of marbles on a linoleum floor.

"Have a seat," Lora instructs me. We sit opposite each other in two oversized, plush loveseats, face to face.

"So I feel as though you are in need of guidance."

"I have some questions, yes."

"What can I help you with?" Lora asks as she curls her legs underneath her on the couch. Her eyes never leave mine. I feel as though she never blinks.

"There's an incident that still haunts me. It happened years ago. I was out for a run. It was raining and a truck came down the road." As I continue, Lora begins nodding her head. "I was pushed off the road. Wasn't I?"

"You were."

"Do you know by whom?"

"By your guardian angel."

"For real?" A prickly sensation erupts as the sweat begins to bead on my neck.

"Yes, for real," she laughs. "Tyler was there to move you. Does that make sense?"

"Uh, yes."

"He's smiling right now at the mention of his name," she says as she closes her eyes. "He wants you to know that he's watching out for you and his little brother."

Stunned, I don't know if I can find my voice. Then I manage a weak, "Wyatt?"

"Yes, you two aren't seeing eye-to-eye right now, and that bothers Tyler, but he understands. This will pass in time," she says while opening her eyes again.

"I'm feeling an older woman figure very strongly around you. Is this someone who's passed?"

"I'm not sure. I don't know of any relatives that have passed yet."

"It starts with an M."

Reminded of the conversation I just had with Maddie, I suppress a giggle. "Marilyn?"

"Yes, that's it. Is she a grandmother or mother?"

"She's my aunt."

"She's definitely watching over you. She's your guardian here on earth."

"Does she talk to...um...spirits?"

Laughing, Lora says, "Yes, she does."

"Do you know who it is?"

"Well, Travis is barking in my ear about being the last person in the world who was told about the baby."

"Seriously?"

"He says he's over it now, but he was really upset that Marilyn didn't tell him about her situation."

Closing her eyes again, she says, "I see a giant, lovable man in your life right now. Does that make sense?"

"Yes."

"Just recognize that I'm affirming the fact that he loves you, though he isn't the love of your life."

Not liking where this is going, I comment, "I love *him*. I feel like he's the guy for me. I can't see anyone else out there to take his place."

Frowning, she says, "I see. I'm just telling you what vision is presented to me." Thunder reverberates through the walls. The soft sound of falling rain begins.

She continues with my reading, saying things that seem unoriginal—I will work with children, I will witness a wedding soon—things that could be attributed to anyone. Soon my reading ends and it is time to send Maddie in.

"I do have one question," I announce as I am being led to the door. "I was at the Friends of kids with Cancer fashion show, and one model told me I had a shadow standing behind me during the show. Who was that?"

"As I mentioned before, you have a guardian angel who watches over you. Next, please," she says as she shuttles me through the door.

"Good luck, Mad. I hope you have a better reading than I did."

"Oh, great, nothing like a little pressure. We'll need to go get a big fat decaf coffee after this."

"Decaf for you; a stiff drink for me."

Slowly she walks through the beads to the waiting Lora. Twenty minutes pass. A half hour passes. Now we are approaching an hour, and I am beginning to worry. Then the beads part and Maddie, with a flushed face, emerges. Lora hands each of us a business card and wishes us peace and prosperity. Without a word, we walk out to the cobblestone street. I decide to head to the Lewis and Clark restaurant and belly up to the bar.

"One decaf coffee with cream and sugar and one vodka and soda, please." I say to the bartender. "So which one of us is going to start?"

"Since you went first, you start," Maddie suggests. I rehash all that was divulged to me on that loveseat. Soon it is Maddie's turn.

The bartender brings over our drinks, and we each take a sip and gather our thoughts before Maddie begins.

"She said she saw a pink cloud, but that the little girl wasn't ready to come down."

Feeling numb, I respond, "Really? What else did she say?"

"She said she had a 'bad feeling' about the father of my child, which wigged me out."

"Did she give specifics?"

"No, but she said that he's having problems with illegal substances and to be very careful now that he lives nearby. What the hell is that supposed to mean? I'm surprised you didn't hear me in the waiting room when I said, 'get the fuck out. He lives in freaking Connecticut.'"

"Yeah, but he's hanging around here. Don't forget, he just did a number on our front lawn." Just talking about it causes my body to inadvertently, convulse. I am beginning to think this Lora is legit. Looking at Maddie, I can see there is more that needs to be said. "What is it?"

"Lora seemed very sad when she asked about the baby. I asked her why. 'This baby girl isn't meant for this earth,' she said. I was like, what the fuck? I didn't think these nut jobs could say anything bad is going to happen. What if she's right? What if she doesn't…" Maddie trails off, lost in thought.

"This was meant to be a fun little excursion for the day; something to take your mind off of things. We need to go watch a funny movie or listen to some stand-up. Something…" I can feel the weight of the psychic readings pressing down on us like a lead blanket

CHAPTER 13
Callie

As the weeks pass, the conversations we had with Lora seem to fade and we're back into our routine. Maddie finds part-time work at a sandwich shop, which keeps her busy from ten to two Monday through Friday. I am thankful for that. This gives her a chance to get out of her head and gives her a reason to get up in the morning.

"Hey, Callie, you have a phone call from your roommate. It sounds kinda urgent," Trevor declares.

Feeling anxious, I take the phone call at the receptionist's desk under the chandelier of bubbles. "Hello?"

"Cal, he's here."

"Who's here?"

"Frankie," she says with a bit of panic.

"At the sandwich shop?"

"Yes. I swear it was him."

"Are you sure? It's been almost a month since he came out here. Surely he's back home by now."

"I promise I saw his car drive slowly by the shop. I'd know his car anywhere."

"I don't doubt that, but it seems awfully strange. How would he even know where you work?"

"What if he's been following me? Have you ever had the feeling that someone is watching you? I've had that feeling for several days. What do I do?"

"Can you have one of the guys walk you out to your car when you leave?"

Sounding like a child, she whispers, "I'm scared."

"You're going to be fine. I'm betting it wasn't even him. You're just a little bugged out from that Lora chick. Just have someone walk you to your car, and I'll be home by five. I'll see if I can get off a little early to be on the safe side, okay?"

Hesitantly, she says, "okay," and hangs up the phone.

What if he has *been watching her and follows her home?* Not paying attention to where I am going, I turn abruptly around a corner, knocking over an IV pole on my way back to the pirate ship. When I try to catch the pole before it comes crashing to the ground, I just make it worse by pushing on it, causing it to knock over a glass pitcher. The glass shrapnel cuts open the unit of blood, causing it to seep out of the bag, all over the ground. Watching this happen as if in slow motion, I see Maddie lying in a pool of blood and it makes my skin crawl.

"I'm so sorry! I'm so, so sorry! I didn't see the IV on my way around the corner. Let me help you clean up," I continue rambling, reaching for napkins from the coffee cart.

Trevor comes to my aid, "Cal, we have protocol to follow when these things happen. It was an accident. We'll clean it up," he assures me while slapping on rubber gloves.

"I'm sorry," I say one last time. I'm pretty shaken up by the time I reach Natasha. "That was the worst."

"Don't worry about it. Accidents happen," Natasha dismisses.

"Yeah, that was bad, but I just had the worst premonition ever." I describe my phone call and vision.

"Whoa. That's your psyche telling you that you need to do something. I'm thinking leaving early is a good idea. I can finish up here by myself. It doesn't look like we're going to be super busy later on anyway. Why don't you leave around four today."

"Okay, thanks."

During my remaining time, I am not fully engaged with the kids and find myself constantly watching the octopus arms tick around the wall clock. By four, I am more than ready to leave. When my last group comes through and are guided off to therapy, I say goodbye and leave.

I am on autopilot during the drive home, feeling as though I have left my body. The car in front of me slows. Seeing the car's brake lights come on ahead of me releases adrenaline into my veins. I am in dire need to get home and see Maddie. *Come on, come ooooon!!* Inching along, I finally get to my exit and enter the apartment complex. Everything seems calm- *the calm before the storm.* I hear voices as I approach the front door. Frankie is inside, and out of control.

In a sinister voice, Frankie barks, "I told you you'd pay for the way you treated me last time. Did you like all my gifts?"

"Frankie, just leave. I'm not going to contact you for any money for the kid, if that's what you're thinking."

"Why should you? It's not my kid."

I walk stealthily closer to Maddie.

Pushing the door open with all my strength, I yell, "Frankie, you're not welcome in my home. Our home. You need to get out before I call the police."

"You're not gonna do that," laughing, he continues, "you can try, but it's not going to work." He is seemingly very amused with himself. I march over to the phone and pick up the receiver to find the line is dead.

Smiling again, Frankie continues, "The phone is dead, just like that little bastard is going to be." Frankie has become a monster. His skin is sallow, his cheekbones sharp, and those crystal blue eyes that once shone bright are clouded and dull. He is out of his mind on something. I call to him as I walk toward Maddie, "Frankie, you don't want to do anything stupid." I speak slowly and deliberately, reaching for the corkscrew that lay on the counter from last night's bottle of wine. He grabs Maddie by the hair and yanks her head back. She begins to whimper. As I lunge at Frankie, the corkscrew lands in the side of his right thigh. In the process, I trip over the purse Maddie must have dropped upon entering the apartment. Frankie laughs as I fall and looks down at his leg. "You think that's gonna stop me?" he says while freeing the corkscrew, still standing with a handful of Maddie's hair. I scream, "Someone help! Call 911! Help us!" I manage to scream a few times as I get up off the floor.

"Shut up!" Pulling Maddie behind him, he slaps me square across the face, causing me to fall once more. He is dragging Maddie behind him on the way out the door when I scream again. My head is spinning with the sound of my pulse pounding in my ears. Sirens shriek in the distance, getting closer, and I'm thankful that this torture will soon end. But as soon as relief floods through my body, the gleam of sunshine reflecting off the rising corkscrew makes my blood go cold. Frankie is on the front lawn with Maddie in his grip. The desperation I see flash across Maddie's face is excruciating as the corkscrew, in one swift movement, penetrates her belly. Maddie doubles over and falls to the lawn as Frankie releases her hair. Watching him rush to his car as the flashing lights arrive, I run to Maddie's side. A puddle of blood surrounds her, and she has gone silent.

Frankie manages to get his car started, peeling out. He is on the road with the cops in pursuit. One officer remains behind to radio for an ambulance. Neighbors have come out of the woodwork to see what all the commotion is about. I run inside to grab a blanket to keep Maddie warm. Returning, I sit and hold her hand until the ambulance arrives. Inside the ambulance, the adrenaline I felt earlier is replaced with shock. "Hang on, Mad. You're gonna be all right. We'll be at the hospital soon, and they're going to get you all fixed up, and Sprout, too," I assure her, caressing her hand with my thumb.

A tear trickles down Maddie's face as she turns away from me. She squeezes my hand, releases it, and begins to sob.

CHAPTER 14
Callie

I'm holding Maddie's hand as they wheel her in for an emergency ultrasound. The dread is palpable. Carefully, the attendants help her move from the wheelchair to the bed while the doctor wheels over the ultrasound machine, briskly. There is a flurry of commotion in the emergency room. Smiling tight-lipped, the doctor rolls up Maddie's top to reveal her black and blue belly. The wound is angry, with puckered skin where the jagged corkscrew was plunged in and removed. I hold my breath. The doctor spreads the jelly on Maddie's belly with the ultrasound wand. The machine comes to life. Tiny little Sprout is on the screen. Everything is there: head, hands, and umbilical cord. I'm hopeful. Continuing to scroll across her belly with the wand, the doctor is in search of life. He finds the four chambers, but says matter-of-factly, "There doesn't appear to be a heartbeat." Letting that sink in for a moment, the shock finally registering on Maddie's face.

"I knew it," Maddie says, staring at her belly, then turning her head away from the screen. Her shoulders begin to tremble, wracked with spasms of grief. Her cries fall in waves followed by tears shed for the unborn child that held promise for her future.

"Would you like to know the sex of the baby?" the doctor asks quietly. Maddie nods, turning her head toward the screen; her eyes intensely following the images on the ultrasound, as they come into view. "These two bright little lines indicate it's a girl."

"My girl," Maddie whispers to the screen as she reaches out to touch it briefly, then places her hand on her belly below the wand.

"I'm very sorry. It looks as though the placenta was ruptured during the attack." Cleaning off the wand and her belly, he unrolls her shirt and says that she can either deliver the baby and let nature takes its course, or he can perform a D & C. She chooses the latter. "Okay. We'll get this procedure taken care of this evening," he says, tapping her knee.

Back home, the light on my answering machine glows with multiple messages. It appears the apartment manager fixed our phone line while we were at the hospital. Thank God for small favors. Charlie called three times. By the third message, he informs me that he is calling my parents. It isn't like me to not return his calls. He must have called my parents immediately after hanging up, because the very next phone message is from my mom.

"Callie, this is Mom. Please give me a call. I just got off the phone with Charlie, and he is worried sick about you. He said he's tried calling numerous times and you haven't returned his calls. Please, when you get this message, please call me."

On the first ring, my mom picks up the phone. "Callista, sweetheart, are you all right? I've been so worried about you."

"Mom, I'm fine, but Maddie isn't." I give my mom the details. She listens quietly without interruption until I am done.

"My word. Will she be coming home tonight?"

"No. The doctor wants her to rest and to make sure she is healing properly from her wound and from the D & C. My heart just breaks for her."

"There really are no words right now. You just need to be there for her. You need to be the strong one."

"I know. I'm gonna take a shower and get to bed. It's been a long exhausting day."

"I bet it has. I'll bring some dinner over for you later."

"You don't have to do that. I have food here to eat. Thanks, though."

"Are you sure? Do you want to come stay here tonight so that you're not alone?"

"No, thanks. I was talking to the police at the hospital, and they said that they have Frankie. It seems he led them on a high-speed chase and his car went off the road, straight into a tree. They say they don't know if he's going to make it. They're doing a toxicology report that won't be out for a few weeks. Good night, Mom. Love you."

"Love you too."

After my shower, I thought I would call Charlie. For now, I let the hot water run over me. The thought of how awful this day has been makes me tremble. *I really wish Charlie were here.* I turn the shower off, wipe off the steam-covered mirror, and look at my reflection. There is a bright red handprint on my left cheek, reminding me of a similar handprint on my skin years ago. *Where were you when I needed you today, Tyler?* The phone ringing makes me jump. Wrapped in a towel, I run out to the kitchen to pick up the line.

"Cal, are you okay? You've had my stomach in knots all day. What's going on out there that you can't pick up the phone and call me back? You should have been home from work hours ago."

"Frankie was here."

"What? What happened?" Rehashing the story one last time I make sure to divulge every detail.

"Oh, Cal. I'm so sorry to hear about Maddie. Is she still at the hospital?"

"Yep, for a few more days."

"Right. Then I'm coming out. Nothing you say will make me stay away."

"Please come out."

Silence

"I'll be there tonight."

Charlie knocks on the door quietly at first, then more loudly the longer he waits. I am not sleeping soundly, and by the third knock, I am at the door.

"Charlie," I exclaim, jumping into his arms and immediately being reduced to tears.

"Shhh, I'm here now. You're going to be okay," he coos. Quietly, he says, "Hey, I'm here. You're safe now," closing the door behind him with his foot. We shuffle to the couch without letting go of each other. At the couch, he picks me up and sits me on his lap, wrapping his arms around me. Slowly, the tears diminish. Handing me a tissue from the side table, he runs the back of his hand over my left cheek, then down my back. "You feel better?" Nodding, I give a big sniff.

"It's late. You need some sleep," he says, kissing my inflamed cheek.

Going to bed, I want to feel connected to something. I *need* to feel connected. Under the covers, he rolls into me and drapes his arm over my shoulder, spooning. Feeling his warmth, smelling his fragrance pulls me in. I roll over to face him and initiate a kiss. It is pressing, and he can sense my urgency. Slowly removing my t-shirt, he gently pulls me into a passionate embrace. Feeling his desire resonate, we make love intensely until we are spent. The feelings of fear and trepidation from the day are gone, and I am able to fall into a deep sleep.

"Welcome home!" Charlie cheers as we walk through the door two days later. Maddie looks solemn but tries her best to seem pleased with the reception.

"I made some dinner for us and bought a bottle of wine."

"I'm not hungry, thanks." Walking past everyone into her room, Maddie closes the door.

Charlie looks worried and says, "Was it something I said?"

"No. I think she just needs some time. I'll go check on her in a little bit. Let's eat while everything is hot. Have you been home awhile?" I ask, pouring a glass of wine for Charlie and me.

"Yes. I gotta head back tomorrow afternoon, though. That three day leave put me behind on my work schedule."

"You didn't have to come out here." I feel a bit defensive now.

"Hey, I came out here because I was worried about you and Maddie. I wanted to," he says with a smile as he continues to eat his dinner.

"I'm glad you came over. I've missed you. I just don't want to keep you from your work."

"It was an emergency. I would drop anything for you. You should know that by now."

"I do. Thanks." I move the food around my plate lazily. I'm not really in the mood to eat. Pushing away from the table, I say, "I'm going to go check on Maddie." As I walk past Charlie at the table, he grabs my hand. "Callie, you know I would drop everything for you, right? You're that important to me."

CHAPTER 15
Jimmy

"Do you take this woman to be your lawfully wedded wife?"

"I do." Jimmy watches Riley as she stands before him in a simple cream-colored dress, carrying a bouquet of sunflowers.

"And Riley Annette Stewart, do you take James Allen Lamply to be your lawfully wedded husband?" Looking at her radiant husband to be, dressed in a navy suit, white shirt and navy tie, Riley says, "I do."

"You may kiss the bride. May I be the first to introduce Mr. and Mrs. James Lamply." The sparse clapping comes from the three people waiting their turn to be married and the clerk from whom they had obtained the marriage license the day before. Holding hands as they leave, they don't let the small reception dampen their mood. Their mood dampens later, while calling home to make the big announcement.

"Hi, Mom. Are you and Dad sitting down? I have something to share with you both."

"Hold on, Jimmy, let Dad pick up the bedroom phone so that he can hear it, as well."

"Okay, I'm on now. So, what's this big news all about?" They're probably thinking that Jimmy has received a promotion at work and is starting to climb the corporate ladder.

"Riley and I got married today." The line goes silent.

"You did what?"

"We got married today. We've been living together for a few years and felt it was the right time to make it official."

"Was anyone there to witness this?" Mom asks in a biting tone.

"No, we decided we wanted it to be all about us. Just us." Feeling a little annoyed that they still had yet to congratulate Riley and himself, Jimmy said, "You could at least say congrats or something."

"Well, congratulations. I hope you are both blissfully happy together," Mom says with a slightly sarcastic tone, "Richard, say something."

"Yes, what your mother said. I have to say I'm a little shocked and disappointed that you didn't even give us the option to witness this very important milestone."

"It's just a piece of paper." Jimmy says, though deep down he doesn't feel this way at all. Surprisingly, since the ceremony he has been wishing for a do-over with all the fanfare. He hadn't expected to feel this way, but he does. What's done is done now.

"Where is the blushing bride?"

"She's right here beside me."

"Pass her the phone so that I can say congratulations to her as well."

Jimmy passes the phone. Mom and Dad say what they are supposed to say. It all feels wrong. Riley passes the phone back; Jimmy says goodbye and hangs up.

"Well, that went about as well as expected. I am surprised that Mom didn't cry, though. She's usually good for that."

"Give them time. They'll come around. Maybe you should call your sister and tell her yourself so she doesn't have to hear about it from your parents."

"Good point." Jimmy waits for Callie to pick up the phone, but surprisingly, Charlie answers.

"Oh, hey, I must have the wrong number."

"Jimmy?" Charlie questions.

"Yeah, who's this?"

"Charlie. I haven't talked to you in ages. How's it going, man? Do you need Callie? Let me see if she's up. Hang on a sec." Jimmy hears the phone clack on a hard surface and then retreating footsteps, a gentle knock, and a door opening. A moment later Charlie is back on the phone. "Sorry, man, Callie's asleep. She and Maddie have had the worst week ever..." Charlie fills Jimmy in on all the upheaval in Callie's life lately, including the nightmare that Maddie just went through.

"But she's all right?"

"Yes, she's going to be fine, as is Maddie, though Maddie may be scarred for life. Want me to pass along a message to Cal for you?"

Jimmy tells Charlie all that's happened to *him* in the last week.

"Whoa! Way to go, man! Congratulations!"

"Thanks. You're more excited than my parents were when they heard the news."

"*Heard* the news? They didn't go up for the wedding?" Jimmy explains how it all happened so quickly.

"Well, we need to come up for a visit and celebrate!"

"Any time! The little woman and I would love to have some house guests."

"I'll talk to Callie and see what we can figure out. I'm kinda stuck going home for the holidays, but sometime soon would be great. It was good talking to you, Jimmy. Take care." As Charlie hangs up the phone, he can't push aside the feeling of jealousy—jealousy over the fact that Jimmy has a soulmate to march through life with. Charlie knows in his heart that he wants that for himself. Someday. When the time is right, perhaps he and Callie can tie the knot and live happily ever after. Right now, living happily every day works for him.

"Rye, you're not going to believe this…" Jimmy relays the conversation he just had. "What do you think about having my family up for Thanksgiving? It might force us to spruce up the cabin."

Feeling hurt, Riley replies, "What do you mean? I've worked really hard keeping a tidy house. We bought some furniture, and I feel like I've made this into a cute little home.'"

Pulling her into his arms, he says, "You've done a great job, but have you noticed that the screened-in porch has holes in it and the roof leaks? All the decorating in the world isn't going to fix that. I need to call some professionals to help. We have a little less than a month, but I think we can do it."

"Where will they all sleep?"

"Have you forgotten that my grandparents live in Franklin, as do all my other relatives? My aunt and uncle live two doors down, though I don't think they are really up to having houseguests. I know Aunt Marilyn would love to have my sister, Mom, and Dad at her house. We'll just host Thanksgiving dinner here. We'll make it like a little wedding reception for ourselves."

"I like parties."

He kisses her on the tip of her nose and releases her. "That you do, and that's one of the reasons why I love you."

CHAPTER 16
Callie

"Married? *Married*? Are you kidding me? They just up and went to the justice of the peace without anyone around? What's he thinking? I bet she put him up to it. She seems to have mind control over him." I am basically talking to myself, pacing the apartment as Charlie sits at the kitchen table, amused.

"You can't blame the guy. He's been in love with her for years. Don't you think it's about time?"

"Oh, great. Take his side. Perfect."

"He said we should come up for a visit sometime." Charlie stands up from the table and walks back and forth from the bedroom to the kitchen, where he finishes packing his duffel bag with his things in preparation for the flight home. "He mentioned Thanksgiving but said he had to clear it with Riley first."

"See! Of course he does."

"I don't know what you're getting all upset about. It's not like he moved out of the country or anything. He *is* only one flight away." Looking at the clock on the stove, he informs me it is time to go.

"If you do go to Vermont over Thanksgiving, maybe you can make a stop over in Connecticut?"

Smiling now, I say, "I'll see what I can do," and kiss Charlie firmly against the lips. "Have a safe flight. Thank you doesn't cut it, but thank you for coming out to take care of Maddie and me."

"There's no place I'd rather be. Tell Maddie goodbye for me when she returns from her doctor appointment. When does she start back up at work?"

"I think next week. They've been really good to her since hearing about the attack. She seems to be getting stronger and stronger each day. See you soon and call me when you get home." With one last kiss, Charlie is gone. My mind is reeling with the news of my brother and Riley. Then, as my mind often does, it shifts gears and starts to dwell on Maddie. Since hearing that Frankie died in the hospital, she's had mixed emotions. One day she's crying, thinking about him, and the next she's calling him every name in the book. Her emotions are all over the board. Walking back into the bathroom to shower and get ready for work, I continue to think about Frankie. His toxicology report was impressive: his blood alcohol level was point two. Cocaine and methamphetamines were also found. That was some combination. The toxicologist said that if the tree that he ran into hadn't killed him, this lethal combination would have.

Maddie has been going in for checkups to make sure her physical wound is healing, and she is going to see a psychologist to make sure her wounded spirit is doing the same. *She's one tough cookie. I have no doubt she'll be stronger than ever after this whole fiasco is over and done with.*

Arriving at work this morning, I wonder which kids I will see today, and to my delight, Pheonix is at the table. As I follow Natasha to the art closet, she says to me that she is cutting the apron strings.

"By cutting the apron strings, you mean what exactly?" I ask anxiously.

"Pheonix is now your kiddo. You're on your own. I submitted the proper forms to the powers that be and informed them that you no longer have to be under my wing. You have proven to me that you are fully capable of working one on one with children yourself. I've mailed you a copy of my report." With a little smile, she adds, "You should be more excited. You don't have to follow my lead anymore."

"I am excited, but I'm nervous. Are you sure I'm ready?"

"I'm sure." I follow her to the art table. "Pheonix, Callie's going to be working with you from now on. Nothing is going to change around here, just that if you need anything, Callie is your girl. I'll be right here working, as well, just with other kids. Sound good?"

"Sure," Pheonix smiles, turning her attention back to the craft at hand. She's working on a pencil sketch of a field with long grass. There's a drawing of a child that looks like it may be her and a tree with its branches bending toward the ground.

"Pheonix, can you tell me a little about the picture?"

Without stopping the motion of her pencil, she describes the tree as being sad and that the child is a little boy. "He's waiting for someone. See here, he's looking in the direction of the brook."

"Interesting. I don't see a brook on the page."

"I haven't drawn it yet," she says with a smile.

"Well, what you've done so far is beautiful. I can't wait to see the finished product."

The rest of the morning passes a little slowly. We make small talk, then Phoenix leaves for her infusion and I am left to my thoughts, wondering if I will do right by her. A tug on my hand pulls me from my thoughts. It's Chunk.

"Callieflower, can you help me with something?" Staring down at this chubby toddler, I think surely I have misunderstood him.

"Hi, Chunkie, what can I help you with?" I ask, as I crouch down to be eye-to-eye with him.

"Can I have a piece of 'struction paper?'"

"Sure. What color would you like?"

"Purple, please."

"You got it." As I search the cabinet for the color purple I notice he has followed me. Reaching up to the top shelf, I ask, "Chunk, what did you call me when you came in?"

"Callie."

"No, before that. You called me Callieflower. How come?"

"I hate the taste of cauliflower. It makes me want to throw up. My mama makes me eat it," he says, making a face. He continues on his rant about strongly disliking cauliflower, so I decide not to press the topic. How odd to hear that term again after all these years. Handing Chunk the purple paper, we sit down at the table and start our project together, but it is hard to keep my mind on the task at hand. I haven't heard anything about Wyatt in a long time, and I begin to invent what his life might be like right now. He's probably in a relationship with some pretty thing he met at the University of Rhode Island. He's probably brought her home to meet his parents and they love her. Maybe they moved in together or maybe they've been married.

"Callie. Uh, Callie. Earth calling Callie," Natasha says, trying to get my attention.

"Yeah?"

"Chunk, why don't you go wash your hands and get all that glue off before your mama comes to get you."

She directs her comments to me now. "You were deep in thought." Feeling my face flush, I look down at the table where

Chunk emptied the entire contents of the glue bottle and began finger painting.

"I'm sorry about that." I stand to get paper towels and rags to clean off the table and continue, "Chunk said something earlier. He called me by my childhood nickname—given to me by a neighbor—which I haven't heard in years. It just got me thinking…"

"Huh, what was it?"

"Callieflower."

"Aww, that's cute."

I explain who called me that and why.

"So you don't know what happened to this Wyatt guy?"

"Not exactly. My parents get Christmas cards from his parents and they always include a picture and a letter. I know that he graduated from the University of Rhode Island with a degree in business and that he found a job in Rhode Island as a Business Systems Analyst. I think he's doing pretty well for himself. Other than that, there hasn't been any mention of a wife so I guess he's still single. My brother says that sometimes when Wyatt goes home to visit, he'll run into him at the grocery store. It's so weird."

"What is?"

"To think he's moving on with his life. Being a grown up and all. It's just weird to think about."

With a chuckle, Natasha moves on to another child who has entered the room. Her last remark strikes me.

"We all move on. We find our path and keep moving in this world. If not, we become stagnant. We have to be allowed to blossom and grow."

CHAPTER 17
Callie

"Do you think I'm not allowing you to grow?"

"Uh, I'm not sure how to answer that. Where is this going?" Charlie asks hesitantly on the other line.

"I just don't want to be keeping you from anything. You should be able to blossom and grow," I say, feeling very serious.

"Cal, if this is one of those times where you start thinking abstractly…"

"Never mind. I was just thinking out loud," I admit, shaking the thoughts from my head.

"How's Maddie?"

"She's starting to emerge again. I'm taking her out tonight when I get off the phone with you."

"Oh, well, don't let me keep you. Tell her I said hello and that she has my permission to let loose tonight. Hey, before I forget. Did you figure out when you're leaving for Vermont for Thanksgiving?"

"Yeah, probably the Wednesday before. It doesn't look like I'm driving up from Connecticut, sorry."

Sounding disappointed he said, "It's okay. We'll see each other soon enough."

"Goodnight, Charlie. Talk to you soon."

"That sounded like a miserable conversation." Walking in from her room, Maddie continues to vocalize, "Why don't you move back to Connecticut already? You look so miserable after you get off the phone with him. You look as bad I used to feel living at home."

"I can't. I'm trying to make some money so that if and when we decide to live together, I'll be able to pay my own way. It just stinks waiting in the meantime." I sigh, "What do you feel like doing tonight? Charlie says you should let loose tonight."

"I got my big girl panties on. I'm ready."

"Atta girl."

A short drive later, we arrive at Harry's West ordering drinks and appetizers. It's not too busy yet, so we have a moment to talk.

"How'd your parents handle the phone call about everything with Frankie?"

"Oh, greeeaat," she exaggerates. "That had to be the hardest phone call I ever had to make. They threatened to drive out here and bring me home, but I told them that I didn't want them to do that. It is my turn to live my life and get back on the right track my way. I have to figure this out on my own, or else how am I going to be able to live with myself? I don't always want to be dependent on someone. I mean, for God's sake, I'm 22 years old. It's time I figure this shit out." Looking frustrated, she takes the last sip of her beer and orders another. "Man, this tastes so good," she says, rolling her eyes back. "I didn't think I'd miss drinking as much as I did. There's nothing like the taste of a cold beer at the end of a hard day."

"Wine tastes pretty good, too, if you ask me," I offer, raising my glass to my lips.

"So what's going on with you and Charlie? Everything kosher between you two?"

"Seems to be."

"Not for nothin', but are you ever going to move in with him?"

"It's possible. We haven't really discussed it yet. We'll get to it." Changing the subject I ask, "Mad, do you think you'll try for another kid someday?"

"Definitely. I really do wanna be a mom some day. Little Sprout was something. I have to say I feel pretty empty without her wiggling around in there," she admits woefully.

"One day you'll make a great mom."

"I have some work to do to get my hot piece of ass again. Thanks to you, I've put on about ten pounds."

"Me?"

"Yeah, you were the enabler with the damn ice cream," she says, with a smirk. "So, what are your plans for the holiday coming up?"

"It seems since my brother got married and all…"

"That's some shit, huh?"

"Now my brother's all grown up and wants to host Thanksgiving. Isn't that something?"

"So you're going to Vermont for Thanksgiving. Really?"

"Yeah, why do you have such a strange look on your face. Like I'm lying or something."

"You haven't thought this through at all?"

"If you mean that Wyatt will be up there, then yes, I have thought it through. We don't know he'll be there over Thanksgiving. For all I know, he has a girlfriend now and is spending the holiday at her house."

"Mmhmm. Have you told Charlie your plan?"

"Yes. Geez, what do you think I'm gonna do up there? I'm happily with Charlie now. Take it easy. I haven't seen Wyatt in years. I've moved on, and I'm sure I'm the last person he wants to see anyway. What are you doing for the holiday? Is the warden condemning you to house arrest?"

"Something like that," she says with a giggle. "They bought me a ticket home. Surprisingly, it's not one way."

"Good. I'm sure your parents will be very happy to have you safe and sound under their roof for a while. Maybe you'll be able to get some much-needed rest. I'll call you over the holiday to give you a reprieve."

"Well, hell-oo, handsome." Swiveling in her bar stool, she follows a tall, olive skinned fellow with a beautifully chiseled face past our seats to where he meets some friends in the back.

"I'm glad to see you're returning to normal."

"It's not like I've dried up and withered away. It might be a while before I get back in the saddle again, if you know what I mean, but it doesn't hurt to look."

"I know what you mean." Looking toward the bartender, I raise a glass to indicate that we are empty.

CHAPTER 18
Callie

Thankfully, I know my limit and start drinking water around nine o'clock. Maddie, however, does not, and continues to drink. She is ready to tie one on, and frankly, I think she deserves to let off some steam. I have to intervene, however, when she walks up to the eye candy in the back of the room and notice him starting to get handsy with her. She is oblivious in this state. I tell the young man that she needs to get home. He doesn't seem too bothered and quickly turns back to his conversation with his friends.

Getting Maddie in the car is a totally different matter. By the time we reach the car, she has stopped to throw up once in the bushes in the front of the bar, and a second time in a planter next to my car. On the ride home, she has to stick her head out the window to keep herself from vomiting. The fresh air seems to help somehow.

This is going to be a rough morning. Thankfully, Maddie has the late shift at the sandwich shop. I, on the other hand, have to get up early. Not feeling one hundred percent myself, I make sure to get the large travel coffee mug filled before leaving the apartment.

"Whoa. What happened to you last night?" Natasha looks on in wonder.

"Maddie was ready for a night on the town. I helped her accomplish that. I have to say she did a great job." Feeling a bit queasy at the mention of last night, I sit down. "I'm betting Maddie is much worse off than I today."

"You haven't seen her yet?"

"Nope, she doesn't have to work until two. Lucky duck."

"I wish I could have slept in today," Natasha says while finishing her coffee and throwing her paper cup away. "I could've used the extra sleep."

In walks a little boy named Clark who I've seen come in a few times to work with Natasha. Quietly, he enters our little pirate ship and begins working on a drawing of a tree using felt tipped markers. Natasha asks gentle questions as he moves along, "What kind of tree is this?"

Clark answers, "I'm not sure. I think it's going to be summertime." He continues with a brilliant sun and green grass but only one lonely dark tree.

"In summer trees are usually full with lush green leaves."

Stopping for a moment to look at what he's drawn, he says, "Well, it's dead."

Looking concerned, she lets him continue.

At the end of the day, Natasha and I walk out to our cars together and discuss our day.

"I think we'll have enough menorahs and wreaths for awards, don't you think?" I ask her quizzically.

"Yep, I think we're in good shape."

Thoughtful for a moment, I ask, "Can you tell me what you saw in Clark's drawing today? I have to admit, I got the willies when he said he was drawing a dead tree."

"He can be very morose at times. He's having a really hard time dealing with his prognosis. It seems he's going to lose his eyesight. He's in the process of learning Braille. His drawings have grown more and more dark these past few weeks. Usually when kids draw a tree, it's an extension of their own person. That's what worries me when he says it's dead."

"Poor kid. It's a reflection of how he's feeling inside, I suppose."

"Right. Usually when a child is working on a tree, on the left side it's the past, and on the right side it's the future."

"Interesting."

"But Clark was working right in the middle of the tree. In the present."

"So right now, he's feeling like he's dying, which in turn is reflected in his drawing? He doesn't really have a choice about his feelings, I guess."

"That's why I feel it's so important that the kids have a choice in the art supplies they use. They don't have a choice in any other part of their lives. I feel like at least I can give them a choice here," Natasha shares.

"That makes sense."

With my keys in one hand, Chinese takeout in the other, and my purse dangling from my arm, I enter our apartment. Closing the door with my foot, I manage to get all the paraphernalia to the kitchen table without dropping a thing.

"That's impressive," Maddie says, looking worse for wear.

"And for my next trick, I'm going to attempt a back handspring, triple sumi with a half twist."

"I'd like to see you try that," Maddie says with a smile. "Smells delicious. I thought I was going to barf at work all afternoon. I think I've made a turn and I'm starting to feel better. I'm actually getting hungry."

"Great, let's eat. How about a glass of wine with dinner?"

Maddie makes a gagging noise. "Nope, not for me."

I set the table with a couple plates, silverware and napkins. I place the food in the center of the table. Maddie gets us each a tall glass of water. We share our days with each other. Maddie produces an envelope with her plane tickets in it.

"See what I got today? I'm headed home the same day you are. Maybe we'll be on the same flight to Connecticut. Have you checked?"

"Not yet. I will, though, and let you know. I hope it works out that way."

The next few weeks pass and Maddie continues to heal. It's nice to see that she is past the dark days for the most part, and she's starting to enjoy life again. The day we are to depart for the east coast arrives, and I am anxious. As luck would have it, Maddie is on the same flight as my parents and me. Once we land in Hartford, Connecticut, Maddie de-planes and we remain behind, continuing on to Vermont.

"Have a safe flight, Schmallie. Happy Thanksgiving."

Giving her a bear hug, I wish her the same. "Don't let the warden keep you down. They're just worried about you. Remember people do love you."

She's off and we're on our way. I feel anxious about renting a car from Burlington airport and driving the remainder of the way to Franklin. It's odd seeing the landscape again after such a long absence. It is still just as beautiful as I remember. Since our move out to Missouri, we haven't made it back. It's going to be great to see Aunt Marilyn, Jimmy and Riley again. We drive the rental up the scenic roads to the town of Franklin and directly to Aunt Marilyn's house. Since Jimmy said his place was too small for everyone, we decided this was best. We're only a few miles from their home. *I've run these roads many times.* Driving into Aunt Marilyn's driveway feels like coming home. Her old farmhouse with the Vermont window is a welcome sight. Her home has been in her family for decades. It has three bedrooms upstairs and one downstairs. Aunt Marilyn sees us drive up and walks out onto the driveway to greet us.

"Aren't you a sight for sore eyes," she says to all of us.

Walking into her welcoming arms, I smell that familiar scent of incense. "It's so good to see you," she says, as her eyes well up.

"It's great to see you, too. It's been way too long. Thank you, so much, for letting us stay with you."

"Are you kidding? I'd be offended if you didn't." My parents have their moment for hellos, and we all walk into the house together. The place hasn't changed in the past few years. I don't know what I was expecting. I do notice that she has rearranged the photographs she had out. The photo of Lilian is prominently poised in front of all the other photos. That makes me smile.

"Can I help you with those bags, Callie?"

"Oh, no, thanks, I can get them. Am I upstairs to the left or the right?"

"To the left. The room with your favorite window," she says with a wink.

Carrying my overnight bag up the stairs, I walk through a cold spot where the air feels as if it has changed. Kind of like walking past a drafty window, yet there is no window nearby. And before I can analyze it any more, it's gone.

As I walk into the room on the left, the floorboards creak with each footfall. The house has to be one hundred years old, at least. The ceiling is low, and on the bed, there is a patchwork quilt with bright pinks, yellows and blues. It reminds me of a child's room. In the corner on a child-sized rocking chair sits a porcelain doll with long blond hair and a pink bow on the top of her head. The thing creeps me out. I've never liked china dolls, and this one...this one makes me feel like I am being watched.

"Um, Aunt Marilyn?" I holler, while keeping my eyes on the doll.

"Yes, what is it, Callie?" she asks, out of breath from rushing to my aid.

"Do you mind taking this doll and putting it somewhere else? I'm sorry to make such a silly request, but these kind of dolls scare me."

Laughing, she picks up the doll and says, "Come on Lilian. Callie doesn't want company." This makes the hair on the back of my neck stand straight up.

When we're all settled in, we have a bite to eat at Aunt Marilyn's, then we drive in the rental car to Jimmy and Riley's. I start getting a panicky feeling as we drive past the old vegetable stand on Riley Road. Turning left onto Camp Road, the gravel spits out under the tires. I can't tell if I am going to faint or throw up. My nerves are on fire. From the top of Camp Road, I see the old turquoise camp, and at the end of the road next to the Black Woods is that familiar red pickup truck.

CHAPTER 19
Callie

"Knock, knock, knock, I wonder if anyone is home at the Lamplys' house?" my mom sings.

With a squeak of the screen door, Jimmy lets us in.

Jimmy hugs each who enters: Mom, Dad, and myself. When I get close enough to him, I say, "I hope your wife is decent."

Pinching me on the back of my arm, he says, "She's fixing drinks, ya' ignoramus." Laughing now, I turn to find Riley in front of the sink pulling ice cubes from an old ice cube tray—the kind with the metal lever down the center with separators for the cubes. With some difficulty, she manages to pull the lever up and out pop the cubes, most of which fall to the floor.

"Do you have wine? I'll have wine, so there's no need to put ice cubes in my glass, thanks." Walking over, I crouch to the floor, help Riley pick up the ice cubes and put them in the sink. "Congratulations, Riley. We're now sisters. Well, sisters-in-law, but sisters none the less." She wipes her hands on a paper towel and we embrace.

"Let's have a toast to the newlyweds," Dad says, raising his glass in the air.

"To Jimmy and Riley."

"To Jimmy and Riley," we repeat and drink thirstily.

The evening is relaxing after Mom finishes scolding them both. Her eyes are filled with tears as she explains how much she wishes she could have seen them walk down the aisle together. Once she says her peace, all is forgiven, and several bottles of wine later, it's time to drive back to Aunt Marilyn's. I can see that Dad is enjoying himself a bit too much, so I start in with water several hours before we get on the road. I have a hard time wrangling the keys from him but manage to do so and corral everyone in the car.

"Thanks, guys, we'll see you tomorrow. What time do you want us over?"

Riley, standing at the door with one arm around Jimmy's waist and the other holding a fresh vodka tonic, calls out, "How about eleven. I'll have some appetizers ready, and then we'll eat around two. Sound good?"

"Perfect. See you then."

Backing out of the driveway, and slowly down the gravel road, I see the Wilsons' house lit up like a jack-o-lantern. I can just make out people in the front room behind the bay window.

Taking a left and travelling up the windy road brings me back to Riley Road. One last right and we're back at Aunt Marilyn's. She's waiting up for us with the porch light on.

Once inside, Mom and Dad go to bed and I sit on the chair closest to Aunt Marilyn.

"Was it a good night?"

"It was. It's just so weird to think they're married now."

"Tyler seems happy."

Wait. What? "Tyler?"

"You couldn't have forgotten about Tyler already, could you?"

"Well, no, but he's been gone a long time. His name rarely comes up around my family."

"He still visits me. Says he's still waiting."

"Waiting for what?" The hair on the back of my neck is standing at attention again.

"Do you know that he and Travis have been so helpful to my Lilian? They've been connected since moving on to the other side."

"Waiting for what, Aunt Marilyn?"

"He says you have a selective memory," she says with a snicker.

Frustration is setting in, "Waiting for what?"

Turning toward me, head tilted to the left as if not understanding the question, she says,

"Waiting for the right decision." She stands. "It's getting late, dear. I best get to bed. Tomorrow is a busy day. Goodnight."

My head is spinning. I slowly turn out the lights and walk up the wooden stairs. Walking across the bedroom's wooden floor produces creaking sounds, as if the pressure of every footfall may cause the floor to collapse, sending me reeling through to the first floor. I quickly change and hop into bed. *I'll brush my teeth in the morning.*

Tap, tap, tap.

Climbing from my bed, I see the most beautiful full moon, its glow creating a breathtaking reflection on the lake. I open my window to see who is making the noise, though I know full well who it is. My heart skips a beat when our eyes meet. I'd recognize those blue eyes anywhere. With outstretched arms, he hands me a bouquet of wildflowers in the most beautiful array of colors. I feel again the cool sensation of being on his fishing boat, traveling at a fast clip to Rock Island in the moonlight. There is a blindfold tied around my eyes, and for a moment, I can't see a thing. I'm frightened, but his soft lips meet mine and all is well. Grabbing my hand, he guides me to the makeshift bed. When he removes the blindfold, I am in awe of the dazzling candles and white gauze curtains attached to each post, floating in the breeze. *I remember this place well.* He takes me into his arms. *I remember his scent.* His next kiss sends ripples of warmth through my body. That familiar tingling sensation creeps into my being, and I am ready for his next move. In a flash, we are on the bed making passionate love. Then a blinding light shines onto us. "Callie?" Charlie utters in disbelief.

"Callie…" The voice grows louder. "Callie." I pull myself out of my haze, feeling disoriented. "Cal, you up?" Mom asks, tapping on my door. "Breakfast is ready."

CHAPTER 20
Callie

Trying to shake the dream I had is almost impossible. I still have a funny feeling in my belly when I strap my shoes on and go for a run through town. I'm going to avoid Camp Road for the time being, at least until it's time to go to Jimmy's. It takes the whole run to clear my head.

"How was your run, dear?" Aunt Marilyn asks, having her coffee at the kitchen table.

"Funny that you should ask. After not sleeping much last night, I had a lot to think about on my run. I just couldn't shut my brain off last night."

"MmmHmmm," Aunt Marilyn muses, eyeing me suspiciously.

"I had the strangest dream. Maybe not a dream…a reenactment of sorts. Something that took place many summers ago." I'm blushing now.

"No need to explain. I think I can figure out whom you were thinking about. It happens when you go back to 'the scene of the crime.' You hold a lot of memories here."

"I had no idea that Wyatt would be on my mind so much. I mean, I realized that I would think about him, but not to the extreme that he'd be working his way into my dreams." Feeling flustered, I continue, "I keep having the feeling that I'm going to run into him while on a run, while down at Jimmy and Riley's, at the grocery store, at the lake, anywhere. How am I supposed to react if that happens? I'm not prepared for this. I had no idea I would be so nervous about it either."

"You two have a history. It's hard not to deny those feelings you had so long ago. He was your first love."

He was my first everything.

"Having firsts with someone is a very powerful thing," she says with a knowing smile, "a lot of emotions are tied up with that. *Did* you run into him on your run this morning? Or at the grocery store, or at the lake?"

"Well...no."

"You seem slightly disappointed."

"I have to admit I am a little bit. When I saw his truck at the Wilsons' house I got that old butterfly bouncing in the pit of my stomach again."

"That's a great feeling," she says wistfully. "Is there something you're worried about?" she asks, concerned.

"No, not really..."

"Callista Lamply, I can tell when you aren't telling me the honest-to-goodness truth, young lady," she teases.

Blushing again, "Yes. I'm worried about how I'll feel. What if my past feelings for him come bubbling up? How am I going to react to that?"

"I guess there's only one way to find out," she says, looking out the front window at the stoplight where that familiar red pickup truck is stopped. I can just make out his blond hair and I feel that old familiar pang. It's stronger than I thought. To make matters worse, there is a passenger with him, a pretty redheaded girl. *That's definitely not his sister.*

Somehow pulled outside, I stand in the driveway. It's like my feet have a mind of their own. I'm trying to get a better look just as the light turns green and his truck rolls past. Our eyes meet.

The squeak of the screen door indicates that Aunt Marilyn is on her way to me. "So, how did that feel?"

Feeling like I want to cry, I mumble, "Terrible."

She puts an arm around me as we stand for a few more minutes quietly in our own thoughts.

"I know what'll make you feel better. After dinner at your brother's house, Aunt Shirley has invited us all over for dessert!"

"We're leaving in a few hours, Cal," Mom hollers out the upstairs window, "don't you think you should shower soon?"

"Be up in a minute."

Aunt Marilyn gives my shoulder a squeeze. "Things have a way of working out in the end. You'll see," she says as she releases my shoulder and walks back inside. *Why do I have the feeling she knows something I don't?*

As I leave the shower, I have the feeling I am being watched again, like someone's eyes are boring right through. *Where's Lilian?* Shaking off the feeling, I get dressed and ready for Thanksgiving. I can smell the stuffing that Aunt Marilyn volunteered to bring to the feast cooking in the oven. It smells divine.

"Need any help with the stuffing? Like maybe a taste tester?"

Laughing out loud, she offers, "Sure, here, take a taste." The spoonful of steaming hot stuffing tastes as good as it smells.

Loading up the car with people and a few side items for the table just feels like the holidays. Our car is happy.

CHAPTER 21
Callie

"Happy Thanksgiving!" Aunt Marilyn hollers to Jimmy and Riley as we walk into the home unannounced. It isn't quite eleven yet, and by the look on Riley's face we shouldn't have rushed.

Frazzled, she asks, "Are you guys always so punctual?"

"It's Thanksgiving, of course we'd be on time. I know how it is timing a meal so that everything is ready at the same time. It can get a little hairy," Mom says cheerfully.

Under her breath, Riley says, "You're not kidding." Her red and white apron is covered with handprints of all the foods she is preparing. Though the house is quite put together, Riley is not.

"Why don't you let me finish up while you go get ready," Jimmy suggests, wiping away some flour from her cheek.

"Good idea. Maybe you can get some volunteers to help out," she says, pouring herself a vodka that she brings to the bedroom.

We all jump in to set the table. Dad pours us all drinks while we wait for the others to arrive.

Justa, my Uncle's dog, arrives before anyone in his group is at the door. He's getting grey around the muzzle and it appears he has a limp. My Uncle Fred and Aunt Shirley follow along with my cousins, John, David, Sally and Steve.

"I hate walking into a place empty handed. Just remember to save some room for dessert later on at my place. I've tried some new recipes today so come prepared to eat." Aunt Shirley instructs.

"Technically, we didn't come empty handed," Uncle Fred corrects, setting down a bottle of cabernet.

"Thanks, Uncle Fred." Turning to Aunt Shirley, Jimmy says, "I'm looking forward to those new recipes tonight." She pinches his cheek and reminds him, "Come hungry."

Soon the small cabin is brimming with relatives. We open the French doors that lead to the screened-in porch since it is an unusually warm November day. We sit outside watching the lake as one can only do up at Lake Carmi.

Dad walks in and turns on football. The fellas retreat to the family room while the ladies all sit in the screened-in porch enjoying the afternoon weather.

"It feels like forever since we've all been together like this. Rit, are your folks coming?" Aunt Marilyn inquires.

"Yes, they should be here shortly." Within minutes, we hear the roar of a car engine and flying gravel. "Sounds like lead-foot Lamply has arrived," Dad announces, fetching a laugh from us all. Nanny and Gramp walk in together carefully as the gravel is uneven and can be easily tripped on. My grandparents appear to be aging before my eyes. Since the scare years ago with Gramp's heart, he's had two bouts of atrial fibrillation, or AFib. "I'm no spring chicken," he says.

When three o'clock rolls around and dinner isn't quite ready we start getting antsy. Holding up two empty gallon jugs Jimmy says, "Why don't you make yourself useful and go fill up these jugs so we have fresh water for the table."

Grabbing the jugs from my brother, I sneer, "Don't let this go to your head," and walk out the door with them. *I know he's enjoying this.* I dismiss the thought; I feel like I am seven again, walking to the water pump for fresh water. What a strange feeling to be doing this as an adult now. A conversation grows louder as I approach the water pump. When I round the corner with the water pump in view, I see who it is and stop dead in my tracks. *Crap! I don't know how to do this. What do I say? How do I strike up a conversation?* The two up ahead stop talking as soon as they hear gravel underfoot. They too have jugs they are filling for the Wilsons' house.

"I didn't realize three o'clock was the designated 'fill your water jug' hour." *What am I saying? Could I be any more lame?* "Fancy meeting you here." *Stop talking.*

"Callie, wow, I did not expect to see you here," Wyatt stammers, looking nervously from me to the red-headed girl next to him.

Thrusting my hand forward and dropping one of the empty jugs in the process, I say, "Hi, I'm Callie, an old friend of Wyatt's."

Taking my hand into her velvety soft hand, she squeezes it gently and says, "It's a pleasure to meet you, Callie. I've heard so much about you."

Giggling nervously, I say, "Don't believe a word of it."

Smiling, she picks up the discarded jug and hands it back to me. "My name is Mary Jane, or MJ as Wyatt likes to call me," she explains, while looking doe eyed at Wyatt. *Oh gawd, has he done a number on this one.*

"It's very nice to meet you, as well. Are you both in town just for the weekend, for the holiday?"

"Yep, Samantha and Brian are here with their son, Tyler. Tommy and Sarah came in this morning, and we're all leaving Sunday evening. How about yourself?" *So civilized.*

"Just for the weekend. I'm leaving Sunday, too."

Uncomfortable silence lingers until Mary Jane breaks it. "Well, Erp, are you ready?" *Did I detect a slight curl of his lip as she called him that?*

"Yep, all full. Time to head back. Have a nice Thanksgiving, Callie. Say hi to the family."

"You do the same. Again, it was nice to meet you, Mary Jane." I hadn't noticed when I walked up, but as they walk away, I see a small bouquet of wildflowers in Mary Jane's hand. *That hurts.*

As I fill the jugs with water, I casually look over my right shoulder to watch the two retreat. I catch Wyatt glancing back at me, and he smiles.

*This is just too weird. I swear, Tyler, if you had anything to do with this...*at the mention of his name, the breeze picks up, just for a moment, then it is gone.

CHAPTER 22
Callie

"There. Don't expect me to do that again," I say, louder than anticipated, setting the heavy jugs on the table. Jimmy is placing the salt and pepper on the table as he asks, "Geez, what got into you?"

"Nothing." I grumble.

"Dinner's ready," Riley sings out from the kitchen as she removes the unnaturally dark turkey from the oven.

Dad turns off the football game and sends everyone to the table, including Justa, who sits at my Uncle's feet.

"Let's make a toast to Jimmy and Riley. Congratulations on your nuptials. We're thrilled to have you as part of the family, young lady—though, not thrilled to have missed it, thrilled all the same."

"Thank you...I think," says Riley. *Is she slurring her words?*

"Jimmy, you certainly have spruced up the place. I remember what it looked like when Mr. and Mrs. Davis owned it. You've really lightened it up and decorated so lovely."

"Thanks, Mom. Rye did most of the decorating. I just put a new screen on and had the roof replaced."

"You didn't get rid of the tin roof, did you? Oh, how I love the way it sounds in the rain."

"Nope, new tin replaced the old."

Smiling, Mom says, "It's lovely."

Though the turkey is slightly overcooked, and the sweet potatoes slightly undercooked, it is still wonderful to have everyone under the same roof again. As the dishes are removed from the table and I offer to clean, I notice Jimmy walk to the bathroom. "Ah, the old 'dishpan diarrhea' strikes again." With a laugh, he closes the bathroom door.

"While you kids clean up, I think Fred and I are going to drive home to get a head start on desserts. Take your time coming over. Play a game of cards or two. We won't be ready for company until after seven." Looking at the clock, he replies, "That gives us close to two hours. You better be ready to eat again!"

"Drive safely," Gramp warns. *Isn't that the pot calling the kettle black?*

My parents clear the remainder of the dishes, and as the last pot is dried, my brother emerges from the bathroom. *How convenient.*

Hours of card playing is about to ensue, and I am eager to play. I'm downright giddy. We start with Spoons, move on to Spades, and round out the evening of cards with a game of Rummy. Good times. Feeling lighthearted as I gather the cards and spoons from the table, we slowly exit the cabin and enter our respective cars.

Driving caravan style to Aunt Shirley's reminds me of all the times we drove that way to the state park, across the lake, on the 4th of July. Such great memories.

Entering Aunt Shirley and Uncle Fred's home is so comforting. It's like being wrapped in a warm blanket. The freshly baked pies, the gooey butter cake, and the key lime torte all smell delicious. I take a sampling of them all, seeing as the meal earlier was underwhelming.

"If the weather is nice tomorrow, would any of you be up for a picnic at the state park around noon?" Aunt Shirley questions.

"I would be. As a matter of fact, I'd love to get a long run in and run to the park if someone can fit me in their car for a ride back."

Aunt Marilyn speaks up, "I've got room, dear. I can drive you and your mom and dad back to my place after."

"Perfect, then it's a date."

Sleeping with a full belly, I am completely content until around two in the morning. The pressure of someone sitting on my bed startles me awake. Though my mind is fully alert, I can't will my eyes open. My breathing is shallow and I'm frozen on my side, away from the voice. "She doesn't really mean anything to him, you know. She's just someone to pass the time with," the man whispers. *Tyler?* "Just know that he'd much rather be with... someone else. I know when he's really into someone. Trust me, brothers talk a lot." I roll onto my back, my eyes fly open, and to my disappointment, the room is empty. Sitting up in bed, I place my hand on a depression on the quilt. It is obvious someone was here a moment ago. *Thanks, Tyler,* I whisper.

The sun is brilliant this morning, filling my room with sunshine. It is an unusually warm November day, making it less of a chore to go for a run. With a skip in my step, I take the stairs two at a time and go to the kitchen to have a cup of coffee before I take off. It is going to be a longer than usual run today, so I want to make sure to get going early enough to let my morning constitution work its way through my system. Coffee usually helps. Seven and a half miles around the lake is going to take some time.

I'm nervous running to the intersection of Riley Road and Camp Road, where I might run into Wyatt and his girlfriend. I don't feel up to making small talk, even if what Tyler says is true. *How can I talk to someone who's been dead for years?* I guess anything is possible up here. Thankfully, there are no interruptions past the dairy farm. Turning right towards Stewart's and along the shore opposite Jimmy and Riley's cabin, I run straight to the state park. Not a soul is around, and I am enjoying the peace and quiet. Not even the cookie cutters are out today. Taking my shoes off, I am eager to get sand between my toes. I find many rocks to throw while I have some time to myself; watching the lake ripple with each rock. I see just a smattering of fishermen out on the lake today. Listening to the quiet, a sound across the lake catches my attention. It is a small fishing boat motor, getting louder and louder. Seeing a flash of red hair glide by on the boat, I know it is Wyatt and Mary Jane. I feel a twinge of jealousy as I follow them with my gaze. Even though they are pretty far off I can tell that they're docking at the end of the lake at Stewart's.

"You made good time." Jimmy says as he sits down in the sand.

"Where's Riley?"

"Right here." Smiling, she sits down next to Jimmy.

"Everyone else should be here in a few." I stand to stretch. "Callie, can you help me get the blanket and basket out of the car?"

Moments later, my extended family is at the state park with all the Thanksgiving leftovers to feast on. A little Frisbee and volleyball action and it is time to leave. Keeping an eye on the lake from time to time, I haven't noticed Wyatt and Mary Jane return. *Maybe I missed them.* No sooner has the thought run through my mind than a fishing boat motor gurgles, churning up the lake. From Aunt Marilyn' car I see, off in the distance, Wyatt extend a hand and help Mary Jane from the boat. In my mind, I can hear him saying "Madame" with outstretched hand. Agonizing, I can't tear my eyes away, knowing what's coming. I watch as they display their affection for all to see. Wyatt picks up Mary Jane in a bear hug and gives her a passionate kiss.

CHAPTER 23
Callie

"Thanks for a great holiday weekend. It's really nice to see everyone," I say to Aunt Marilyn Saturday night.

"You okay, Callie?"

Aware that she will know if I lie, I start with the truth. "Not really. I feel like I need to see Charlie. I'm only a seven hour drive away."

"Doesn't your flight land in Connecticut tomorrow for your connection?" Aunt Marilyn asks curiously.

"Well, yeah, but I'm supposed to be at work on Monday morning at nine."

"Couldn't you change your flight for later in the evening or take the red eye out Monday morning?"

"He doesn't know I'm coming," I say, revealing that I have thought about this already.

"Why does he have to know? Wouldn't it be fun to surprise him?"

Feeling excited now, I think, *why not?* So I get on the phone and change my flight to Monday morning at six A.M. Now to tell my folks what I am going to do. I decide not to tell them until we are on the flight to Connecticut. When we deplane and look at the screen for our connection, my parents begin to walk, but I stand still.

"Cal, you coming?" Dad asks.

"No. I decided I'm going to see Charlie. I'll be flying in tomorrow morning at six. Don't worry about me. I'm going to take a cab from the airport to the Canfields' house, and when I get back to Missouri, I'll take a cab home. It'll be fine." Kissing each of them, I say, "Fly safe. I'll call when I get home."

Looking slightly confused, they say okay and leave. They don't have a choice. There isn't much time before their connector departs.

After getting directions from Hartford to Bethel at the car rental, I am on my way. Finally feeling like this is the right decision, I feel happy as I exit Highway 84 for Route 25. One hour and three minutes from the start of my drive, I am in the Canfields' driveway. My feelings of happiness transformed into anxiety. I walk up the steps and press the doorbell. The voices inside cease as Mrs. Canfield answers the door.

"Oh, my goodness. What a surprise! How are you Callie? Please come in!" We embrace quickly and soon the faces around the living room come into view: Mr. Canfield, Charlie's sister Laura, Charlie and Liz. *Wait, Liz?* I haven't seen Liz since we lived next door to each other in college. What is she doing here? Feeling very confused, I look to Charlie for an explanation. I am struck by the odd, guilty look on his face.

He trips all over his words, "Callie, it's so great to see you. Liz is here! Funny story. I was out at Bethel State Park walking the grounds when I literally ran into Liz. She stumbled over a rock on the trail and tripped right into me. We started talking. This was about Tuesday of this week. I asked if she was doing anything for Thanksgiving, she said no, so here she is."

"Thanksgiving was Thursday. Today is Sunday." Feeling unusually calm, I wait for a response.

"Yeah, she came over in the evening after her family's dinner, they eat in the afternoon, and we eat at night, so she came over. She didn't want to make the drive back that night. It was late so she stayed here; 'til Sunday." His face reddens.

Liz rises from her perch and hugs me. "Hi, Cal. It's great to see you. You look great. He's a big oaf. With all his rambling, I'm sure you're getting all kinds of wild notions running through your head." Looking around the room, I notice everyone has stopped moving and all eyes are on us. "I slept on the couch. I'm leaving right now. They were kind enough to let me hang out awhile." She looks to Mr. and Mrs. Canfield, "Longer than I expected. I hope I didn't overstay my welcome."

"Never. Any friend of Charlie's is a friend of ours." *That sounds familiar. That must be the pat answer for all parents in the parenting handbook.* Suddenly I feel very sarcastic.

Watching Liz hug everyone goodbye, I feel like an imbecile.

"I'm sorry, Liz. This just caught me offguard. Especially after the weekend I've had. It really was good to see you. I hope I'm not rushing you off."

"Nah, it's nothing. I'm sure my parents wonder if I've been taken hostage. It's time for me to go home. Take care. I hope to see you sooner rather than later."

"You should come out to visit sometime. You could reconnect with Maddie. I'm sure there's a lot there that needs to be caught up on."

"Oh, I'm all caught up in that department. I saw her while she was here for Thanksgiving. As a matter of fact, you just missed her. She left about an hour ago to fly home. She stopped in to see Charlie and me. What details I didn't get from Maddie I got from Charlie, so I'm good."

"Oh. Okay...Well, I guess that's it then. See you soon." I feel extremely uncomfortable.

"Bye, everyone. Thanks for the wonderful weekend."

"Bye, Liz. Come back soon," Mrs. Canfield says as they embrace.

Turning to a room full of eyes, I suddenly wish I had stayed on the plane with my parents. I have made everyone feel uncomfortable with my unannounced visit.

"Hey, I didn't mean to mess up your afternoon. I should have called first. 'He'll like the surprise,' they said. 'They'll be happy you stopped in,' they said." I am talking with my hands now, putting air quotes around my comments.

Drawing me close, he says, "I *am* happy you're here. We all are." It feels so good to be in his arms. His parents busy themselves with Laura. They walk into the kitchen out of earshot.

"How long can you stay?"

"I'm on the red eye tomorrow morning. I just wanted to see you. It was really bugging me that you were a seven-hour drive away. I mean, I was flying right into Hartford. I was *this* close. How could I not stop by."

"Well, I'll take what I can get. Wanna take a walk? Or better yet, let me take you to the state park I work at. It's really beautiful this time of day."

On the way to Bethel State Park, he keeps touching me. He has his hand on my shoulder, then back on the steering wheel, on my knee, then back on the steering wheel. *I guess he is happy I'm here.*

"For real, a few days ago, I was out here walking the grounds, and out of the blue, Liz falls right on me. What are the chances of that happening?"

"Why was she in Bethel? New Haven is about an hour away."

"She said she was out here antiquing, but it was such a beautiful day that she decided to go for a run."

"Liz doesn't run," I say with a scoff.

"She sure looked like she was running to me. Maybe she took up running after college?" Pulling into the state park, I observe that it's actually called Huntington State Park, which is in Redding, Connecticut. The park borders Bethel, Newtown and Redding. We drive down to the nearest parking lot and follow one of the trails to the lake. At the edge of the lake there stands the most majestic weeping willow tree I have ever seen. Its expansive trunk indicates that it is well over 50 years old. The branches are full with most of its low hanging leaves and the bare, neighboring trees are stark in comparison. We sit on a bench beside the lake just under the highest branches of the willow tree. The branches wrap around us as if standing guard like protective soldiers.

Clasping hands, we sit and watch as a family of ducks swims by: mama duck with four downy ducklings. The littlest one lags behind as the mother bleats out for it as if to say, "Hurry up, son."

"Now there's a mom that takes charge," he says, as the mother duck circles around and uses her beak to propel the duckling forward. "I can see you being really good at that."

"Pushing a duckling in the water?" I joke.

"You know what I mean," he smiles, glancing down as he rubs his thumb over my thumb. "I've been thinking lately."

"That's dangerous."

"Can we be serious for a minute?" he asks, making me feel like I want to crawl under a rock.

"Sure, sorry. You're making me nervous. What's going on?"

"I don't mean to make you nervous. I was just thinking about us moving forward. What do you think about moving back to Connecticut with me?"

"I like where this is going. It's just that I finally found a job I love and I'm starting to make friends. My family is in Missouri now, and I have Maddie out there with me. What if you move out to Missouri? We have state parks there, too," I encourage, sounding hopeful.

"Yeah, I could, I suppose. It would certainly be a change for me."

Feeling excited now, I turn to hug him. "This could be really great! You could move in with Maddie and me. It'd be like old times." He smiles at my enthusiasm.

"It might take a little bit to get a transfer to another state park and to get my stuff packed up. I could plan on moving in January? Does that work?"

"Sounds great!" With yet another hug, encased in his arms, I look up and watch the branches of the willow tree sway in the breeze. Its wispy leaves and branches whisper just low enough that the voices go undetected. Goosebumps form on my arms.

"You must be freezing. You're trembling."

"Am I? It feels like winter is on its way." Walking back to the car, I can't shake the chill that has seeped into my bones.

CHAPTER 24
Callie

"Merry Christmas, Charlie! Only a week to go now. Are you ready?"

"I was born ready."

"I'm excited. Maddie's excited, too, though she says we'll be kicking her out soon. She swears."

"Tell her not to worry. I won't kick her to the curb just yet."

"Her birthday is January 6th. I'm so glad you'll be here for that."

"We should do something fun that day. Let's make a plan. Any ideas what she wants for her birthday?"

"She'd like a man in her life, but I'm nixing that idea for you."

"Funny. Let me think about that. I know, what about some earplugs or some headphones. The room next to hers will be loud for the first few days." Laughing, he continues, "I'm going to leave January 2nd so I don't have to drive with all the crazies on the road over the holiday."

"Good thinking. Drive safe. You need to make it in one piece."

"Will do. Talk to you soon."

After hanging up the phone with Charlie, I think about the last comment I made, *'she'd like a man in her life, but I'm nixing that idea for you.'* I'm feeling uneasy. Ever since Thanksgiving, that moment of surprise at Charlie's house, I can't quite ignore the feeling that Charlie and Liz may have crossed the line of friendship. *It feels like I was the one that got the surprise.* Picking up the phone, it's time to figure out just what went on that weekend. It can't wait until Maddie returns.

"Hey, Mad, how's it going? Did you have a nice holiday?"

"Hay is for horses," Maddie says with a laugh.

"Did I catch you at a bad time? Do you have a minute?"

"Yeah. I mean, no. What's up? You know I'll be back in a few days right?"

"I know. I was just thinking about something and had to call and ask you a question."

"Uh-oh. That usually gets you into trouble but shoot."

"So when I was back in Connecticut in November. Remember, I surprised Charlie?"

"Yeah."

"And you were there visiting Charlie before I got there."

"Y-eah," she says, drawing out the word hesitantly.

"And Liz was there."

"I'm not sure I like where this is going," Maddie says uncomfortably. "If you think I'm doing the horizontal mambo with Charlie, you are sorely mistaken."

"What about Liz?" Pressing my line of question.

Pausing a second too long, there is now an elephant in the room.

"Cal, I don't know what's going on there. It was a bit awkward when I arrived for a quick hello."

"That's it? That's all you're going to say? You didn't talk to Liz while you were there?"

"Well, I did, but really, it's none of my business. She did say that nothing was going on, but if I had to guess, I would say that if things don't go well with you and Charlie, you might have a replacement."

"Great. Thanks," I say flatly.

"Don't worry about Liz. If you and Charlie are happy, then you have nothing to worry about. I mean, the man *is* moving across the country and into our apartment, which says a lot."

"What does that say to you?"

"It says *I'm a free-loading sack of shit.*"

"Come on. It does not," I say, smiling.

"Oh, right, it says *I want that sexy mink in every possible position 24/7.*"

"Please, I'm not sexy."

"Who's saying anything about you?"

Laughing heartily now, "Thanks, Mad."

"Now, stop worrying. I gotta get off the phone. I'm getting *the look*. See you in a few."

While Maddie is home for the Christmas holiday, I stay the night Christmas Eve at my parents' house. Stubby snuggles in next to me through out my stay. Jimmy and Riley have come down for a visit and my grandparents remain up in Vermont. It's been a nice holiday, and I have to admit Riley is a nice addition. I am growing used to the idea of her being in my family. Jimmy and Riley decide to stay with my parents for four days and on the night before they return to Vermont, I call to invite Riley out for a drink.

"Do you think you could come out for a drink with me before you leave tomorrow?"

Sounding unsure, she replies, "Yeah, I guess so."

"Don't sound too excited," I respond, feeling slightly irritated.

"Should I ask Jimmy to come along?"

"Nah, just us girls. I don't get much time to hang out with only you. I'll be over around eight tonight to pick you up."

"We still haven't packed for tomorrow's flight, so it'll have to be an early night."

"No problem. I'm not going to sweep you away for an all-nighter, just a few hours. I'll have you back by ten. I promise."

Hesitantly, she says, "Okay."

Why is this so hard? I'm making an effort here, and she's dragging her feet the whole way. I invited her out in hopes that I could get to know her a little bit better. It's sad to say that over these past several years, I haven't had any lengthy conversations with her, ever. Not that I sought her out. We were acquaintances, though she married into the family. *I'll bridge the gap tonight.*

As the eight o'clock hour nears, I feel more and more apprehensive about our date, but having to make good on all promises, I hop in the car and drive to my parents' house.

I walk in like I own the place. Mom and Dad are watching a movie on TV with Stubby snoring between them. "Hi, guys. Is Riley ready?" The sound of my voice startles the slumbering pug. A sound escapes Stubby's mouth. Something between a snort and a sneeze as he lifts his head resonates.

Jimmy walks up to me and whispers, "She's a little nervous about tonight. She feels like you're up to something."

"Ha, no, not up to something. I just want to get to know my sister-in-law better. Is there a crime in that?"

"Nope let me go get her for you."

Out walks Riley with her hair done, makeup on and a pair of skin-tight jeans, white blouse unbuttoned so that you can see why Jimmy married her, and cowboy boots. Not at all used to seeing this side of her, I say, "Wow, Riley, you clean up real nice." Feeling underdressed in my faded blue jeans, Rolling Stones t-shirt, and my "dressy" earrings, I walk to the door.

"I thought we'd go to Krieger's for a beer. Are you hungry? Wanna order something to snack on?"

"I just ate an hour ago, so I'm not hungry, but a beer sure sounds good."

Walking into the bar and grill, I sense all the fellows turning to check her out. Feeling a bit out of place, I just sit down and look over the drink menu.

"Maybe I'll have a martini, they sound so grown up."

"I'm going to have a beer with a sidecar."

"Sidecar? What's that?"

To the bartender, who now has his eyes on her cleavage, she says, "Make it a tequila, Cuervo gold." *She means business.*

"And you miss?"

"I'll have a lemon drop martini, please."

"May I see some ID, ladies?" He turns to make our drinks.

"So a sidecar is a shot, I take it."

"Yep, and Cuervo is my favorite."

"Do you get a chance to get out on the town much at home?"

"Not a whole lot. Sometimes I go out with Megan, my sister, after work at Stewart's. Sometimes the guys that stock the shelves join us. It's a fun group, but we don't get out a ton."

"So how's married life?"

Slow to respond, she drinks the shot before answering.

"It's fine."

Fine? "How do you mean?"

"Well, I'm not the most domestic person. Keeping the house clean and cooking isn't really my thing. I do like to make my husband happy," she says, batting her eyelashes.

"That I don't need to hear about."

"Do you think you and Charlie will be next getting married?" Suddenly I feel a weight on my chest.

"Um, I don't think so, no. Not right away."

"You're smart. Take your time and think about it." This sounds ominous. "Here's the thing. I just can't see myself staying with one guy the rest of my life. I mean, Jimmy for the rest of my life, the end."

Hello, have you forgotten who you're talking to here? That's my brother you're talking about.

"Well, this conversation isn't going exactly as I thought it would."

"No disrespect to your brother. I'm just thinking out loud here." Looking down now, I notice that her left hand is bare.

"Where's your wedding ring?"

"It needs to be sized, so I didn't put it on. It floats all over my hand, and I feel like I'm going to lose it."

How convenient. Closing in on ten o'clock, I remind her that she needs to go home and pack for her flight. I pay the bill and we leave.

CHAPTER 25
Jimmy

"How was your night?" Jimmy asks Riley as she undresses for bed.

"It was fine. Your sister wasn't as much of a wet blanket as I thought she would be." Taking off her earrings, she slips her wedding rings back on.

"I think we're all packed now. Time to get back to wedded bliss," Jimmy says, full of hope and enthusiasm. He nuzzles her neck as she sits on the side of the bed, setting her alarm clock. "Whaddya' say we get a little crazy in this room tonight. It would feel so naughty doing it under my parents' roof," he says mischievously, making a swipe at her breast.

Batting him away, she says, "Nah, I've got a headache." She gets under the covers and rolls onto her side away from him.

Feeling dejected, he rolls over and goes to sleep.

Flying home the following day, Riley remains quiet. Jimmy is concerned but thinks maybe it was just spending time with his family that made her uncomfortable. Once back in their own territory, things return to normal and their work schedules are back on track.

"Hey, I have the late shift tonight, and I think I'm going to go out with Megan to see how her holiday went. Okay?"

"Sure. That'll give me a chance to catch up on some work anyway. Have fun." with a peck on the cheek, he is out the door, and she lets out a sigh of relief.

Later, at Stewart's, Lyle- a stock boy- asks if Megan and Riley want company at JD's Pub, and they tell him to come along. In the process, Lyle invites his friend Drew, so the four of them go out for drinks. The place is kind of quiet, seeing as it is a Monday night and only open until 11. They decide to order a round of beers and Riley's favorite sidecar, Cuervo. Everyone is feeling happy and getting comfortable with one another. Drew puts some coins in the jukebox and turns on some familiar song. The girls start singing at the top of their lungs, and the guys join in the act. Lyle orders another round for everyone. Standing up is becoming a problem for Riley. Megan tries to talk some sense into her, "Rye, I think you've had enough. We should get going. It's almost eleven. Won't Jimmy be wondering where you are?"

"My vanilla husband? Yep, he'll be wondering where I am."

"Vanilla?" asks Lyle. "I'm more of a rocky road kinda guy." The look in his eye reveals that he is getting ideas in his head about Riley, and Megan knows it is time to go.

"I like rocky road ice cream," Riley slurs, and plants her hand on his inner thigh.

"Okay, Riley, you like rocky road ice cream. Very good. I'm glad we established that now let's go." Megan tugs her sister's hand off Lyle's thigh and pulls her to the exit. "Thanks, guys, for a fun night. I gotta get this one to bed."

With smoldering eyes, Lyle says under his breath, "I'd like to get that one to bed."

Hearing this comment, Megan says, "Easy, fella. She's a married woman."

Fumbling with the keys to the door, Megan helps Riley get the door open. "Rye, I'm gonna walk home. Are you okay?"

"Yes, right as rain," Riley says, stumbling into the bedroom. Megan quietly closes the front door and walks back to her grandma's cabin.

Hiccuping, Riley flops into bed fully clothed.

"Riley, are you drunk?"

His answer comes in the form of a snore from the pillow beside him.

When she wakes the following morning, a hot cup of coffee waits for her on the nightstand with two aspirin beside it. *He's too good to me.* As she gets ready for work, she realizes she is already late. They open at nine and it is almost ten. *No time for a shower today.* Rushing, she detects people waiting at the door as she pulls up, one of which is Lyle.

"Sorry, sorry, sorry. I overslept." Pushing past Megan, Lyle and a few regular customers, she unlocks the door and turns on the lights. Quickly, she turns on the coffeemaker and grabs an apron.

"Next time, cut back on the sidecars, all right?" Megan snaps.

"Thanks for the advice, Mom," Riley barks back.

"Girls, let's not fight. There's enough of me to go around," Lyle interjects. Megan just rolls her eyes. "We should go out again sometime. Whatcha think, Riley?"

Too busy to really acknowledge the attention she is receiving, she mumbles, "Mmmhmm."

"Great. Next week we'll do it again."

Giving him a sideways glance, she notices how his pants fit his rear end rather nicely. "Sure, next week. Now get back to work." He winks back at her. She loves the attention and is not sure why, after two years of employment, he is just now starting to flirt with her. She just goes along with it. It feels good being the one the boys fawn over.

Hours go by as the daily routine rolls on. She goes on break, and Megan mans the register. Stepping outside for some fresh air, she walks out as Lyle is walking in. "Oops, sorry. Did I hit you with the door?" Riley asks, showing concern.

"Nothing bad," he says rubbing his forehead. "I'm sure it'll knock some sense into me." She walks up to him to inspect his forehead, standing a breath away from him. She can smell the spearmint gum he is chewing. She places her hand on his forehead where a small bump is beginning to form. "It looks like it hurts." She looks directly in his eyes, then slowly her eyes go to his lips, willing them to kiss her. Leaning ever so slowly, she places her hands on his shoulders as he leans his head in. His lips are warm and inviting. There is a moment when she thinks *don't do this,* but then her body says *go big or go home,* so she leans in forcefully and attacks his mouth with her own. It is a fitful kiss, full of lust. His hands are on her backside, squeezing. There is nothing gentle about it. The door they are leaning against is pushed forward as Drew comes out with the garbage. Lyle and Riley separate, and without a word, Riley takes his gum from her mouth, tosses it in the trash and goes inside.

CHAPTER 26
Callie

"Charlie, look at this one. It's so precious," I coo at the teacup poodle.

"Maddie doesn't need precious, she needs a dog."

"I know. What about this one," I ask, pointing at a golden retriever.

"Too big. The apartment complex won't allow it."

As the woman working returns from the back with a Boston terrier puppy, both Charlie and I look at it and say, "That one."

He has a body that wrinkles with all its loose puppy skin. His black and white fur has adorable markings. Both eyes are encircled in black with white down the bridge of his nose. One ear is white and the other black. He is just perfect.

"Best birthday gift ever," I say, cradling the new puppy in my arms while Charlie drives us home.

Walking in, I set up his new little bed in Maddie's room on the floor. I put the food and water dish in the kitchen. All we need is for Maddie to get home.

"Hi, guys."

"Happy birthday, Maddie!" The commotion wakes up the puppy, who has been curled up on the couch next to me. He jumps down barking.

"Who's this little guy?"

"He's your birthday present from Charlie and me."

"For real? He's mine?"

"Yep. All you have to do is name him." Maddie thinks for a minute, crouching down to pick him up. He licks her on the chin.

"Sprout."

My eyes well up immediately; I am unable to speak.

Charlie responds for both of us, "Perfect."

Months go by. We are one big happy family: Charlie, Maddie, Sprout, and me. Maddie starts going out more, spreading her wings, making friends and even, on occasion, dating. Things are looking up until mid March.

"Hi, sweetheart, it's Mom. Um, we have some bad news." Pause...

"What? Is it Jimmy? Dad? Aunt Marilyn?" Silence "Mom, spit it out."

"Gramp died this morning."

"What? What happened?"

"Old age happened. He died of natural causes. Dad got the call earlier this morning to let us know. Please clear your schedule for next week so that we can go to his funeral as a family." She continues with the particulars and how Nanny is faring, then hangs up the phone.

Sitting down next to Charlie, I relay the phone conversation.

"Ah, I'm sorry to hear that. He seemed like a spunky old man when I met him."

"He was. We're going as a family next week to spend time with Nanny and go to the funeral. Eesh, I really don't like funerals," I say, as my body gives one convulsing shake.

"Will you be staying with your Aunt Marilyn?"

"Yep. I'll be seeing my whole family while up there."

"Well, we'll keep the home fires burning while you're gone. Me, Maddie, and Sprout."

"Good to know. Guess I should start making calls about flights."

The week passes, and we are on our way up to Vermont, driving from Burlington Airport to Franklin. It gives me that funny feeling all over again. *Will this ever stop?* My parents are quiet on our drive from the airport to Aunt Marilyn's. They talk softly about the possibility of selling Gramp's camp. This hasn't occurred to me.

"Couldn't Nanny keep it for a while?"

"Honey, she's too old for the upkeep. I think it's inevitable," Mom admits somberly.

The conversation abruptly stops, and I am officially depressed.

At Aunt Marilyn's, we take our respective rooms and prepare mentally for the upcoming funeral. I am not big on funerals; to put it bluntly, I suck at all things death related. The funeral is less than 24 hours away, and already I am dreading going. As I do in anxious situations, I strap on my shoes and go for a run.

The crisp spring air fills my lungs and renews my spirit. I feel alive. By the time I return to the house, I am feeling better.

Pulling up to the Franklin United Church, every relative I know, and some I don't, have arrived and are walking in. *Why exactly do we wear black to funerals? When I die, I want people in bright colors. Shouldn't it be a celebration of life?*

The minister that served as our pastor in Vermont for so many years begins the service.

CHAPTER 27
Callie

..."The life of Mr. Rupert N. Lamply was a colorful one that spanned 90 years. Mr. Lamply was born in St. Albans, Nov. 27, 1900, the son of the late Leonard and Elizabeth Lamply. He was a member of the last class to graduate from the former St. Albans High School, and on Sept. 14, 1924 was married to Wilma who survives him.

"Mr. Lamply lived most of his working life in St. Albans where he worked as a purchasing agent for the Union Carbide Corporation, retiring in 1971. Prior to his association with Union Carbide he worked ten years for the Central Vermont Railroad. Following retirement, Mr. and Mrs. Lamply loved to vacation in Florida where they vacationed for 23 winters. In addition to his wife, Wilma, of 65 years, he leaves two sons and their wives, two brothers and sisters-in-law, seven grandchildren, ten great grandchildren and several nieces, nephews and cousins.

"Mr. Lamply was a feisty one." Several in the congregation laughed lightly. "It seemed that he had a sparkle in his eye just waiting for someone to challenge him in any way. He welcomed it. Correction, he longed for it..." The minister continues with the beautiful eulogy.

From the church, we drive to the interment at the South Franklin Cemetery in our family plot. Nanny chooses not to stand near the casket and sits in the back of Gramp's beloved Cadillac, which dad drove to the service. The minute I sit in the back of the car, I smell that familiar scent of Listerine. *Hi Gramp* I say to myself.

"Are you sure you want to stay in the back of the car?" I ask Nanny gently.

"Yes, I'm sure. He knows I'm here."

Leaving the gravesite and walking toward the car, my eyes are transfixed on an old red pick up truck. My parents continue to mill about, talking with relatives, not quite ready to leave. Searching the sea of faces, I notice one on the edge of the gravesite that makes my heart skip a beat. He gives me a half smile.

"Wyatt," I say softly as I approach him.

Hesitantly, Wyatt leans in for a quick hug. The familiar feeling of his arms around me providing the comfort I need. "I'm sorry about your grandpa."

"Thank you," I say, looking into his clear blue eyes with a hint of sadness. "I'm so surprised to see you here."

"When my parents called to tell me Mr. Lamply had died, I felt like I needed to come and pay my respects. He was always kind to my family and me. We were neighbors for years, after all."

"I know. It's just that…" I stammer, looking to him for help. He doesn't budge. "It's just that the way we kinda…ended. I didn't really think you'd want to be here."

"I don't wish bad things for you, Callie. Sure, right after we broke up, I did. I was really hurting…I don't want to talk about it."

"Okay. Well, thank you for coming. It means a lot to me and my family."

"Tell your grandmother I'm sorry for her loss," he turns and walks to his truck. I watch as he climbs in and drives away, feeling a tug at my heart.

"Wasn't that nice of Wyatt to come say goodbye?" My mom says quietly.

"It was a nice surprise," I say, feeling overwhelming melancholy.

"It shouldn't be a surprise, he comes from good stock." She squeezes my shoulder, kisses my forehead and says, "We should get going. Don't want to keep Aunt Shirley waiting."

CHAPTER 28
Callie

"I'm glad you're back, Cal," Charlie says, giving me a squeeze. "Everything all right?" He shoots me a worried glance.

"Fine. It wasn't as bad as I thought it would be," I trail off.

"But? I feel like there's something more."

"Nothing more, no but."

"Okay. If you feel like talking about it, I'm here," he offers, walking into the kitchen.

"There's nothing to talk about. I just buried my grandfather. Nothing more." I start to feel irritated.

The evening continues, and by nightfall, I am exhausted from the events. I am tossing and turning in bed when Charlie comes in. He crawls under the covers, gives me a kiss goodnight, and rolls over. A few minutes pass without my being able to shut my brain off.

"Okay, there is something. Wyatt was at the funeral."

"Oh?" He says, seemingly unaffected.

"I was a little surprised to see him there."

"I bet." with interest, he now rolls onto his back, fluffing his pillow in the process.

"Anyway, that's what was on my mind earlier. There's nothing else, just that."

"Okay. I'm sure that was a surprise since you haven't seen him in years."

That isn't exactly true. I saw him over Thanksgiving. *Why didn't I tell Charlie that?*

Months go on with work for all of us. Sprout is getting bigger. He is the sweetest dog. He especially loves going on runs with me in the morning, his little legs barely able to keep up. Everything is status quo for quite some time. I'm busy working with my art therapy patients at the hospital, Charlie works at Queeny Park and Maddie makes ends meet at the sandwich shop. It's as if we have three different worlds living under one roof.

"Hey, you wanna go get a bite to eat tonight?" Charlie asks me excitedly one evening.

"Sure," I say, leaning in for a kiss.

"Hungry?" he asks, reaching for the car keys.

"Famished," I say, holding my stomach. Our small talk causes an unsettling feeling in the pit of my stomach.

"Great. Let's order then we can talk." The unease I feel reminds me of the few times my dad would come home over the course of my childhood, carrying an atlas. *Let's go out to dinner.* He would say. *I have something important to talk to the family about.* A dead giveaway that we were about to move.

"What is it you want to talk about?"

"Cal, I got offered a great job with Newtown Park and Recreation," he informs me excitedly. "This would give me a chance to be close to my family again, and you could be a therapist in Connecticut. I've looked into art therapy programs, and there are several jobs you could apply for. As a matter of fact, I've contacted a few hospitals in the area to inquire about a position for you."

I am not happy with this conversation at all. My face is screwed up tight.

"What's that look for?"

"You did what?" Incriminating tears begin to well in my angry eyes. "Charlie, you had no right to *inquire* about a job for me. I love my job. I'm very happy here working with the kids I have now. I really don't want to uproot myself when these kids need me. They may not be here for very long, but while they are, I want to be here to help them on their journey," heat rises from my neck to my face.

"I've been very patient throughout all this. Starting with Maddie and her situation. I love Maddie, I do, but when were you going to tell her it was time to move out so that we could have our own place?" he asks sternly.

"I'm not ready for her to move out. She needs me."

"What about me? Huh, Callie? What about me? I need you. I've been here for a little over a year, in a new town, a new state with a dog and two roommates. This isn't really what I bargained for. I was hoping we could have a fresh start in Connecticut. Is that too much to ask?"

"Yes, it is. My family is here. Maddie is here because of *me*. I love my job and I love where I live. I'm not willing to drop everything and move back to Connecticut. Can you understand that?" Frustration sets in.

"No. I really can't. I felt like it was finally our time. Maddie is finally on the right track. She could find a roommate to help her with rent. Your family will always be near whether up in Vermont, Connecticut, or Missouri. It's time for *us* now. We're not getting any younger. Damn it, Cal, I'm excited about this new job and the prospect of us starting a life together in Connecticut."

"New job? I thought you said that you were offered a job, not that you took it already."

"I took it. I accepted it as soon as the offer came through. I thought you'd be on board and everything would be in place."

"Well you thought wrong. I'm not leaving, Charlie. I'm sorry."

Exasperated, he reaches for my hands and says, "I am."

The tears that collected earlier now run down my cheek. "When?"

"I start June 1st, before the summer season kicks in."

That's three weeks away.

Our food arrives and he eats in uncomfortable silence, not noticing that my food is being tossed around my plate in circles, uneaten.

"I know this is hard for you to wrap your brain around, but I've given this a lot of thought. We can still do the long distance relationship thing. It'll be hard, but we've done it before."

I don't feel the sincerity in his voice.

"Sure, we can," I say, feeling as though this is the beginning of the end.

CHAPTER 29
Callie

With Charlie gone, there's a strange vibe in our apartment. I can feel his presence is missing. We continue to talk often on the phone, vowing to visit each other soon. As the weeks turn into months, I realize that we are not making an effort to see each other, but that neither of us want to say the words to end it. I can't help but feel insignificant.

I have begun to hang out with Natasha and the staff after hours more often, getting more and more involved with Art from the Heart, Friends of Kids with Cancer programs, and the art therapy that I love. We are rolling into fall as a new intern starts working at the hospital with us. His name is Jason. He's in his twenties, young, attractive and very friendly. He is a very flirtatious guy and makes all the girls at work feel beautiful, including me. Jason is from Missouri and has jet-black hair that's neatly coiffed, and green eyes. His six-foot tall athletic build is always neatly framed in the latest styles. Sitting down on a coffee break one day, Jason comes and sits next to me.

"So tell me your story."

Laughing, I begin, "I was born in Pennsylvania, moved to Connecticut, spending most of my summers in Vermont visiting family. I followed my family out here to Missouri. Don't even ask me what high school I went to because it was in Connecticut," I say with a smile.

"And your story?"

"Born and raised in West County. I'm an only child. I had lymphoma as a kid, and I've always had an affinity for the arts, so naturally, art therapy was in my future."

"That's quite a history. Are your parents still around?"

"Yep, they live in the same home that I was raised in. Great people, my folks."

"They must be. They produced a very carefree spirit that loves working with kids and art."

He blushes ever so slightly. "My 'carefree' spirit has gotten me in trouble a time or two. My boyfriend can attest to that."

"Boyfriend? You mean you're gay," I blurt out.

"So they say," he laughs.

"Huh, I never would have guessed."

"Really? Is it because I don't have your stereotypical flamboyant behaviors or over-accentuate my words? It's true, much to my parents' chagrin."

"Well, Jason, I hope we become fast friends because I'm in desperate need of a shopping companion."

"So, just because I'm gay you think I'd want to go shopping?"

Feeling as if I've stumbled and am unable to right myself, I stammer, "I'm sorry, I just thought I was being funny. I didn't mean to offend you."

"Sweetheart, I'd love going shopping with you. Your outfits certainly do need a little sprucing up, and Jason is just the man to help you out."

"Well, thank heavens you came into my life, Jason, and just at the perfect time!" I smile. We continue talking, and I find myself sharing way more information than I thought possible with a near stranger. I'd only known Jason for less than a week, and he already knew my life story.

"So now Charlie is back in Connecticut, and I'm single again. It feels weird not having him around anymore. We never really officially broke up, but I have a feeling he's dating, though he probably wouldn't admit it."

"Well, then you need to get back on the saddle again."

"Geez, between you and Maddie, I hear that a lot."

"Maddie is your roommate?"

"Yep. You'll have to come over for dinner some night. Bring your boyfriend, if you'd like."

"Love to! When?"

"How about Friday night?"

"I'll let Ryan know," he says with a smile.

"I gotta get back to the kiddos. If Chunk is here already then I'm sure he's into something."

I like him. Dinner should be a trip.

"Does he like red or white wine? I don't know anything about wine other than I like to drink it. Should I get the appetizers out now?" Maddie is full of nervous energy.

"Mad, you're acting like we're going on a double date or something. It'll be fine. Jason's a great guy. I think you're really going to like him. I'm so curious about his boyfriend. I wonder what he looks like? I wonder what his personality is like?" Through the window, Maddie notices two men walking up to the front door. "I'm curious to see which one is a power top."

"A wha?"

"Hi, fellas, I'm Maddie," she says hugging each. Turning to me as I pass to give a hug she whispers, "definitely Jason."

Ryan walks in with a bottle of white wine, wearing a pair of skinny jeans, cuffed at the ankles and an oversized, grey, long-sleeved shirt that he wears untucked and unbuttoned with a darker grey silk scarf wrapped once loosely around his neck. Jason is wearing a pair of fitted dark jeans and a button-down hunter green oxford that brings out the color of his eyes. He looks very handsome. Jason has just introduced us when Ryan asks for a corkscrew. We poor the wine and begin enjoying ourselves. We eat appetizers of Havarti cheese and salami on crackers. Butternut squash alfredo is the main course of the evening. The apartment smells delicious.

"Wow, who made this?" asks Ryan.

"That would be me," I say happily.

"Well, my compliments to the chef!"

"Thank you! I'm so happy you're eating it. You never know what the food is going to taste like around here. It's hit or miss. You just happened to get a hit." Pouring more wine, we all sit around the table chatting. I stand to clean, and Jason says, "Sit, sit. Ryan and I will do the dishes. It's the least we can do after such a lovely meal."

Looking at Maddie stunned, I say, "I'm not going to argue with you. Thank you. I think I'll just sit a bit longer and have some more wine."

Jason smiles. Maddie and I sit at the table as Jason and Ryan clear the dishes and begin working side by side at the sink, interjecting into the conversation while their backs are turned.

"So Maddie, have you found Mr. Right yet?"

"Nah, I'm not looking for Mr. Right, I'm looking for Mr. right-now."

"I've had plenty of those," Ryan admits through the side of his mouth.

"I'll have to introduce you to some of my straight friends. I think you'd like a couple of them."

"It doesn't hurt to keep my options open. Maybe you could find someone for Cal, too."

"Possibly. I do have a musician friend that all the ladies fancy. I'll introduce you to him next time we get together, though I don't think Callie's quite finished with the fella she has," he says, placing the last dish to dry on the counter. "Well, ladies, this has been wonderful, but we need to get home and let the dogs out. Thank you so much for dinner. It was truly a treat to meet you, Maddie," Jason says hugging Maddie. Ryan comes in for a hug, as well, and just like that, our evening is over.

"Oh, I like them a lot," Maddie says, smelling her shirt where the remnants of Jason's cologne clings.

CHAPTER 30
Callie

"All set for tonight, Callie?" Natasha asks me as I load multiple pieces of framed artwork into the back of my car.

"As ready as I'll ever be," I say with slight panic.

"You're going to do great. You don't have to speak to the group if you don't want to, I can do all the talking."

"That's a relief," I exhale. "I'll see you there around five?"

"Sounds good. Do you need help with any of the artwork? I think I could squeeze maybe one or two more pieces in my car if you need me to."

"Thanks, but I think I got it."

Driving home, I think about all the patients that I've worked with this year. *I really want to buy Pheonix's dragonfly painting.* In my apartment, the light from the answering machine blinks in Morse code. With a sigh, I press play.

"Hi, Cal, it's Charlie." Pause. "I just wanted to hear your voice. The holidays are around the corner, and I was wondering where you were going to be this year. Can you call me when you have a minute?" Before he hangs up his end, I can hear him waiting on the line. Breathing. After a minute he hangs up.

Feeling fatigued by the message, I press delete on my way to the shower.

Having just enough time to get to the event, finding a parking spot proves to be a challenge. My car nearly regurgitates all the artwork when I open the trunk. Thankfully, Jason is here to run to my aid.

"Geez, it would have been a disaster if these beautiful pieces of art shattered right in front of the venue."

"True. You're very lucky that I'm early. That rarely happens," he chuckles.

As we carry the pieces in by the armload, Ryan comes over to help. I bark orders for them regarding where to place the artwork and placards. Looking around the room, I feel pleased with how it all turned out. All of Natasha's artwork is meticulously laid out. We smile at each other from across the room. People scurry about, getting the glass blowing, face painting, and hand molds all set up. Many vendors set up around the artwork with samples of food for everyone. The room is buzzing when in walk our first guests of honor, our art therapy kids. Arianna looks absolutely majestic with her red ballgown and tiara atop her fuzzy head. She is beaming. Natasha meets each patient with a hug and poses for photos with them.

"Pheonix, you look beautiful," I greet Pheonix as she walks her frail young body in awkwardly, pulling on the hem of her dress.

"Thanks, Callie."

"I'm ready to bid away tonight!"

"Good luck. My grandmother is here tonight."

A feeling of dread spreads over me. "I wouldn't outbid your grandmother. That would be wrong."

"I can make a drawing for her any time. She doesn't even need to pay for one."

That makes me feel a little better, but I'm still unsure. As the evening progresses, I keep circling the table to see the bids coming in. *Damn. Someone keeps outbidding me.* And then I see her: an unassuming older woman with snow-white hair. She is eyeing me as I march back to the clipboard and write a new bid. I walk away but keep an eye on the woman. She walks right up to the clipboard and outbids me yet again. *That must be Pheonix's grandmother.* An announcement is broadcast over the P.A. system, "Bids for auction items numbered 30-46 will be closing in five minutes."

Trying to seem nonchalant, I circle one more time and write down $150.00 higher than the previous bid. As Grandma makes her way back over to the table, something unusual happens. Pheonix must have been watching our shenanigans. She cuts her grandmother off at the pass and pulls her aside.

"This closes the bidding for auction item's numbered 30-46. Items number 47-63 will be closing bids in five minutes." That makes me the winning bidder. A smile spreads across my lips as I turn to see Pheonix smiling back at me.

I feel honored to take home one of her pieces as I leave the auction, knowing she had a hand in my win. She's such an amazing young woman. Without any notice, the tears begin to well in my eyes.

"I know, my beauty does that to people from time to time," Ryan says playfully. "Just ask Jason." Ryan is definitely the more outgoing of the two. Full of life. Jason is much more subdued. They make a perfect couple, actually, complimenting each other's personalities.

Spotting Pheonix's grandmother, I place my things in the car and walk briskly over to her.

"Excuse me. My name is Callista Lamply. I'm an art therapist that works with your granddaughter, Pheonix at the hospital," I say, extending a hand. She takes it into her warm hands and holds on a fraction longer than I anticipated. She smiles as I look into her sparkling auburn eyes. "I know who you are, dear. It's a pleasure to meet you. Pheonix has told me so much about you. I know my granddaughter is terribly shy at times, and you probably wouldn't know this, but she really admires you and the work you're doing here."

The unexpected compliment brings on the tears yet again. Wiping away the moisture, embarrassed, she pretends she doesn't see them.

"If you're coming over here to apologize for buying her artwork, please save your breath. I can get my very own masterpiece for free. I was playing with you a little bit to see just how far you would go with your bid," she admits with a twinkle. "Until Pheonix told me to stop."

"Oh, you're good. You've definitely perfected the art of maintaining a poker face." I say with a chuckle. "It was very nice to meet you," I shake her hand one last time, then walk back to my car.

CHAPTER 31
Riley

Thinking more and more about being married to one man the rest of her life has really been dragging her down. Riley can't get it out of her head. *Sleep with the same man forever and ever? I can't.*

The holidays are over, and Riley is bringing the holiday decorations into the back storage room when Lyle spots her. Riley and Lyle have been stealing kisses from each other for months now, but it hasn't progressed any further, much to his dismay. Riley overheard Lyle tell Drew he was going to help Riley put the holiday decorations away and to not come looking for him. He'll be back when he'll be back.

As Riley walks into the storage room closing the door with her foot, Lyle catches it, turns and locks it. "What's going on, Lyle?"

"You looked like you needed some help with these decorations."

"Um, no, I got this, but I do need help with something."

"Yeah, what's that?" he asks, slinking toward her with a steely grin.

"I'm having a hard time getting out of these jeans. Do you think you could help with that?"

Instantly, the buttons on his button-down jeans are in imminent danger of bursting from the fabric. He surreptitiously begins groping her, leaning her over the plastic Santa. Releasing the pressure from his jeans, the act lasts all of five minutes of furious bumping and grinding.

As if they hadn't just defiled the plastic Santa, she turns away from him, zipping up her jeans, and leaves without a word leaving Lyle stunned yet wanting more. Riley watches him as he emerges buttoning his jeans and goes back to stocking the shelves, following her every move throughout Stewart's.

The sound of the bell indicating someone has entered causes Lyle to turn. Riley can hear the patron enter and strike up a conversation with Lyle. To her surprise, she realizes it's Jimmy. *That was a close one.*

"Hey, man, can I help you with something?" Lyle asks with a grin.

"Hey, uh, I'm looking for Riley. Is she around?" Jimmy asks, unsuspecting.

"I think she's on the ice cream side," Lyle says, as Riley is smoothing her hair, looking surprised.

"Hey, babe, I was in the neighborhood and thought I'd come by and see how my wife was doing?"

"I'm doing fine. What do you really want?" she says, visibly irritated.

Feeling like an outsider, Jimmy says, "Just thought I'd come by and say hi. That's all. I guess you're busy. I'll see you at home later."

"Yeah, about tonight…Megan and I are going out for happy hour, so I'll be a little late."

"Hmm. Okay. Just the girls again?"

"Yep. We're going back to JD's Pub."

"Okay. Don't be too late," he says, leaning in for a kiss which she hastily accepts before backing away.

After Jimmy leaves the building and is driving away, Megan asks, "When were you going to tell me we were going out tonight?"

"Right now."

"What's gotten into you, Rye? Don't you have any respect for yourself or your marriage?"

"I think it was a mistake; I'm not meant to be married."

"If you have that kind of attitude, then no, you probably shouldn't be married. Have you talked to Jimmy about how you feel? You probably should, before you go off with someone else."

"No," she says, glancing over at Lyle sweeping by the back door.

"Oh, Jesus. You've already gone and done it, haven't you?" she asks, looking accusingly at Riley.

"What? No, I haven't done anything."

"Bullshit."

"Come on, Megan, why would I do that? I have a perfectly good husband at home."

Disbelieving, Megan says, "You do, and you should remember that. He's a good man, Riley. Just think about all the shit you've been through with him."

"Are we through with the lecture now?"

"It's your life. You can screw it up if you want, but remember, it's more than just you that you're screwing with."

A few hours later, Megan and Riley sit at a high-top table having a beer. Riley seems preoccupied, searching the room every few minutes for someone.

"Rye, who are you looking for?"

"No one."

They are on their second beer when Riley spots Lyle in the corner of the bar next to the restrooms. Megan is positioned with her back to the restrooms and doesn't notice him in the back of the room.

"I've gotta use the little girls' room. Order me another when you're done."

Walking past Lyle, she reaches out for him and they go to the restroom, locking the door. As they reemerge, Megan turns in time to see them part as Lyle slaps Riley's backside. Giggling, she sits down with Megan.

Completely at a loss for words, Megan just stares in disbelief. What has her sister done? What has Jimmy done to deserve this?

"Oh, come on, Megan. It's all just fun and games. I'm not hurting anyone because Jimmy's not going to find out."

"You disgust me," she says, standing up to walk away.

"Just keep your mouth shut. I don't want to hear that you've been talking to Jimmy," she says, menacingly, poking her sister in the chest.

Swatting her sisters finger away, Megan spits, "Find your own way home. I'm sure Lyle would gladly drive you."

"Fine. I think I will. He's a heck of a lot more fun than you right now."

Feeling low, thinking she and Megan rarely fight, she walks to Lyle's table and sits down.

"Can you take me home?"

With a lustful glare, Lyle asks, "My place or yours?"

"Yours."

Riley comes home at one in the morning to find Jimmy sitting up, staring blankly at the TV screen.

"Where have you been?"

Feeling trapped, she says, "At JD's, I told you."

"Why did Megan get home hours before you did? I called over there looking for you because it was getting late and I was worried." Feeling resentful, she says, "I'm fine. There's no need to worry about me," She coos as she walks over to him. "I just had another friend drive me home is all. I hadn't seen my friend in a long time and we wanted to catch up, but Megan was tired so she left and we stayed." *When did lying become so easy?* "Are you jealous?" she whispers.

"Riley, tell me the truth." She can see that he is starting to believe her; this is much easier than she thought. Walking to him, wrapping her arms around his neck, she says, "That's the honest to God truth. You can even ask Megan."

"She didn't mention this *friend* when I spoke to her on the phone."

A fleeting moment of panic passes, "Well, that's silly." Riley can sense that she is starting to wear him down. "She was sitting right there with us. How could she not remember? Come on, baby, it's late. Let's not argue," she proposes, somehow managing to deflate the situation. She grabs his hand and walks him into the bedroom.

CHAPTER 32
Callie

"Callie, it's Charlie again. Can you give me a call so we can talk?" I just sit here listening to his message. I don't have the patience to talk it through. *I'll call back later on.* I've been saying that for a month. The last time I called he wasn't around and I left a message for him. That was over the holidays. *What's wrong with me? I can't leave him hanging like that. I owe him an explanation.* Maddie and a new man walking through the door interrupt my thoughts.

"Hey, Cal, this is my friend, Zachary." she smiles at him.

"Hi, Zachary, nice to meet you," I say, shaking his hand.

"Call me Zach," he says releasing my hand, "I've heard a lot about you."

"Hopefully all good."

"Of course," he grins.

"We're gonna grab a bite to eat, wanna join us?" Maddie asks hopefully.

"Yeah, I might be a while, though. Charlie called again…"

"Ah, well, we'll be at Gitto's for a while if you wanna come by," she says, nervously waving goodbye and mouthing the words *good luck* as she closes the door.

Oh boy. Here we go, I think as I dial Charlie's number. After three rings, Charlie answers out of breath.

"Hello?"

"Hi, Charlie, it's Callie," I say, feeling nervous for the first time in a long time.

"I was beginning to think you were avoiding me. How's art therapy these days?

I draw a picture with my words, explaining the artwork I purchased at the Art from The Heart program.

"Sounds really cool. I hope to see it soon."

"Yeah, maybe."

"Callie, what's going on with us? It's felt really strange these last few months. Really since I moved back home. Is this long distance stuff making you uncomfortable? I know, you miss the Toddle House," he said, trying to induce a laugh from me.

"Ha, yep, you got me. It's the Toddle House."

"Seriously, Cal, what's going on? I'm not a mind reader. Can you tell me what you're feeling? Just be honest with me."

"I think we need to take a break," I blurt out unexpectedly.

"Okay. I was kind of expecting that."

"Charlie, I don't want to hurt you. I have a habit of doing that to people I care about, but I mean it. You've been really great. You deserve someone that can dote on you, spend time with you, and cherish you because you deserve it. You really do," I ramble on.

"Cal, I'm gonna give you time to come to your senses. You'll see that we belong together. Truly, we are cut from the same bolt of cloth. Just because we live in different states right now doesn't mean we can't make this work in the long run."

"Charlie," I caution.

"We can have a break for a few months if you want, but I think it's a mistake. I think you'll see sooner than later…How about come springtime we meet up and reevaluate."

"Okay, springtime. Around April," I say, feeling deflated.

"Can I still call and check up on you?"

"Charlie, if you keep calling me, then it's not technically a break."

"I know, but old habits are hard to break."

"Talk to you in the spring."

"In the spring, we'll celebrate by going to the Toddle house," he says with a sad laugh. I feel in my heart of hearts that that isn't going to happen.

Months have rolled on with work. Maddie's relationship with Zach has blossomed and they are taking it to another level by finding a place for themselves and Sprout. On a rare night at home with just she and I, Sprout on her lap dozing as she rubs his back, we talk about what the future holds.

"I'm looking at a place not far from here, closer to Zach's work. We're looking at renting a little ranch style home," she says, beaming.

"I'm so happy for you, Mad, I really am."

"That wasn't very convincing."

"I'm going to miss our little family and our little Sprout, that's all."

At the mention of his name, Sprout's head perks up. "Well, you can come visit or I can bring this little shit-storm to you on weekends if you want. I'll share custody with you," she laughs.

Hugging her tightly, I say, "Oh, Maddie, I'm gonna miss you."

"Hey, don't get all leaky. I'm only a five-minute drive away. Hell, you'll be running by my place every morning."

"I'm so happy you found your forever guy," I say, releasing her.

"You can help me pack if that'll make this process easier on you. You'll be so sick of me and my shit by the time I'm packed up you'll be dancing the jig when I finally walk through that door."

"I doubt it," I somberly add.

"So what's going to happen between you and Charlie? He sounds like he really wants this to work out between you guys. At least over Thanksgiving he sure sounded so ready to settle down. What's changed?"

Feeling a pang of jealousy at the mention of her visit, I say, "I don't know. Things are changing. I feel like now that he's back in Connecticut, our relationship is different somehow. We tried the whole 'living together' thing and that was fun for a while, but I started to feel smothered. I'm not sure why. He's such a great guy, I'm beginning to think we make better friends."

"Ew, the 'F' word."

Smiling, "I know. I'm terrible. Did I lead him on somehow?"

Shaking her head, she says,"So what are you going to do come April? Damn, this is like the same conversation we had involving Wyatt years ago. Deja vu. Remember that?"

"I do. Why is history repeating itself?"

CHAPTER 33
Callie

"Charlie, I just don't think this is going to work out. We've been together for years, and I think we've run our course." facing myself in my bathroom mirror, I continue, "Charlie, you're a great guy, but you really deserve more than this." *Why do all of these explanations sound like an after school special?*

The phone rings and breaks my concentration. I glare at it. Will it to stop ringing. It continues. The answering machine picks up.

"Callie, it's Charlie. I really do think you're avoiding me now. I've called you several times in the past few weeks to set a time so that we could discuss things—have an adult conversation—and you haven't returned any of my phone calls. What is it? If you think avoiding me is going to deter me from continuing to call, you're wrong. We need to talk. Call me."

The machine flashes red with the impending message. Since he called weeks ago, I haven't had the courage to call him back and say the words I need to say. *We're over.* I have tried to hint around by saying things that were, to me, obvious, but he just doesn't pick them up. I'm going to have to put my big girl panties on and call. It's like ripping a Band-Aid; it'll only hurt for a minute. *But first I should eat something. Surely I can't break up with the guy on an empty stomach.* So I make dinner. Then I decide it is a nice night to take a run through the neighborhood. *I don't want to go to bed all sweaty. I should shower.* Before I know it, it's ten o'clock, and in my mind, too late to call Charlie. *I'll call tomorrow.*

I am restless from a terrible night's sleep, knowing that I should have made that phone call the night before. *After work today I'll call him. I mean it.*

"Whoa. What happened to you?" Natasha asks, concerned.

"Nothing…yet."

"What's that supposed to mean exactly?"

"I have to call Charlie tonight and break up with him."

I explain my feelings about the situation and she commiserates with me.

"Well, that doesn't sound like a whole lotta fun, now does it?" The kids begin trickling in, and soon my thoughts of Charlie move to the back burner. I have stopped thinking of him until my ride home when my mind is racing and my palms are sweating. Once at home, I give myself no excuses and go directly to the phone. My hands shake as I dial the number. One ring, two rings, three rings. *Phew, must not be…*"Hello?"…*home.*

"Hi, Charlie, it's Callie. Is this a bad time?"

"Cal, it's never a bad time when you call." *This is not going to be easy.*

"So, you've probably been wondering why I haven't called you back in a while."

"Yes, the thought crossed my mind."

"I'm just going to come out with it. Charlie, I think we need a long-term break."

"You mean months apart isn't a long enough break for you?"

"Well, no, actually. I was thinking a permanent break so that you can find someone else. We make such good friends. I think we should just *be* friends." Silence. "Is this making any sense?" Continued silence. "Charlie, are you still there?"

"Yes."

"So, I guess the bottom line is I think we should break up."

"Why?" he says sounding childlike.

"Charlie," I say, feeling exasperated, "we have just grown apart. I'm not ready to settle down. I'm not ready to move to Connecticut. I'm not ready to leave my family, and I don't want to waste any more of your time waiting for me to move."

"What if I don't mind waiting? What if I think you're worth the wait?"

"You'd be waiting a really long time. You're closing in on 30. It's time for you to move on."

"I'm nowhere near 30. I'm 27," he replies, sounding hurt.

"Please don't make this any harder for me."

"Is it someone else? Did you find someone in Missouri?"

"No. I don't have much of a social life. I run. I work. I eat. End of story. There's no one else."

"Then I'll wait." This is not the response I am looking for.

"There's no need. Please find someone to move on with."

"I'll talk to you soon. We should meet up somewhere."

"Are you listening to me at all? I want to break up."

"Bye, Cal." The line goes dead. *What just happened there?*

As I open a bottle of wine, the phone rings. *Why would he call back so soon?* "Charlie, I meant what I said. We need to break up."

"That sounds awful. How did the guy take it?" Jason asks on the end of the line.

"Oh, Jason. Hey. Sorry about that. I just got off the phone with Charlie."

"And you broke it off? Tough night?" Jason asks gently.

"Yes," I sigh.

"Great! Well, not great, but it sounds like you might need a night out on the town. I called to tell you that Ryan and I are going down the street to listen to Singer Songwriter Night at The Wolf if you'd like to join us."

"That actually sounds fantastic. I'll be there in thirty minutes."

"How you holding up? Maddie's gone, and tonight you broke up with Charlie you're having a red letter day!" Jason feigns excitement.

"I would say this will go into the record books as one of the worst days," I admit, taking a bite of my black bean burger.

"Thankfully you came to the right place." Jason waves over Ryan, who had gone to the bar to get drinks for the table.

"Thank you, Ryan. Just what the doctor ordered," I say, as he hands me a glass of wine with a smile.

"Turn that frown upside-down. You're going to love this music tonight. Tonight's singer is yummy," Ryan enunciates the word, causing a giggle to bubble up and out of me.

"Music to my ears," Jason says, rubbing my shoulder.

"Please welcome to the stage Duncan Campbell." applause erupts from around the sparse crowd.

Turning toward the stage, I watch as Duncan sits behind an upright piano and begins to play an original piece. His voice is velvety smooth, and immediately I feel myself relax. He sits on stage with his shaggy, shoulder-length, light brown hair—wearing his well-worn denim jeans, flannel shirt, and flip-flops. *Interesting.* When he is finished with his first song, he turns to thank the audience and I see his eyes. They are the most unusually, beautiful gray I have ever seen. *Interesting indeed.*

CHAPTER 34
Callie

One humid spring morning, the ring of the phone startles me as I stand in the shower. It rings, then stops, then rings a few more times. Someone is trying to get ahold of me; it's evident. On the next round of rings, I'm out of the shower running for the phone.

"Hello?"

In a rush of excitement, Maddie rambles excitedly, "Cal, he did it. He proposed this morning. Out of the blue, Zach proposed! Can you believe that? Not for nothing, but I thought for sure you'd be the first one getting married. He wants to marry me even though he knows everything—I mean everything—about me. I told him about my past with drugs, rehab, Frankie, the baby, everything, and he STILL wants to marry me. Ain't that some shit?" she finishes, finally taking a breath.

"Oh, my gosh, congratulations! That's so exciting!" I feel just a twinge of jealousy once again. "When? Where? Have you told your folks?"

"You're the first person I wanted to call."

"Awe, I feel honored."

"Speaking of being honored, would you be my maid of honor? I can't think of anyone else in the world that I would want standing up there with me," she says, sounding emotional.

Between tears, I say, "Of course I would. That is truly an honor."

"Mrs. Zachary Grayson. Maddie Grayson. Mrs. and Mr. Zachary Grayson. That sounds so good," she says, reminding me of a schoolgirl with a crush doodling the many ways to say husband and wife on a piece of notebook paper. Her enthusiasm is infectious.

"We'll have to celebrate soon. Right now, I gotta get going to work. Love ya', girlfriend and I'm so happy for you," I say, meaning it this time.

"I'm not sure when they'll get married," I explain to Natasha as we wash the paintbrushes between groups.

"I love a good party. Can I come to the bachelorette party?"

"Sure. I don't see why not. She doesn't have a whole lotta girlfriends around here. A few girls at the sandwich shop, but that's about it."

"Great! I'm an excellent party planner. I'll help with whatever you need."

"I have no doubt," I smile.

Pheonix walks in looking much weaker than she had the previous weeks.

"How's everything going, Pheonix?"

"Okay."

"Did you have a tough treatment today?"

"Yes."

From the way she looks over at her worried mother, I can tell there are things to be said. Watching this conversation without words makes my stomach sour. I press on with our artwork, asking Pheonix, "Would you like to use chalk today or paint?"

"Chalk, please."

As I bring down the construction paper, she says, "Black, please."

A chill runs down my spine. "All right."

She uses pastel chalk over the black construction paper to draw a tree. Not just any tree, but a weeping willow.

"That's an interesting tree, Pheonix. Can you tell me a little about it?"

"It's me."

"It's a beautiful tree," I say, looking at the downcast branches. There are many branches, each of them look sparse and brittle, clinging to the ground.

"This year, I wanted to make a piece of art that's from *my* heart," she says, while intensely working on her tree. Again, I peek at the mother, who is wringing her hands.

When Pheonix has grown tired and is done working, she asks if she can rest in "the cave." "Of course you can," I say, with a worried smile.

Her mom walks her over to a couch and helps her lie down. The cave is a room behind the art area separated by a wall. Long couches and a big screen TV furnish the room teenagers prefer to go during treatment. It's quiet and dark; a place for some solitude.

After a long tiring day, I talk with Natasha as we clean up the art supplies.

"I'm worried about Pheonix."

"I know you are. So am I," Natasha frowns.

After thinking for a moment, I continue, "Tash, do you feel like you're still connected with the kids after they pass away?"

"I do," she says without hesitation.

"How so? I mean I know I've had some strange experiences in my life after people I've known have passed on. Like one time, my friend's brother, Tyler, died in Lebanon back in 1983. He was in the military, Marines actually, and he was killed while he was sleeping in his barracks. It was really an awful time for my friend."

"What did you experience?" Natasha asks, as she hands me some glitter paint to put away.

"This is going to sound crazy, but he pushed me off the road out of the way of a truck. I truly believe I would have been seriously hurt, or worse, had he not pushed me off the road." I laugh, "even as I say it out loud, it sounds like I'm crazy. Sometimes I even hear him. Not often, just occasionally."

"I don't think you're crazy. One time I had a patient, Jon. He liked to go to the cave, like Pheonix does. But he was nearing the end, and he was receiving a lot of IV fluids to keep him hydrated. He'd have to use the restroom a lot. In and out of this room he would go all afternoon. You know how this door is handicap accessible? You press the square and it slowly opens and closes?" I nod my head, looking toward the door.

"Well, I went home one day after seeing him one last time. I just had a feeling he was going to pass away soon. I was in my kitchen cleaning up after dinner, and I saw this blur, this flash of color run past me through the kitchen and out of the house. I just knew it was Jon and that he had passed, so I checked the clock. It was 8:05 P.M. When I went to work the next day, I explained what I had experienced to one of the nurses, and she verified that he had passed away at 8:05. It felt like he was running through to say goodbye one last time." She smiled at the memory.

"For the next three weeks as I worked with patients in the art room, the electronic door would open and close all day long without anyone coming or going. Every time it would open, I would say, 'Hi, Jon.'"

"Whoa. That's really cool… and creepy."

"It is," she laughs. "So it's possible you'll hear from Pheonix again, if that's what you're wondering. If you're open to it and you're aware of what's going on around you."

"That's exactly what my aunt told me."

"Smart lady," she winks.

CHAPTER 35
Callie

On my way to the art room to work with Tabitha, I walk into a conversation that Tabby's mom is having with Natasha.

"I can't go back to that area. Her father was in a concentration camp. Can't go back." She speaks with a thick Croatian accent.

Tabby is a quiet, sweet, four-year-old girl. The only hair she has lays in thin wisps of brown, barely visible on her tiny head. She's focused on the clay in front of her, making different foods. In between conversing with Tabby's mom, Tasha asks Tabby questions about her creations.

"Is that spinach?"

"No. I need the big spatula. I want to make a ginger man." Natasha hands Tabby the utensil.

Tabitha has clear cell sarcoma. She was diagnosed right before her second birthday with a sarcoma that was causing tumors on her kidney. It has since metastasized and moved into her brain. She's undergoing chemotherapy to eradicate the tumors.

"We think it'll work this time," Tabby's mom says as she turns toward the door. Another nurse enters, checking on Tabby's treatment. "We love Molly, don't we?" She prompts Tabby.

"No."

"Haha, yes, we do. She's always on time and she's really good at assessing kids," Tabby's mom continues to speak to Natasha and I. "Tabitha doesn't like the nurses during this process, but after we're finished, she loves everyone." Lost in thought for a moment, she gazes at Tabby. "This is our last chance."

I look at Tabby and notice a very subtle change come over her. "Do you want to go lie down?"

"No."

Tabby's face is even paler than moments ago, which doesn't seem possible. Her eyes well up, redden, and her frown deepens.

"I want to play on my iPad." This is her mom's queue to help her leave the room, and go lie down. As they are leaving the room Tabitha looks over her shoulder and says, "Don't mess up my pizza!" referring to the clay creation she just completed.

Handing the clay pizza to me, Tabitha's mom says, "Let's let Callie hold that so that Mama can carry you." As the mechanical door opens, we hear a wailing child from down the hall. I look at Tabby and her mother; it takes everything in my being to compose myself. As Tabby lays her head on her mother's shoulder, a crescent shaped scar becomes visible just above her left ear. Seeing this draws a quiet gasp from my lips. I try to cover it up with a cough, but her mother turns and looks at me with aching sadness.

Glancing over my notes from the time I began working with Tabitha, I read that Tabby's mom has taken one picture a day to track the changes to her daughter over the past two years. She used to be a bright, rambunctious little girl, but since the diagnosis, her energy has declined rapidly, along with her mobility. She often fights it by trying to walk on her own but is unsteady. As of a few weeks ago, she can only go three steps without falling.

Later in the day, I have the privilege of working with Hannah, a young teenager, on a piece of art. She uses white craft paper and charcoal. She is drawing four small pictures on one page. She has sectioned off four squares, and in each square she has drawn a house. In one, there is a simple house with a tree out front, snow on the ground, snow on the branches and roof. Smoke is coming from the chimney. The second drawing is the same house and tree with small flowers on the tree and on the grass in front of the house. I begin to see a pattern. She is drawing the seasons and has two more to complete her work of art. As she begins the third house, a change comes over Hannah. She seems listless. "Hannah, everything okay?" She is having a difficult time replying due to shortness of breath. I have seen this before. I open the mechanical door and holler for the nurse who quickly comes in and verifies that Hannah is indeed having a toxic reaction to the chemotherapy. Because her immune system is so compromised, an ambulance is called and she is brought to the emergency room at the hospital next door. Unfortunately, that means that she will have to start this round of treatment over again with a new chemo.

"It always scares me when patients have a reaction," I say, trying to shake the ominous feeling.

"I know it's hard to watch. Good thing you know what to look for. If not, she could have had more serious reactions to come," Natasha explains.

"Watching Hannah, I begin to think her poor body isn't going to be able to take much more of this."

"I have a feeling you're right."

Sure enough, a few weeks later, Hannah is back. Her mother is with her and she sits quietly finishing her artwork of the seasons. Oddly enough, she has gone from beautiful drawings of winter and spring to a scene of destruction for summer, leaving the fourth square blank. The summer scene is the same house, but the tree no longer has the beautiful flowers. There are no leaves and the house is in the middle of a terrible thunderstorm. Lightening is all around, striking the house and the tree; all telltale signs that the cancer is consuming her. She tires quickly. Her mother helps her to the couch behind the wall. It seems the time has come. Hannah's mom is prepared with Hannah's favorite spiritual music and presses play on the recorder for her to listen to as she passes on. As Hannah lies there taking her last breath, her mother comforts her with the music. She lies with Hannah on the couch, stroking her hair, telling her how loved she is. It is an intimate scene I feel compelled to be a part of.

After the moment passes, and with it Hannah's life, the hospital staff comes over to handle Hannah's body. Her mother sits on the couch where moments ago her daughter had lain. She sits listening to the same song on repeat. Reaching down to turn off the recorder, Hannah's mom notices not only that the recorder is in the off position, but that it isn't even plugged in.

The fragility of life gives me pause. As I sit in the silence of my apartment, alone, the thought of being by myself at the end of my life evokes the depressing image of myself on my deathbed, with no one around to hold my hand or stroke my hair. Sure, my folks are around, but not forever. It's time to invest some energy in myself and work on forging a new relationship. *Or an old one,* a voice whispers in the stillness.

CHAPTER 36
Callie

"All right, Mad, you ready for your big night?" I place a veil on her head and attach lifesavers onto her t-shirt—front and back with needle and thread.

"As ready as I'll ever be. What are you doing to me?" She giggles.

"This was your idea, not mine. 'Suck for a buck?' Really? Where do you get these ideas?"

"It looked like fun when I saw someone else doing it."

"I wish I lived in your little world," I point at my forehead, smiling.

"Be glad you don't. I wouldn't want to tarnish that lily white mind of yours."

"Lily white? What's that supposed to mean?" I say, feeling slightly offended.

"It's *your* little world I need to be a part of. My mind is in the gutter and yours is in a happy little bubble floating on a breeze."

"I see. Well, for your information, I have nasty thoughts, too. Just not as often as you do." Bringing out the wind-up, walking penises, I continue, "It's nice to be in the gutter sometimes," I confess, releasing a tiny, plastic, bouncing penis across the table.

"That looks just like a penis, only smaller."

"What did the penis say to the condom?" Maddie asks, trying hard not to laugh.

"I don't know, what?"

"Cover me, I'm going in."

"Ha! Nice one."

"What do you get when you cross a penis and a potato?" I counter, smirking,

"Hmm. I give up. What?"

"A dictator."

"Enough," I manage between laughs. "I have to get these little guys into gift bags for all the girls. How many girls are there in total?"

"I think we have nine or ten."

"I'll make up ten bags just in case."

"What else is going into these bags?"

"Some very clever straws, chapstick, lollipops, and a few more goodies."

"What time are we leaving?"

"In about 25 minutes."

Finishing up the bags, I hear a car pull up out front and know it is time.

The gleam of the shiny black limousine out the front window catches me in the eye, causing me to blink. It has pulled up out front, a gentleman wearing a uniform and black cap, looking very official, waits with the door open.

"Looks like it's time, Mad."

She grabs her purse, pulls open the door, and gasps. "You got this for me? I've never been in a limo in my life! How cool is this?" She hugs me and leaps out the door.

I bring out the box of gift bags, and the driver opens the door and takes the box from me so I can enter. Maddie and I sit in the back with big grins on each of our faces. Uncorking a bottle of champagne, Lester, the driver, pours us each a glass, then proceeds to close the door and follows my handwritten directions to each of the guests' houses. Once all ten of us are in the limo, we head to our first destination—dinner. Maddie wants a good steak, so we eat at Annie Gunn's, where we consume many drinks, and great food. Our next stop is an all male review at a place called Boxers and Briefs on the east side. This is definitely a first for me, but apparently, right up Maddie's alley.

"Yeah! Now we're talking!"

Ten to twelve male dancers rotate between the rear bar and the horseshoe bar. Above the bar sits a workable shower in which workers, and occasionally patrons, sometimes shower together. The dancers walk around in underwear, but when dancing, get completely naked on the dance floor or the bar. I feel utterly out of my element. Maddie calls to me, "You can close your mouth now, Callie."

"I've never seen anything like this before," I say, wide-eyed.

Some of the girls in our group are getting a dance from one strapping young man, and a few others try desperately to get Maddie to enter the shower with a hulk of a man. Before I can talk her out of it, she is soaking wet, this man simulating all sorts of wretched things on her, causing her to laugh heartily the whole time. While the ladies wait and watch the show Maddie puts on in the shower, I pass out the goodie-bags. Bouncing penises everywhere. By the time Maddie emerges from her shower, all the lifesavers have been consumed. Finally enjoying myself with the girls, the hours fly by. I glance at my watch. We're closing in on 3 A.M. Knowing our limo time limit is about to expire, I corral all the girls, some of whom have given out their numbers to dancers, and we drive home. Finally, it's just Maddie and me in the limousine.

"That was a kick ass night, Schmallie," it warms my heart to hear her use the nickname she gave me many years ago.

"It sure was, Schmaddie. Worth every penny to see you let your hair down…in the shower no less."

"How about that? That was some shit!"

At her new place, the house is dark save one light on in the window to guide the way. "Sleep well, girlfriend. I'll talk to you soon."

"Love you, Cal," she says with a hug.

And now there is one. The limousine driver, Lester, drives me back to my house where I pay him and thank him for taking care of us throughout the evening.

"That was a good night, Miss Callie. I hope you enjoyed yourself."

"I did. Thanks, Lester. I hope we weren't too crazy for you."

"Nah. It's not crazy until someone vomits in the back seat. Thankfully, your girlfriends kept it in check. Well, most of them," he smiles. "At least the bachelorette was squeaky clean at the end of the evening."

"Yeah, there's that. Thanks again, goodnight."

CHAPTER 37
Jimmy

Pulling her clothes on in the back seat of Lyle's beat-up Jetta, she says, "No, he doesn't suspect anything. It's fine. Who cares about him anyway? You're the one who makes me feel so alive." she kisses his lips before exiting the car.

Lyle climbs out of his car, rushing to Riley's car window. "Why can't you spend the night with me tonight if it doesn't matter?"

"Because in order to make this work, I have to be home at night. As it is, he'll be wondering why I'm an hour late. I'll have to make up some lame excuse again. The good news is that I've discovered I'm really good at lying."

"Does that mean you're lying to me?"

Riley reaches out to him, and pulling him down by his shirt collar, kisses him open mouthed. "Never."

Jimmy sits at the dinner table with a peanut butter sandwich and a bag of chips as the door opens.

"Hi, baby. Whew, what a day. When I was done and ready to close up, being the klutz that I am, I knocked over a carton of worms and had to spend the next hour washing the floor. Gross work."

"MmmHmm. Bummer," he says flatly as he eats his dinner.

"Are you upset with me?"

"You've been really busy lately. We've hardly had any time to ourselves. When I'm in bed, I'm usually alone. When I eat dinner, I'm usually alone. When are you going to make time for me?"

"I can't help it if my job is keeping me busy."

"Have you been drinking tonight?"

"I had one glass of wine from the back cooler after I cleaned up my mess, why?"

"I feel like you've been drinking a lot more than usual."

"Are you saying I have a problem?"

"No, no, I'm not. I'm just worried about you."

Riley walks over to sit on his lap. He pushes his chair away from the table.

"Awe, I love when you get all fatherly. I'm okay, really. No need to worry."

He detects an odor about her but can't place it. Dismissing the thought, he says, "Wanna go to the movies with me tonight?"

To placate her husband, she says yes.

For the next few weeks, she slows her visits with Lyle to throw Jimmy off her trail. One evening, Lyle is closing up the shop with Riley. They have been eyeing each other the entire shift and she knows what is to come. As soon as they lock the door and turn the closed sign on, Riley is on Lyle like stink on a skunk. As they part ways, they fail to notice a car in the adjacent parking lot. Jimmy slumps down in the driver's seat, undetected and fuming. He decides to give her a five-minute head start and enough time to cool down. He needs to formulate a plan. He can't be absolutely certain about what Riley is doing, but he has a pretty good idea.

"Hi, baby," she strolls up to him with a kiss as he enters the house. When she comes within an inch of his lips, Jimmy turns his head.

"What's wrong?"

"Oh, I've got a cold. I don't want you to get it." Two can play at this lying game.

"Oh, that's thoughtful of you."

"How was work today?" he asks evenly.

"Fine. You know what happened at the end of work today?" *Here we go.* "The fire alarm went off, and I had to call the fire station to say that it was a false alarm. Isn't that weird? Never had that happen before."

"Huh. Strange." Plotting his next move, he says, "I'm gonna go out with some guys from work at 8. I'll be home late. Don't wait up for me."

Thinking that sounds strange, she says, "Oh, okay. Maybe I'll see if some of the girls wanna get together."

"Yeah, you do that."

Having no intention at all of going out with the guys, Jimmy camps out at the end of the gravel road just waiting for Riley to leave the house. Eventually, she does. He follows close enough to see her car in the distance, but far enough that he won't be spotted. Driving through Franklin, past the church, she makes a right and goes to JD's Bar. *This must be where they're going to meet up.* A Jetta pulls up, and she hops out of her car and into his. *Clever: leaving her car to make it look like she's at the bar with Megan. She must think I'm an idiot.*

He follows at a safe distance. They pull into a field behind an abandoned barn. Soon the windows steam up and Jimmy can only see shadows bobbing and weaving in the back seat.

The car shakes. Jimmy watches with a white-knuckle grip on the steering wheel. Once the shaking ceases, the windows roll down. As Jimmy follows them back to JD's, he finds it hard to breath. In the parking lot, Lyle leans over to kiss her passionately. The sight nearly rips Jimmy's heart out and stomps it into the ground. Riley opens the passenger door and walks to her car when she spots him. Jimmy is leaning against the hood of the car, arms folded over his chest. She stops in her tracks, not knowing what to do or say.

"What excuse are you going to come up with this time?"

"I…well…we…Jimmy."

"You disgust me."

Lyle flees the parking lot.

"Your boyfriend clearly doesn't want to defend your honor. How's that feel?"

"He's not my boyfriend."

"Really? You don't even have the decency to call him that?"

"Jimmy, let's go home. You're thinking irrationally."

"Am I?" he laughs.

She finds it difficult to formulate a sentence as he watches her start and stop speaking twice.

"Find somewhere else to sleep tonight. You're not coming back to my house."

Jimmy drives off feeling as if he is having a heart attack. *How did I let this happen?* He grabs a beer from the fridge, walks to the back porch and sits, contemplating what to do next.

CHAPTER 38
Callie

The morning of Maddie and Zach's wedding falls on the beginning of a beautiful October day. The sapphire blue sky is gorgeous through the crisp autumn air.

At the end of my morning run with Sprout, I pass Maddie and Zach's place. With all the wedding preparations taking place, no one is home at the moment. *What a cute little house they share.* Sprout takes a left toward the home—creature of habit.

"Sorry, little dude, you gotta come with me for a while. Mom and Dad are going on a trip."

He cocks his head sideways, looks at me, and sneezes.

"I don't like it when she's gone either," I commiserate.

Back at my apartment, the answering machine's blinking red light catches my eye.

"Hey, Cal, it's Charlie. Have a minute? I was hoping you'd call. Maybe I could be your plus one to the wedding?" His message continues while I leave the room to shower.

I pull on my burgundy velvet bridesmaid dress with cap sleeves, slip on my matching shoes, which appear out under the tea length dress, grab my clutch, and I'm out the door. No need to do my makeup or hair because it will be done at the church before the service. We will meet at 11:00 and have a light lunch while having our hair and makeup done. Charlie's message comes creeping back into the forefront of my mind. *He wants to be my plus one? For real? What will it take for Charlie to get through his thick skull that we are through? No more Callie and Charlie. No more messages left on answering machines. No more plus one.*

I am the first to arrive. Maddie is walking around in a white bathrobe with 'Bride' written in silver embroidery on the back—a gift from one of the girls at her bachelorette party. Her hair is pulled loosely into an up-do with baby's breath and bobby pins holding the style in place. Her makeup is heavy on the eyes but light on the lips. It'll look great for pictures, which they plan on taking before the ceremony.

"Cal, I'm so glad you're here early. I wanted to give you something. Stay here."

She runs in her slippers into the closet and back out, holding a small silver box with a burgundy ribbon tied around it. "Do you want me to open it now?"

"No. I want you to open it tomorrow," she says sarcastically, rolling her eyes. "Yes, now. It's for you to wear today."

I open the box, revealing a silver chain with a small solid, silver heart, slightly off-kilter. Stamped in the center is a tiny, delicate dragonfly.

"How did you…?" I start, incredulously, unable to complete my sentence.

"Oh, man…did I totally fuck this up? Was it supposed to be a butterfly? Oh, shit, I bet it was supposed to be a butterfly." Sure that she has made a mistake, she reaches for the necklace. "I can fix this. I'll switch it with one of the other girls' gifts."

Moving the necklace away just as she was about to swipe it, she looks at me confused.

"It's beautiful," I squeak.

I turn over the necklace to read the inscription on the back of the heart, 'Love you, Schmaddie.' Rubbing the inscription with my thumb, I'm touched. "I love you, too," I say, and we embrace.

"Thank God! I would have had to get a nail file out and scrape that shit off," she says of the inscription. "Now stop it. If you continue to cry, you're going to make me cry, and then my makeup will have to be scraped off." This makes me laugh through my tears.

Slowly, the other girls come in dressed identically, and each of them receives a trinket from Maddie, however, I am the only one with a necklace. We have a light lunch of tuna or chicken salad and soup along with an abundance of champagne.

"Callie, you look beautiful!" Maddie's mom says as she finishes with her hair and makeup. I thank her for the lunch and go to the chair to have my hair done. My hair is pulled up loosely on the sides with a comb that has baby's breath wired into the tines. My makeup is a little on the heavy side for my liking. *I'll just wipe a little off when she's done.*

Maddie leaves the room to meet up with Zach alone. They want a moment together before the festivities begin. In her absence, I help the florist hand out the bouquets to the girls. Mine is slightly different than those of the other girls. We all carry calla lilies wrapped in white satin, but mine has three burgundy calla lilies interspersed within. When we are called to the altar to have pictures taken, Maddie's appearance takes my breath away. Her sleek, satin gown is stunning. Swarovski crystals, sequins, silver beadwork and embroidery are sewn into the bodice. Her neckline is a beaded "V" shape with beaded straps, an A-line silhouette and beaded buttons on the upper part of her skirt. It looks gorgeous against her olive skin. Her flowers are a bouquet of deep burgundy calla lilies that match the bridesmaid dresses, wrapped in white satin, which compliments the ensemble beautifully. What catches my eye are the flowers interspersed. Small pops of color from an array of wildflowers. *"For the pretty lady."* Wyatt's words echo in my mind.

Each of the groomsmen wear black tuxes, each adorned with a single white calla lily as a boutonniere, except for Zach's; his boasts a single burgundy calla lily. After taking pictures, it's time to move out of the sanctuary, as the guests are about to arrive. The back room is abuzz with wedding excitement. I hug Maddie and Zach, tell them how great they look, and how happy I am for them.

The last wedding I attended was Samantha and Brian's. It seems eons ago that I attended that wedding of Wyatt's sister. The smell of the flowers triggers the image of a drunken Wyatt professing his love for me on the dance floor. In a flash, I'm pressed against the wall of the cloakroom with his hands gripping my hair. Remnants of panic bubble up, and just as quickly, the image is gone. Looking forlorn at Maddie and Zach, *how did I get here? When will it be my turn to be happy?*

"I wish you would settle down with someone soon so that we could be barefoot and pregnant at the same time," Maddie whispers in my ear as we hug.

"Yeah, that'd be something," I say without emotion.

The wedding coordinator leads us down a hallway to the front of the church to line us up for our procession. Two by two the procession begins. I am the last to walk with my partner down the aisle before Maddie and her dad. The doors open and I walk, telling myself to slow down. Looking through the congregation, I find familiar eyes smiling back at me. Jason and

Ryan look so handsome. Ryan is already crying as I sway down the aisle. Jason rubs Ryan's back for comfort, handing him a tissue he retrieves from his pocket. Ryan wipes his eyes, blows his nose and leans into the strong shoulder of his partner. I turn my attention to Zach. He looks nervous as the trumpeter's blast announces Maddie's arrival. The doors open and an audible gasp escapes many lips. Zach wells up, which in turn makes Maddie get teary. I can hardly see as my eyes cloud.

The service is lovely, and the sentiments in the bride and groom's vows are beautiful. After fixing the train of her gown several times, my job is finally done as the trumpeter, again, blasts his horn, announcing the end of the service. Maddie and Zach lead the way, then my partner and I begin our walk. I recognize a pair of eyes behind Jason and Ryan, and I wait nervously in the receiving line for him to make his presence known.

"Hi, Cal. You look beautiful," he says, hugging me briefly.

"Hi, Charlie," I say, uncomfortable in his arms.

"I know. I was just as surprised as you were when I got the invitation to the wedding."

Why would you come to the wedding of my best friend?

Liz rushes forward, blurts, "Hi, Callie!" interrupting my thoughts.

"Wow…Liz?" Surprised and irritated, I say this looking at Charlie.

"Charlie brought me along. I didn't have a date, so he thought, since we were both back in Connecticut, we could travel together."

"Huh…that's great," I utter with disdain.

My mind reels. *Charlie and Liz are together?* Caught up in disbelief during the reception, I fail to notice a change in the music. The DJ stops and a new voice rises from the silence, accompanied by piano, playing the beautiful song that Maddie and Zach are dancing their first dance to. I turn my head, lock eyes with the musician on the stage. It's Duncan Campbell, the musician from The Wolf.

CHAPTER 39
Callie

I'm surprised to see Duncan at the wedding. I can't stop staring. Our eyes lock several times and I blush, trying to avert my gaze. It doesn't work. Eventually I look back over, and there he is, still looking in my direction. *Man, he can sing.* I swoon, listening to his melodic, breezy tunes. After the first dance, he continues to play while everyone dines on prime rib and chicken. Dinner's detritus is removed, and then the happy couple is brought to center stage to cut the cake. Dessert is distributed to all. Soon after the live music stops, and the DJ is back at work with the dance music. Duncan materializes by my side. *You are one fine specimen.* Those gray eyes make me weak in the knees. He pulls the chair out beside me and sits down in my partner's seat. The entire wedding party sits in one long table, alternating between bridesmaids and groomsmen overlooking the dance floor. My groomsman has gone to kibitz with some of the others in the wedding party.

"Hi, Callie, I'm Duncan." His seductive eyes never blink.

"Hi, Duncan, I'm Callie." *Oh, geez.*

"I think we've established that."

Blushing wildly, I say, "Yeah, I guess we have."

"I saw you at The Wolf the other night. You were sitting with Jason and Ryan.

"I was, that's right. Great guys those two," I manage, fidgeting in my chair now. *What am I, 12?*

"So I'm all done performing, and you're all done with your duties. Whaddya say we get outta here."

Flabbergasted, I reply, "The party's just starting. I can't leave now."

"Why not?"

"Because I'm the maid of honor, that's why," I explain, sounding righteous.

"I see. Well, when you're done being the maid of honor, let me know."

"I don't think I'll be done any time soon," I say, beginning to perspire.

"Well, that's true. You are tremendously busy with your duties at the moment," he offers, smirking. "Catch ya' later."

The dancing picks up now that the bridal party is involved. I do my best to keep up with my partner for the evening, but decide that his dance moves are far too advanced for me, so I waltz my way to the bar.

"Hey, Cal. You got some partner out there," Liz laughs.

"Yeah, he's something all right."

"Who was that dreamy guy you were talking to at the table?"

"Duncan Campbell. He's a local musician that I've listened to a time or two," I say, feeling irritated by her questions. "Are you guys dating?"

"What? Me? No."

"He looked like he was interested. You can't deny the body language."

My end of the conversation ceases briefly. *Where is this going, exactly?*

Turning to look her square in the face, I feel a resilience surface I've never felt before

"Liz," my eyes darken as I stare at her silently for a heartbeat. "Just stop," every word calculated. "Shut up. Just cut the shit." Breathing deeply, I continue speaking with a measured tone. "We don't need to do this *small talk*. It didn't take you long to fill my shoes where Charlie is concerned. I don't really want to know when you two became a *thing*. Just stop talking to me like you're still my friend. Friends don't do what you're doing so just move along. We'll pretend this conversation never took place." Her shallow breathing picks up in its intensity. I know I have hit the nail on the head. As she walks swiftly to Charlie's side, animated with hand gestures, I walk to Duncan with all the strength I can muster.

"Look out, Rico Suave is on the prowl," Duncan says, watching the groomsman I'm paired with for the evening.

"Kiss me."

Turning to look at me with fascination, he asks, "where?"

"Right here, where we're standing."

"Yes, but which body part?" Without answering, I reach up on my tiptoes to entwine my fingers in his hair as he wraps his arms around my waist. He draws me near with fire in his eyes, and we exchange a fervent kiss. I release him and walk to the bar leaving many tongues wagging in my wake.

The evening comes to a close and *my dogs are barking*. I say my goodbyes and congratulations and limp to my car. Duncan is leaning against his car, legs crossed at the ankles, tie undone just enough to exude sex appeal. I'm elated but try to play it off.

"What? You're still here?" I ask as I throw my shoes in the car. Sauntering over, he says, "That was some show you put on in there. I thought you'd like to get a night cap to fill me in."

"As lovely as that offer is, I'm exhausted."

"Then some coffee?" he petitions.

My resistance wanes, "Maybe one cup." With a grin, he motions me to ride with him, so I grab my shoes and walk to his car.

We find a pancake house that is open late and sit at a booth by the window. The streetlights cast shadows on the sidewalk as if ghostly patrons walk by. Sleep sounds delicious at the moment, but I've piqued Duncan's interest.

"Duncan, how do you know Jason and Ryan?"

"Oddly enough, my brother used to date Jason. It was a nasty breakup, but I thought Jason was a cool guy. My brother was being unreasonable. I guess I chose Jason after the split," he chortles "don't get me wrong, I love my brother but when you're wrong, you're wrong. You know what I mean?" he says with a wink.

"Yes, too well," I say, thinking of Charlie.

"So tell me your story." he takes a sip from his coffee mug, and I can't help but be drawn to his full lips. As I speak, he continues to drink his coffee, licking the lip of the mug slowly after each sip. I tell him about my recent breakup with Charlie and how he isn't really getting it through his head that I really did mean for us to break it off for good. I explain Liz and my assumptions about her and Charlie. Duncan listens intently. His eyes never deviate from mine. For good measure, on his last sip, he runs his tongue across his top lip. *Check, please!*

"Whaddya say we take this after-party to my place?"

Within minutes, we are at his home and in his bed. It all happens so quickly and furiously that I'm not even sure how we got here. I am panting, with a glaze of sweat on my brow. This is all so surreal. Getting up to dress, he asks, "Where you going?"

"I was thinking you should drive me home so you can get some sleep."

Reaching for my wrist, he says, "Stay. It feels really nice having you here. I can bring you to your car in the morning after some more coffee," he offers, raising his eyebrows up and down.

"Okay, if you're sure."

He pats the side of the bed I was in moments ago, "I'm sure."

I lay down beside him, having a hard time getting to sleep. He, on the other hand, is sawing logs within minutes. *I can't sleep here.* After tossing and turning, I decide to stealthily slither out of bed and into the kitchen where I get dressed and call Jason to rescue me. It takes four rings before he picks up the phone. "Hello?" he answers, sounding as if he has a frog in his throat. "Jason, it's Callie. Can you come get me?"

"Callie? I can hardly hear you. Where are you?"

"I'm at Duncan's. Can you pick me up?"

There is a moment of silence before, "You dog!" Then in the background I hear Ryan asking who it is and why I am calling. Jason relays the story. At this point, they're both howling.

"Jason, seriously. Come get me," I hiss.

Between chuckles, "Okay, okay, don't get your panties in a bunch. Oh, wait…what panties." More laughter. "I'll be there in five."

I grab my shoes and my handbag and wait by the door listening to Duncan's soft snores from the bedroom. I leave him a brief note and walk out the door as the headlights flash the front of the house.

"Hey there, Cinderella, you're turning into a pumpkin," he grins.

"Oh, shut it. You've had your fun, just drive me to my car."

"Yes, ma'am. Go home and get a good night's sleep because it sure looks like there wasn't any sleeping going on over there."

We pull up next to my car. I open the door and thank him for the ride. He starts to speak again as I close the door, get in my car and drive off.

CHAPTER 40
Callie

I'm met with the flash of the answering machine the next morning as I roll out of bed. *Damn answering machine.* My thoughts flash to the previous night, making a spectacle of myself as I threw myself at Duncan.

"Hey, Cal. Just thought I'd call and check on you. I mean, we are still friends and that's what friends do, right? Give me a call when you get a chance."

Has he always sounded this whiney? I'd have to call at another time. I am dealing with a Mack Daddy of a headache at the moment, and this message isn't helping. The timer on the coffee maker goes off and the smell of coffee permeates the room. Just what the doctor ordered.

After drinking one cup of coffee, I quickly realize caffeine isn't going to do the trick. I need a healthy dose of Mom. She loves figuring out my life. I'm like a human Rubik's Cube that only she can solve. I pull on my sweats and drag a brush through my unruly shoulder-length hair, make a ponytail, and I'm off.

"There's my fluffy little girl," Mom teases, giving me a welcoming hug.

"Hi, Mom." We sit with our coffees in a booth out of the main stream of walking traffic in a local coffee shop.

"So tell me all about it. Was it beautiful? Was Maddie so happy? Did Zach look handsome? Tell me everything," she demands, leaning in.

I describe in detail the day of the wedding from soup to nuts. "It really was a beautiful wedding and reception." I go on to describe the cake and the dancing and the music. "And Duncan Campbell was there. Do you know him? He's a local musician they hired to play during dinner. He's really good." Mom smiles. "What?"

"Oh, nothing. It just looks like my daughter has moved on."

"Oh, it's nothing like that. I met him. We talked at the reception. We'll probably see each other again. This town isn't *that* big," I explain, playing it cool. She looks at me with that knowing smile. *How does she do that?* My parents have always had this uncanny way of reading me like an open book. "Okay, yes, I think he's cute, and yes, we've seen each other outside of the wedding. I wouldn't call it dating yet but it has potential." She nods her head and smirks. "Moving on ... how are Jimmy and Riley doing?"

"That's an interesting question. I haven't heard from Jimmy in about a week, but when last we spoke, it sounded like there was trouble in paradise. I'm hoping to call him tonight and find out what's going on. If I hear anything, I'll let you know."

All in all, it is a nice chat, but it is time to leave. I have stuff I need to get to; important stuff, like a run and a nice long nap.

I'm dreaming when my phone rings. Before I can reach the phone, I miss a call from Duncan.

I pick up the phone to return his call, "Hey, Duncan. What's going on? You called?"

"Yeah, where'd you run off to last night?"

"I couldn't sleep and you were already out like a light, so I called Jason to come get me."

"Huh, okay. When can I see you again?"

"When's your next gig?"

"Wednesday night at The Wolf. Can you come by?"

"I'll see what I can do. I had a great time last night."

"Me, too. I look forward to seeing you on Wednesday." That was it. He hung up. I'm not sure what I was expecting, but our conversation was a bit ordinary. I'll just have to go have a listen on Wednesday night.

During work on Wednesday, I keep thinking about the upcoming evening. Would I have Duncan come over after the show? After all, I cleaned my apartment. Who am I kidding … I shaved my legs, which would be such a waste. Or would I go back to his house? Guess I'll just play it by ear. Leaving, I mention my plans to Natasha.

"I'd love the company, if you can make it."

"Uh, let me check my calendar and see what I have planned. Mmm, nope, nothing. I'm free. What time should I meet you there?"

"I think he goes on at 7. I'm going to get there by 6:30 so that I can get a drink and some dinner. Wanna meet me at 6:30 then?" I am grateful that she says she will drive herself, just in case.

"Sounds great. See you then."

Driving home, I mentally go through my closet, assessing my choices for the night. I don't want to come off as too needy or aloof. I have to be somewhere in between. I decide on faded jeans, a loose white t-shirt, and a loose black vest with black ankle boots. These clothes make the statement: I'm available, yet hard to get. I take a quick shower, dry my hair with a towel, then let it air dry, indicating that I am not making a big fuss about tonight. After applying minimal makeup, I leave the apartment with my damp hair curling as it dries.

"Dang, Cal. You're looking hard core." I immediately regret my choice of wardrobe.

"Thanks, Tash. Thanks for that moral boost."

"Aw, come on. You can't fluster that easily. I have just never seen this 'edgy' side of you before."

"Because I've never worn this together. Do I look ridiculous?" I ask, feeling vulnerable.

"No, no, it doesn't look ridiculous. It looks bad ass." Tash smiles.

We walk into The Wolf together, and I order a glass of wine and a black bean burger. As we enter the adjacent room where the live music is performed, I spot Duncan. He is cozied up in the corner with a cute little blond thing. His body language certainly says that he is available. *Great.* Without making eye contact, we sit at a table in the opposite corner. This is like watching a train derailment; I cannot avert my eyes. He has his hand in her hair at the base of her neck. He looks like a giant octopus next to her with his hands on her knee and neck. As I take my first bite of burger, I nearly choke when he goes in for a kiss. *Are you kidding me?*

"You okay?" Natasha says, while patting my back. Seeing the reaction on my face, Natasha turns, spotting Duncan. "Scumbag," she utters under her breath.

Trying to put two and two together, I say, "We just saw each other that one night. It's not like we're going to get married. We're not exclusive. Heck, we haven't even started a relationship."

"Still.... " Tash says.

I continue watching them, fascinated by their movements. She wraps her foot around the leg of her chair and leans into his hand while he continues to caress her neck and knee. He glances at the clock and realizes that it's time for his gig to start, so once again, he leans in, kisses her mouth, and walks to the stage. The lights dim. Duncan picks up the guitar leaning against the upright and strums. The melody is melancholy in nature, and the words he sings are soulful. It's a touching song about his one true love. Sitting on a stool, crossing one leg over the other, he drapes the guitar over his knee. His signature flip-flops dangle from his toes. He locks eyes with the blond in the corner as she sways to the music. When the song is over, the audience claps enthusiastically. Next he moves to the piano. This song is more upbeat. Sweeping the crowd with his eyes, he finds me. The mix of emotion that washes over his face is a sight to behold. I am pleased and hopeful with his continued stares.

CHAPTER 41
Jimmy

"So how's married life treating you?" Callie asks, knowing the answer.

"Did mom put you up to this call?"

Debating whether or not to tell the truth, Callie says, "Yes."

"Great."

"So really, what's going on? Mom's worried about you."

"Cal, I don't think you really want to know."

"Come on. Try me."

Exhaling, Jimmy begins to tell the sordid tale.

"Oh, man … you're right. I don't wanna know."

"Too late now. Cat's outta the bag," he says, sounding tormented. "I told her to not come home the last time we spoke, and she hasn't been back since."

"Do you know what the next move is?"

"Yeah, something I thought I'd never have to think about."

Interrupting his thoughts, I say, "Murderer for hire?"

"Ha! That thought did cross my mind … but no. Divorce." I am feeling guilty that I haven't mentioned the conversation I had with Riley at the bar a while back.

"Ah, I'm sorry to hear that, Jimmy. Honestly. This whole thing really stinks."

"Yeah, it does. Guess I should contact a lawyer."

"Probably a good idea. It should be a pretty easy case, though."

"Right. Thanks for the call. You can share with mom now. It'll make it easier for her to take coming from you."

Jimmy knows the next call is going to be difficult. Discussing his wife's infidelities with a lawyer is not something he's looking forward to.

The phone conversation with the lawyer lasts close to an hour, and by the time Jimmy is done talking, he is exhausted. Describing his wife going off with another man just feels so wrong. It physically pains him in a way he isn't expecting. He is upset about losing his wife. He is upset about losing his lover and best friend. *Why didn't I see this coming? I should have. She was with both Tyler and me at the same time; it shouldn't come as a shock. The fact that we were married doesn't mean a damn thing to her.* He sits with his head in his hands in the screened-in porch when he hears the front door open. Looking over his shoulder, he realizes that he doesn't have the energy to confront her. He watches as she scurries from room to room, gathering her belongings and shoving them in a large suitcase. She stands in the middle of the room, surveys the small cabin looking for anything else she may have forgotten, then walks toward the screened-in porch. Jimmy braces himself.

"Oh!" Riley gasps as she clasps her chest, "You scared me. I didn't think you'd be home in the middle of the afternoon." Jimmy notices the scent of alcohol in the air.

In a monotone voice, Jimmy replies, "I had some stuff to do around here."

"I see. I'm guessing you don't really want me around here. So…"

Not bothering to get up, he concedes, "Yeah, you guessed correctly."

"I'll come back another day if there's anything else for me to pick up. In case you're wondering, I'm staying at my grandma's, but I'll stay outta your way," she says, stumbling over the ottoman of the rocking chair.

"Perfect," Jimmy says, disgusted.

"Hey, you're the one who *had* to live in a house on this lake. 'It's a cute fixer-upper', you said. 'We can start our family here', you said."

Standing now, he says, "I think you should leave."

"You think you're so high and mighty now because I made a mistake. Once you come down off your high horse, you'll see that this is fixable. Lyle doesn't mean anything to me." This unhinges Jimmy; his anger begins to bubble over.

"Rye, leave." He walks to the door and opens it, ushering Riley out.

"How dare you push me out of my house. What do you think you're doing, anyway? You'll be sorry if you push me out. Once I'm out this door, I'm not coming back no matter how much you grovel."

"Grovel? GROVEL? What gives you the impression that I would want someone like you back in my life? I should have seen this coming years ago. You didn't want to marry me. You didn't want to start a family with me. Why don't you just leave; head down to the bar and continue on this bender you're on since that's what you're really good at."

"How dare you," she seethes, winds up and backhands him across the face with her left hand. Her wedding ring leaves an angry scratch from his cheekbone to his chin. Her eyes fly open in surprise. The scratch is unintentional, but to Jimmy, it perfectly depicts the demise of their relationship. Raising his hand to his cheek, he just smiles a sad smile at Riley.

"You'll be hearing from my lawyer," he informs her, calmly guiding her out the door.

"Jimmy. I'm sorry, I didn't mean to…"

He closes the door, not wanting to hear what it is she's sorry for. *Didn't mean to what? Didn't mean to hurt me?* Enough is enough. Time to move forward.

Several weeks pass. He feels the worst of it is over. He has boxed up some of her clothes, CD's, and a few pictures that were on display on the wall. He leaves the boxes on the driveway for Riley to pick up at her convenience. Jimmy's lawyer assures him that the papers are drawn up and should be signed by Riley by the end of the week. Things are looking up until his lawyer calls back.

"Hi, Jimmy. I have some good news and some bad news. Which would you like first?"

"Bad news."

"May I suggest the good news first?"

"Okay, good news then."

"It looks like Riley will not be contesting the divorce."

"She shouldn't. It was her fault all this happened in the first place. What's the bad news?"

"She can't sign off yet because of a little snafu."

"What could possibly be the snafu? We've established that she was a cheating drunk. What more is there?"

"She's pregnant."

Shock registers and his mind goes blank. He feels his knees buckle as he lands roughly on the chair beside him.

He always wanted to be a dad, even dreamed of a day when he could play in the lake with his son or daughter. Then panic takes over. What if the child isn't his? What if it's Lyle's?

Afraid to ask the next question, Jimmy summons the courage. "Is she keeping the baby?"

"That seems to be the plan. I haven't heard of any other suggestions. You have a voice in this. Would you like me to discuss the possibility of terminating the pregnancy?"

"No. If there's a chance that this child is mine, I want it. We'll just have to do a paternity test to see if it is," he speaks flatly.

"Yes, that would be recommended. It can be performed while she is pregnant if you choose not to wait until the child is born."

"That would be best for my peace of mind."

"Do realize that there are some risks that go along with the procedure. That being said, it does pave the way for legal and medical benefits for the child once paternity is established."

"Got it. I would like to know as soon as possible."

"We'll see what the medical professionals say as to an appropriate time in the pregnancy to perform this procedure. I'll be in touch soon."

Cradling the phone, Jimmy is in shock. This has never entered his mind as a possibility. *Well, this certainly makes things interesting.*

CHAPTER 42
Jimmy

"I have some good news and some … " Jimmy has grown accustomed to this form of banter with his lawyer, but is in no mood today.

"Bob, just tell me. I'm on pins and needles over here," he interrupts.

"Congratulations, daddy, it's a girl."

Stunned, "A girl? I'm going to be a dad? For real?"

"For real. Congratulations!"

"A girl. Holy shit, a girl," he says, stunned.

"Now, we do need to discuss parental rights. With the current state of Ms. Stewart's wellbeing, I think it may be in the best interest of the child if we lobby for you having sole custody. How do you feel about that?"

"Yes, okay. I'm not sure how Riley will take that news, but yes, I think that is best for all involved."

"We can write into the document that she can earn back time with her daughter if she takes certain steps to rehabilitate and proves to the court that she no longer drinks alcohol. I can send you all the documents stipulating that."

"Sounds good. Thank you."

Hanging up the phone, he is on cloud nine. *I'm going to be a dad … to a little girl …* Overcome by emotion, he crumbles into the chair and weeps. Once composing himself, he picks up the phone.

"Cal, you need to sit down if you're not already."

"Uh-oh, what? Okay, I'm sitting, give it to me."

"How does being an aunt sound?" Jimmy has to tear the phone away from his ear with all the screams piercing through the phone. Once Callie calms down, Jimmy explains everything that has happened since they last spoke.

"So I'm now looking into sole custody."

"Probably a good idea. Do you know if she's still drinking?"

"We've taken steps to ensure that she's not for the safety of the baby."

"Good. Wow. I can't believe I'm going to be an aunt. And you're gonna be a daddy! That's crazy!"

They talk about names, what she's going to possibly look like, and what her personality will be like. "Naturally, she'll be feisty, like her aunt."

"Naturally," Jimmy jests.

"Have you told Mom and Dad yet?"

"Uh … no."

"If you think I'm going to do your dirty work, you are sorely mistaken, mister."

"Ah, come on, Cal. I need your help with this one."

"As much as I would love to be the bearer of this news, you are on your own. You do have to call me later and let me know what she says."

"Right."

"Good luck with that. Seriously though, I'm sorry about the divorce. That's gonna stink on ice."

"What are you, ten?"

Laughing now, "In my little world, I am. Get going or you won't do it. Pull the Band-Aid already."

More time passes, and Jimmy is able to put the hurt and uncertainty behind him. Everyone in the family appears to be warming to the idea of a new little Lamply running around town. The vernal equinox of 2006 comes along, and with it, a new baby girl. Jimmy calls Callie at 4:54 AM on March 20th, out of breath and excited.

"Callie, she's here. She's beautiful. You should see her. She looks just like you. It's creepy really," he laughs. "she'll probably be just like you, too. I'm not sure the world is ready for another Callista."

"Please tell me you didn't name her Callista."

"No, I wouldn't do that to her. We named her Claire Prudence Lamply. Claire was Riley's mom's name, and Prudence was just a name that I've always liked. I'm going to call her Prue for short. Isn't that cute?"

"Really cute. How's Riley feeling?"

"She's exhausted. She called me at 2 this morning saying that her water broke, so I rushed over to her grandmother's cabin and brought her to the hospital. I guess the baby wanted out, because by 3:45, Riley was dilated ten centimeters and ready to push. She popped out at 4:01. We've been staring at her and passing her around to Riley's grandmother and sister. We've talked it over, Cal, and Riley has agreed to let me raise her. Can you believe that?" He spoke in a hushed tone. In the silence following his statement, the sounds of soft-soled shoes squeak down the hall where the monitors and the murmur of the voices at the nurses' station are muted through the phone.

"Wow, Jimmy. Are you ready for this?"

Without hesitation, he says, "As ready as I've ever been." Callie sits, beaming at her brother's remarks. She's impressed with all he's had to overcome and end up stronger for it. "Mom's coming up to stay and help for a few weeks. I'm taking a paternity leave of absence for 12 weeks. Unfortunately, it'll be unpaid, but I think I'll be okay with the savings I have. Dad said he'd gladly help out if need be, but I think we'll be fine."

"You're amazing, Jimmy, really, I mean it. I can't wait to see Prue and hold her."

"She's beautiful, Cal, just beautiful," he says with a sniff. The muffled sound of a newborn's cry carries out of the room.

"Get back in there, Daddy, your daughter needs you. I'll be up to visit as soon as I can. Congratulations, big brother." Hanging up, Callie lets a sigh escape her lips. If only I could be that lucky, she thinks. *Your turn will come.* The faint sound of Tyler's voice echoes through her mind, making her smile.

CHAPTER 43
Callie

It's late afternoon, and I'm out watering the roses I planted in Gramp's honor. Something catches my eye. Beneath the primrose bush is a toy. As I get closer to investigate, it appears it's a plastic insect. Not just any insect, but a red dragonfly with blue wings just sitting there. Picking it up, I look around to see if any kid is near the yard that may have dropped or thrown this plastic toy. As far as I can see, there's not a soul around. Placing it back under the roses, I'm stumped as to how it got there.

The screen door is open, and through it, Natasha's voice filters across the yard, leaving me a message on the recorder. I quickly get inside to try and catch her, but she's no longer there. Dialing her number, the tiniest of electric currents run through my fingers. *That's odd.*

"Hello?" Natasha speaks nasally through the receiver.

"Tash, it's Callie. Sorry I wasn't quick enough to answer your call." An audible sniff echoes in my ear. "You okay?"

"Callie, I'm sorry to have to tell you this over the phone," she says, as her voice cracks.

"No. Don't say it. Please tell me you're not calling about Pheonix," my voice wavers.

"I'm afraid I am. Pheonix passed away last night at home with her family surrounding her as she took her last breath. I'm so sorry." Natasha is finding it difficult to remain composed.

I stand there with the phone at my ear, yet I feel out of my body. *Pheonix? It can't be.*

"Callie, are you still there?"

"Yes. I'm gonna go now. Thanks for letting me know."

"Do you want to talk abo…" Natasha's sentence is cut off by the disconnection of the phone.

Stunned, I find myself back outside staring up into the brilliant blue sky. *Why?* Slowly I walk to the rosebush and pick up the plastic dragonfly once again, now fully realizing who sent it to me. This realization breaks the floodgates wide open and I'm reduced to tears. I crumble in the front yard, as my legs can no longer carry my weight. The dragonfly looks at me with a knowing stare. Unaware of time and space, I sit and stare at this toy until the streetlights illuminate.

I'm on autopilot as I drive to work. I'm able to perform my daily activities at the hospital, just barely. After ignoring my lunch break, Natasha sets a yogurt in front of me. Placing her hand over mine, she says, "She wouldn't want you ignoring your health. You should go home," Natasha says, gently rubbing my back. "Light a candle, take a bath, take it easy and let yourself grieve. We will all miss her."

"She seemed to pass so quickly," I say, not embarrassed by the tears rolling down my cheeks. I look at Natasha with bloodshot eyes, "Why does it hurt so much?"

"You two were kindred spirits; connected, linked souls. It happens sometimes. There's a connection that no one can explain. It just happens."

I stand sniffing loudly and gather my things. As I walk toward the door to leave, Pheonix's last piece of art releases itself from the wall and floats to the floor. As if a window is open with a breeze pushing its way through the room, I bend over to retrieve it. When last we worked together, she had the picture half finished. Somehow in the weeks between visits, she has finished it. My hands tremble as I look at each item on the paper; the silver wings of the dragonflies that flutter across the darkening sky; the mist that hovers above the grassy field; the light cast down through the mist; the weeping willow tree and the two figures standing facing one another. It's beautiful. I turn the paper over to find an inscription that reads To: Callie *BELIEVE* Love, Pheonix. Feeling eyes on me from all corners of the room, I continue through the door without looking back.

CHAPTER 44
Jimmy

July 2006

Walking in a sleepless haze to the nursery, Jimmy is physically and emotionally exhausted. Standing beside the crib, looking down at his baby girl as she whimpers for comfort, he marvels at this exquisite being. He reaches down, picks her warm, wiggly body up, and breathes in her scent. He carries her to the rocking chair in her room, places the bottle to her lips, and watches as she nourishes herself. Setting the bottle aside, he places Prue over his left shoulder and gently pats her back, hoping to produce a burp. As he continues to pat her back rhythmically, there isn't even a hint of sunlight on the horizon; it is still the dead of night.

"Okay, baby girl. It's time for you to go nighty night. Daddy needs his rest." kissing her forehead, he places her on her back and winds up the mobile of dragonflies, which lazily fly above her head. He turns on the soft dragonfly night light in her room and quietly retreats. He is still amazed at the beautiful mural Callie painted of whimsical dragonflies and fairies in an enchanted forest. In the distance of the forest, there lies a castle with beautiful weeping willows surrounding it. Not realizing what an artist she is, he was a little leery when she said she wanted to paint Prue's room as a gift to her new little niece.

The job had taken several months due to the fact that she lived so far away. Callie managed to come out several times while their mother stayed to help Jimmy. It was great to have family around those first few months, but now that Prue is nearly four months old, they are on their own.

Jimmy returned to work the week before and is starting to get into the new routine of being a single dad. The hard part is getting up for the middle of the night feedings, but that's going to end shortly. Though he dreads the day that he will let her cry through the night, he knows it has to be done. Just, not yet.

The soft purples and blues were perfect paint choices. Somehow Callie had used a glittery paint on the walls in places that captured the light, making it a magical place.

He climbs back into bed, listening to the baby monitor at his bedside as his daughter goes from restless to silent with only the sound of her sweet rhythmic breathing in a matter of minutes.

He sleeps soundly until he is roused by his alarm and the sound of light giggles coming through the monitor. He knows he has to get ready and feed Prue breakfast before the sitter arrives. Hoping for a quick shower before his day begins, he takes the monitor into the bathroom.

In Prue's room, he is greeted by his baby girl's beautiful smile. His heart melts as she lies in her crib reaching for him. Smiling at her, he reaches in to pick her up and notices that the mobile is still spinning as if just wound up.

"How's Daddy's favorite girl this morning?"

Squealing with delight, she begins to kick her legs with enthusiasm.

"Great! Let's get you ready for Becca, sweet girl. We don't want to keep her waiting."

Becca has taken on the position of caregiver during business hours. She is a 24 year old single woman that hasn't graduated college in four years like all of her other friends. She is paying her way through school, and it is taking her a lot longer than anticipated. This nanny position with Prue is helping to pay for her schooling.

Prue is happily eating her cereal as Jimmy scoops spoonful after spoonful into her eager mouth, "Here comes the airplane." Hearing the doorbell, he reluctantly places the spoon on the high chair next to the bowl and leaves to answer the door. "Guess who that is," Jimmy asks in a singsong voice as he exits the kitchen.

Hastily, Jimmy opens the door and greets Becca with a hug. If he weren't so sleep deprived, he would linger on their hugs but knows this is neither the time nor the place. "Come on in. Prue's just finishing her breakfast." He walks quickly back into the kitchen and stops in his tracks as he looks at his sweet little girl covered in cereal. She has been using the cereal as moisturizer in his absence. She continues to rub it into her skin and her hair, oblivious to the stares of Jimmy and Becca.

Laughing, Becca swoops in, "I got, this Mr. Lamply. You go ahead and do what you have to do. I'll get this little monkey all cleaned up," she smiles. It's obvious she adores Jimmy's daughter, and the feeling seems to be mutual as Prue reaches up for Becca. "Come here, you little rascal. Let's get you in the tub. We have a play date in an hour, and I'm pretty sure they didn't mean this when they asked for us to bring a snack," she says, scooping cereal from Prue's PJs and tossing it in the trash.

"Okay then. It looks like you have everything under control. Give me a call if you need anything today. Take care of my little girl."

"Will do Mr. Lamply."

"Hey, Becca. About this 'Mr. Lamply' business. You can just call me Jimmy, you know."

"Got it. Have a great day, Mr. Lamply," she says with a twinkle in her eye. Jimmy walks to Prue, who is splashing water all around the tub and kisses her gooey head.

"Bye, sweetheart. Be good for Becca."

"She always is," Becca replies, as Jimmy stands lingering, finding it difficult to leave his daughter. "She's in good hands, now go," Becca chastises.

Walking out the door to work today is a little easier than the day before, and a little easier than the day before that. He is getting into a routine with Becca and Prue, and he feels lighter than he has in years.

CHAPTER 45
Callie

As seasons change and winter returns, I find myself combing through the many Christmas cards my parents receive during the holidays. In the basket I search for the card I'm holding now and wonder why I didn't end up walking down the aisle with Charlie.

"I think you may have broken his heart," Mom says quietly as I place the picture back in the basket. "Over the past several years, Charlene and I have kept in touch. She said that Charlie never really got over you."

"Gee, thanks for that, Mom," I say sarcastically.

"She said that he never really understood why you broke up or when it was actually over. He figured since the phone calls were getting farther apart and you just stopped returning his calls, that pretty much meant it was over."

"I tried to break it off with him several times. He just wouldn't take no for an answer. It just felt like we had grown apart. I do miss him sometimes, but that's just because he used to be so much fun to hang around."

"For what it's worth, he seems very happy with Liz. She's pregnant with their first child. Charlene is thrilled to be a grandmother." Looking wistful, Mom continues, "I'm looking forward to the day a little one is running around here yelling me Nana." *Nothing like turning that knife in my back, Mom. Liz? Really?* I knew that Charlie and Liz had been seeing each other.

I do recall Liz visiting Charlie the Thanksgiving I drove down to surprise him. I guess the surprise is on me. Still, it pains me to hear Mom's words.

"Huh," is my only response. What am I supposed to say? I am happy for him. Isn't that what we want for everyone? Just to be happy? *I'm happy aren't I?* Duncan and I have dated irregularly for over two years. He isn't settling down anytime soon; I know that, and he knows that. We're just keeping each other company for the time being, keeping it simple. It seems all my friends are settling down except me. *Maybe I was born without that gene?*

I often wonder what would have happened if I'd moved back to Connecticut with Charlie. If I would have had that happily ever after I'm looking for? Somehow I doubt it.

"I wonder why Maddie never told me that Liz and Charlie were serious," I questioned.

"Probably didn't want to hurt your feelings … you can get emotional sometimes."

"Pssst. Shhhyeah right."

"Honey, you know you do. You're just like your mother," she smiles in my direction.

"Sometimes I am, but it's warranted."

"Exactly. Precisely why they didn't tell you."

"Okay. I get it. So how long have they been married?"

"They just got married in September."

"Wow, they certainly moved fast on the baby front."

"No time like the present," she says with a singsong voice.

As if on cue, my cell phone begins to ring.

"Hello?"

"Hey, beautiful." Just hearing Duncan on the other end makes me blush wildly.

"Hi yourself. Where have you been the last couple of weeks?"

"Oh, you know, here and there." I know better than to ask too many questions. I really don't want to know who he has been with and when. It's too upsetting, and it is the holidays. "I was wondering if you would come to my holiday gig this week. I was told to bring a date."

Feeling flustered, I ask, "What day?"

"Saturday night."

"Sure that sounds like fun."

"Great. You can meet me there around 7. Cool?"

"Why not. I have nothing going on that night." *Why am I trying to play this thing so cool?* If I had my way, he'd dress up in a pair of black pants, a jacket and maybe a tie. Heck, I'd be happy if he just put on some dress shoes for a change. In this little fantasy, he'd pick me up with some flowers in hand, give me a kiss hello, then walk to the car and open the door for me. The best I may get from Duncan is a pair of "dressy" jeans, essentially a pair without holes in the knees.

True to form, Duncan is in his dressy jeans, flannel unbuttoned with a navy t-shirt underneath and his dress shoes for the occasion: Birkenstock sandals. Feeling overdressed, I sit in my red and blue plaid maxi skirt, blue t-shirt, and white cardigan.

The good news is when I walk into the private party at Harry's West, Duncan sees me immediately and waves a quick hello. Unfortunately, he turns and begins chatting with an adorable blond in a black leather mini dress. *How can I compete with that?* After his first set, the person in charge of the party begins making announcements that don't pertain to me, so I mosey up to the bar. I make small talk with the bartender, who looks up from our conversation and says, "Hey, man, whatcha drinking? You sounded great up there."

"Thanks, I'll take a Bud. I just came over to talk with this pretty lady right here."

Feigning ignorance, I ask, "Oh, yeah? Who might that be?" With that he leans in for a kiss. Not just a light 'this is my hello' kiss, it's a 'let's go back to my house and stay awake until 3 in the morning' kind of kiss. It takes me off-guard. Catching my breath, I say, "That was some 'how do you do.'"

Laughing, Duncan sits down at the bar. "How'd you like the set?"

"You sounded great, as usual." I smile as he places his hand on my knee.

I can feel the buzzing of my cell phone in my pocket but am too mesmerized by the soft grey eyes staring at me to pick up the phone.

"I've got one more set to get through before I take you home with me."

Again, my phone comes to life. Once more, I ignore it as I enjoy the attention from Duncan and begin visualizing just what may transpire in about an hour. My phone buzzes for the third time.

"Hold that thought. It seems someone is in dire need to speak to me," I say, while reaching into my pocket for my phone. Duncan leans in and nuzzles my neck as I answer the phone.

"Hello?" I manage, finding it hard to concentrate.

"Cal, it's Nanny, honey…" My mom's voice is being drowned out by the crowd, so I tap Duncan on the knee, point to the phone, and then to the door.

"Hold on a sec, let me get outside. I can hardly hear you." I find a quiet spot just to the side of the building.

"What's going on with Nanny?"

"Sweetheart, Nanny passed away earlier today." I hate being at the age where people I love start to die.

"Oh, my gosh, I'm so sorry to hear that. Is Dad okay?"

"Yes, he's doing all right. You know she lived a long life. She *was* 93," Mom says, trailing off.

"I know, but it's never easy. When are the services?"

"They're working on the plans right now, but probably sometime early next week. Can you get a few days off to go to Vermont?"

"I'm sure I can. Just send me the information and I'll be ready to go." No longer feeling too excited to hang out in a bar, I go inside to say goodnight to Duncan. Walking numbly through the crowded bar, not able to locate him immediately, I find comfort in the thought that Pheonix is up there with my grandparents drawing beautiful pictures for them. The tick of a wall clock in this loud bar draws my attention. *I never noticed that clock before.* It's a clock in the shape of a refrigerator. On the hour, the door of the fridge opens with the sound of falling beer cans. I walk around the place until I spot him. He is clinging to the blond he was eyeing earlier in the evening. *Shocker.* Walking slowly over, I watch as he whispers something in her ear, making her blush right before my eyes. Then as if for my pleasure, he leans in for a doozy of a kiss as I stand in front of them. He is still unaware of me, so I clear my throat.

"Duncan, I have to leave. Don't get up. Really. It looks like you're preoccupied." "Everything all right?" he asks while playing with the blonde's hair.

"No. My grandmother passed away," I say flatly, irritated by the blonde's presence.

"Wow, I'm so sorry," Blondie says from her perch, sitting there wrapped around Duncan like a ring-tailed lemur. *Oh pulease.* Ignoring her, I continue, "I'll be leaving for Vermont with my family next week."

Peeling blondie off his leg, he stands up to console me. As much as I want to walk away from him, the human contact is just what I need. Without realizing the pent-up emotion, I begin to well up. His strong arms hold me close as he strokes my hair and soothes me until my tears subside. Regaining composure and breathing normally again, I squeeze his torso and back away. "Whew. I was not expecting that," I say, laughing at myself as I wipe my nose with my sleeve. "Anyway, I'm gonna get going."

"Give me a ring when you get back into town, babe." As he resumes his position with the blond, I have a strong suspicion this will be our last contact. I thought I could play it cool and be that girl who just goes with the flow, but deep down, I know I want something more. Something stable and secure. This life as a musician's girlfriend isn't cutting it for me. I feel more like a groupie, and that goes against all my morals.

Walking out of the bar, I take one last glance over my shoulder to find Duncan deep into Blondie's mouth. *They're made for each other.* As I reach the door to exit, I hear the clock announcing the top of the hour with the sound of crashing cans. I turn to watch as the refrigerator door opens, revealing the contents that, fixed on a hinge, spill from the inside. Riding on top of the lead can is a dragonfly.

CHAPTER 46
Callie

This is your captain speaking. We're cruising along comfortably at 39,000 feet, so I have turned off the fasten seatbelt sign. Feel free to move about the cabin. When seated, however, please fasten your seatbelt at all times as we may unexpectedly experience turbulence... The captain drones on as I sit looking out the window at the sea of clouds beneath the plane. Another funeral. An end to an era.

"Cal?"

"Huh?" I ask, as I turn my head towards my mom.

"What do you want to drink?" The flight attendant holds her pen at the ready.

"Oh, nothing. I'm good."

The flight attendant extends a bag of peanuts before moving on to the row behind me.

"Thanks."

"What were you thinking about? You've been so quiet since we got on this connection."

"Just about life. Not really being where I want to be. Don't get me wrong, I love what I do and I really do love where I am physically in Missouri..."

"Are you speaking romantically?"

"Yeah, I guess that's what I mean. I just thought by now I would be settled down. Maybe have a kid or two. Death really makes you think about life."

"Funny how that works," Mom says as she puts an arm around me and squeezes my shoulder. "You'll find your guy when you least expect it. He's out there waiting for you," she consoles with a far-away look in her eyes.

"Thanks. So," I say, shaking my head, "who's picking us up at the airport, Jimmy?"

"No, we're renting a car and driving up to Aunt Marilyn's house. She's really looking forward to your visit. She loves spending time with you kids."

"I'm looking forward to seeing her, as well. How's she doing?"

"Pretty good, all things considered. She's gettin' up there. She's in her 70s now."

"Really? You'd never know it by looking at her."

"Good gene pool," she says with a wink.

Dad's snoring interrupts our conversation, making us both laugh.

"How can he do that?"

"He's out as soon as he sits for any length of time. It doesn't matter what's going on around him. The man drives me crazy." I smile at her chastising.

Pulling into my aunt's driveway, I'm back at my home away from home. I carry my bags up the stairs to *my* room and find that the familiar creepy doll is still around. This time, however, the doll is in the hall in a child-sized rocking chair rather than in my room. I walk over to it and turn its head around so that I won't have to look at its glassy eyes.

"Don't you know it's impolite to stare, Lillian?" I say as I walk to my room to unpack my things. The view from the catawampus Vermont window looking out into the world catches my eye. Traffic has stopped at the streetlight below. There, crawling to a stop, is that old red pickup truck. I would recognize the Wilsons' truck anywhere. I strain to get a closer look. It appears to be Mr. Wilson behind the wheel. *But if the truck is here, that means Wyatt is here.* Butterflies wildly bump in my belly. Thinking he must have come up for the funeral makes me excited for tomorrow's service, then immediately I feel disgusted with myself. I whisper, "Just remember why you're here, Callie," fogging up the windowpane.

Back in the living room, happy hour in honor of Nanny is in full swing. Each person has a Manhattan in hand. Mom cautiously drinks hers. It is quite obvious this isn't to her liking, but for Nanny, she'll choke one down. The face she makes with each sip makes me giggle.

"Raise your glass for Wilma," Aunt Marilyn says.

"Cheers," is spoken in chorus. Clinking of glasses and looking into each other's eyes is in Lamply fashion. Nanny would be proud.

The evening ends promptly after dinner when Dad excuses himself. I know he is tired and emotionally drained. I retire to my room. Walking past the doll in the hallway, I notice her glassy eyes staring at me as I pass.

"Good morning, Callista. Would you like some coffee?" Aunt Marilyn asks sweetly.

"Yes, please. Lots of cream and sugar. Light on the coffee."

"Got it," she smiles.

We sit at the kitchen table.

"What has you up so early this morning?"

"Just couldn't sleep. My mind just wouldn't shut off, as usual," I say, taking a sip of my coffee. "I'm terrible with all things death related."

"It's just part of the circle of life, I'm afraid."

"Does dying scare you?"

"Oh, no. I'm actually very excited! Not that I want to drop dead right now, but when it does happen, I'll be excited to see who's waiting for me on the other side," she says excitedly as she looks over my head. Before I can say any more, my mom and dad enter the room.

Within the next two hours, we are showered and ready for the service. Jimmy walks in and greets my dad first, then the rest of us.

"How's it going, Jimmy?" I say with a hug.

"It's going. Riley won't be going to the funeral. She has to work today," he says, sounding upset.

Sitting through the start of the service, I keep surveying the crowd for Wyatt. I don't see him in the congregation and I stop looking when the minister asks for anyone to come forward to speak. Several of the old neighbors come up to speak. My dad speaks, which leaves everyone in tears. In closing, he says, "Please stop by the house for happy hour in honor of Mother this evening. Nothing would make her happier."

We follow Dad out of the church into the waiting limo to take us to the burial ground, our family plot, where Nanny was being laid to rest next to my Gramp. The service lasts about

20 minutes, coming to a conclusion with sprinkling dirt onto her casket. Many people come to pay their respects. Some with walkers, some with nurses, some unbelievably, drove themselves. As I'm turning to leave, I hear the unmistakable rumble of that old pickup truck. It comes to a stop at the wrought iron gate, and in walks Mr. and Mrs. Wilson, followed by Wyatt. My stomach drops.

"Thanks for coming out today, Sam, Mary. It's nice to have friends around our family during this difficult time," Dad says as they hug one another.

"Of course. It's hard to believe that both are gone now. They lived a long active life."

"Very true, Sam. It's hard to be sad when Mother lived to be 93. That's one long life."

"Yes, but it's never easy when people pass on," Mrs. Wilson says.

"They're never truly gone," A voice speaks up from behind us. Aunt Marilyn is walking past the tombstone, running her hand over the top with a smile. The hair on my neck is standing on end. As a breeze picks up, Aunt Marilyn looks up and closes her eyes. "Tyler says I'm right." *Oh boy.* Mrs. Wilson blanches at the mention of Tyler's name. Dad jumps in.

"Okay. Well, we're going to get going. Please come by for happy hour in honor of my Mother this evening," Dad says, escorting Aunt Marilyn to the car. Wyatt looks in my direction and waves as I get into the backseat of the car.

"Marilyn, you really need to pick a better time to mention the dead."

"Tyler wanted to be heard, so I spoke for him. I can't control when they have something to say." Tapping me on the knee, she says, "and he really wants you to tell Wyatt." Feeling a bit confused, I ask, "tell Wyatt what?"

"About hearing from Tyler. He thinks Wyatt would like to know this."

"I don't think that'll be well received. You saw how well Mrs. Wilson handled that information. Besides, I rarely see Wyatt anymore."

"You'll have an opportunity tonight."

"We'll see," I reply, hoping my aunt is right. Sitting in the back seat with my aunt, I daydream out the window and picture Wyatt running up Camp Road after me, breathless. Then instantly, as I begin to feel warmth in my chest, the scene takes a turn in the coatroom again. The warmth I feel turns cold. *People can change, can't they?*

CHAPTER 47
Callie

"To Mother or Wilma or Nanny. However you knew her, please raise your glass," Dad says, raising his own and looking up to the ceiling. "I'm sure you're up there cruising with Dad in his Cadillac. Cheers." The sound of glasses connecting fills the room. Under her breath, Aunt Marilyn says to me, "He's looking in the wrong direction. She's sitting on the stairs over there," and raises her glass to no one, but briefly I smell the scent of Chanel No. 5.

As the last glass clinks, there is a knock at the door. In anticipation, I open it only to greet more neighbors and friends. People filter through the house eating finger foods brought over by neighbors. Aunt Sally's desserts line the counter along with the fixings for any type of drink you desire. Scanning the contents on the counter, I am unaware that some more guests have arrived.

"Anything look good?" My heart skips a beat. I turn around slowly to find Wyatt standing a foot away.

"Hi, Wyatt. Thanks for coming." We each lean in for a hug. *Did that last longer than it should have?*

"I'm sorry to hear about your grandmother. She was a nice lady."

"She was. She was a saint being married to my grandfather for so many years," I laugh.

"How's your world?" I ask nervously.

"Good. Pretty good. Yep, keeping busy," Wyatt says uncomfortably.

Small talk is not my forte. Feeling the moment is right to start in about Tyler, I miss my opportunity as Wyatt continues.

"Feels like these funerals are coming closer and closer together. It seems like just yesterday we lost Tyler."

"It does. How long has it been?"

"Eleven years, but it feels like yesterday," he repeats.

"I'm sure it does." There is a lull in conversation as we each shift on our feet.

"I've been meaning to talk to you about Tyler. There's something I want to tell you."

"There she is," Wyatt interrupts. "Mary Jane, you remember Callie?"

"Yes, I do. It's nice to see you again. I'm sorry for your loss," Mary Jane says with a quick hug.

Placing his arm around Mary Jane, he says, "What was it about Tyler you wanted to tell me?"

"Oh, nevermind. It's not a big deal. Maybe another time. Have a drink and enjoy the food. Thanks again for coming. It means a lot to our family."

"Callie, you okay?" Wyatt asks, concerned.

"Yeah, it's been a rough day," I say, needing to remove myself from the room.

"Hey," Wyatt says, removing his arm from Mary Jane and walking after me. The look of disdain in Mary Jane's face is evident. "Hold on a sec." I feel the need to flee as panic sets in. *What's wrong with me?* Wyatt follows me out to the driveway. I'm breathing deeply, trying to slow my breath and keep the tears from flowing. "Cal?...Callie-flower?" Wyatt calls to me and I lose it. I walk around the garage out of view from the masses, as Wyatt continues to follow, and I crumble to the ground. He sits next to me and waits patiently for my tears to stop. As he waits, he picks dandelions from the grass along with any other weeds he can find. Every few minutes, he looks in my direction with concern. My breath returns to normal as I lean against the garage with my eyes closed. I feel a tickle on my chin and open my eyes to find a bouquet of weeds tied together by long blades of grass in Wyatt's outstretched hand. Reaching for them, he says, "For the pretty lady." I have to laugh at that. Wiping my eyes, I manage to smudge all remnants of makeup down my face. "Ha, not so pretty, but thanks."

"You'll always be pretty in my book," he says with a wistful look in his eye.

"Thanks, Wyatt. I'll be okay, you should head back inside."

"Yeah, I should," he says standing, reaching for my hands to help me up. He pulls me into his arms for a hug. It feels like home.

"Wyatt?" Mary Jane's voice calls from the open door.

Wyatt looks down at me from his embrace, and for a second, just a brief moment, I think he's going to kiss me. "Take care, Callie. I am sorry about your grandmother. I know grief can hit you in the strangest moments. If you ever need anything I'm here for you. It doesn't matter what we went through. I'll never forget the compassion you showed when Tyler died." He releases me, steps away and the moment is gone. "I hope to see you again. Are you here for the weekend?"

"Just a few days. Take care, Wyatt." He rounds the corner of the garage.

"There you are. Everything okay?" Mary Jane asks.

"Everything is fine. Just taking a moment to reflect on the past."

"Can we leave now? Callie's Aunt Marilyn was talking to me about your brother, Tyler. She said that he was laughing at the weeds you were collecting."

"What?" he asks, sounding startled.

"Yeah, she gives me the creeps."

"Give me ten more minutes?" he asks.

Placing his arm around her waist, guiding her back into the house, he turns to look at me as I come into view. He gives me a look of amusement and alarm.

We pass the evening with a smattering of neighbors until it is hard to keep my eyes open. I excuse myself and go upstairs to bed. After brushing my teeth and getting into my PJs, I hop into bed. The moon filters in through the crooked window at the roofline. Just as I am rolling over to fall asleep I hear a crinkle of something in my bed. Feeling around in the moonlight I find the edge of a piece of paper under my pillow. Now full of curiosity, I turn the nightstand lamp on and unfold the paper.

Dear Callie,

I feel like I'm 16 again writing you this letter. I am truly sorry you have lost both of your grandparents. Like I said earlier, I know what you're feeling. It's so hard to experience loved ones dying. After seeing you at your grandfather's funeral and now today at your grandmother's funeral, I felt it necessary to get something off my chest. It wasn't your fault. I've known this for a very long time. Being bull-headed has not served me well and I apologize. That night many years ago when Sarah told me about Charlie, I should have listened to you. I should have taken the time to understand your feelings, and I didn't. We were so young. I often wonder what would have happened if I had been patient. If I had let you work through your feelings. Now we have both moved on and started our lives. We'll never know, I guess. I regret many of my actions to this day. It seems being at a funeral puts things in perspective. I just didn't want to leave this earth without telling you that I am truly sorry for the way I treated you back then. I know it's too little too late. Maybe sometime in the future we can grab a coffee and talk about it. Just know that it's been bothering me for years. I wish you all the best.

   -W

I read his note over and over again. Shocked by this revelation, I sit up thinking for hours. Finally overcome by sleep, the last thing I remember is hearing a voice say, *it's not over.*

CHAPTER 48
Callie

Flying back home to Missouri is exhausting. I can't get Wyatt's letter out of my head. I read the thing at least 15 times before landing in St. Louis. *What am I supposed to take away from this letter?* I'll definitely have to call Maddie and discuss.

My phone lights up as I walk into my apartment. I press the play button on the machine, kick off my shoes, and lay down on the denim couch to listen.

"Hi, beautiful. I hope your visit to Vermont went well. Call me when you get this message. I'd love to see you." Duncan makes my insides melt. It is always nice to hear that he'd love to see me, but I know that Duncan only calls when he wants something. And I know what that something is.

The second message is from Maddie, who wants to see me, and wants me to call ASAP. It is urgent. "It doesn't matter what time of day, just when you get this, call me." She doesn't sound upset, but she doesn't sound like herself either. Gauging from the clock on the wall, she'll still be awake. It's only ten.

"Hi, Mad. What's so urgent?"

"Callie, where've you been?"

"My grandmother died. I had to fly to Vermont and go to her funeral."

"Oh, that sucks. I'm so sorry."

"Thanks. She lived a long life. So tell me, what's going on?" There was a pause on her end. "Mad, you okay?"

"I'm knocked up."

"What? Wow! That's great news! Zach must be so excited for you guys!"

"He is."

"Aren't you?"

"I'm scared shitless. What if something happens to the baby this time around? What if I go in for an ultrasound and there's no heartbeat? What if..."

"Stop right there. Just stop it. Zach will be by your side the whole time. I'm here for you. You have a lot of people that only want the best for you. You're going to make a great mom! Nothing is going to happen to this nugget this time. Don't be afraid, Mad. It's all going to work out."

Maddie is taking deep breaths. "I know it is. I really feel it is going to be fine. I'm afraid to get excited."

"I know you are. How far along are you?"

"I'm about eight weeks."

"That's awesome! Are you feeling all right? Any morning sickness?"

"Yes. And the cheese stench of Zach's feet makes me wanna puke."

Laughing, I say, "That's a good sign, right?"

"That's what the doctor says."

"Great. We need to get together so that I can see this nugget you're starting to grow."

"Let's do that soon. I miss your stupid face."

"Call me in a few days, and we'll get together. I'm a little scatterbrained at the moment with the whole funeral and all."

"I get it. I have the whole pregnancy brain thing going on."

"I'm gonna get going. I have to unpack and do some laundry before I get back to work tomorrow. Great news about the baby, Mad. I'm so happy for you two! Love you."

"Bye, Schmal, love you, too."

As soon as I hang up, I remember the reason I wanted to talk to her in the first place. I completely forgot to tell her about Wyatt. It was too late to call her back. I'd just have to wait until we met up and tell her in person.

I unpack my things, throw dirty clothes in the washer, and as I sit waiting for my clothes to clean, I empty the contents of my carry-on bag. Out falls Wyatt's letter. As I sit on the laundry room floor rereading his letter, I begin to think maybe I should write Wyatt back. It has been years since we have corresponded this way, and for the moment, I'm excited. Then reality sets in. He has a serious girlfriend. I have a serious boyfriend. Well, not serious. As a matter of fact, Duncan is the farthest thing from being serious. I really can't even lump him into the boyfriend category. If I'm busy, he's out with another girl. If he's busy ... I'm sitting at home. *That's it, I'm writing him a letter.* Having found a notebook in the kitchen junk drawer, I begin to compose my letter.

Dear Wyatt,

This feels very strange, yet all too familiar. I wanted to let you know that I got your letter. What a surprise that was! I feel like we have so much catching up to do. I'll start by saying that Mary Jane seems very nice. I'm glad to see you happy. I, too, have moved on in life and I'm with a guy named Duncan. He's a musician and lives nearby. I'm not sure if you keep in touch with Riley or not, but if you don't I'll give you a little update. She and Jimmy got married, then divorced not long after. They had a little girl in the process, but unfortunately, Riley has a drinking problem and would rather spend time with the companion of a bottle. Jimmy ended up with full custody. It's been very difficult, but as he puts it, he wouldn't have it any other way. He loves being a dad, and he's really great at it.

After graduating from college, I moved to Missouri to follow my family and continue my education with a master's degree in art therapy. I got a job at St. John's Mercy Hospital in the pediatric cancer center. It's the toughest job yet the most rewarding at the same time. I've met some really interesting families along the way. I lost my first patient about four years ago and have since lost seven more. It's really the worst. But it's such a gift for me to have time to spend with them at the hospital. They're sweet, troubled souls. It's my dream job. It's really strange, though, I still feel connected to them even after they have passed on. Kind of like your brother. You had asked me what I was going to say to you about Tyler when we were on my aunt's driveway. Well, it's hard to put into words, but let me try. Tyler is more or less my guardian angel. I feel it. I know it. I hear him. Don't think I've lost my mind completely. There's something I've wanted to tell you for a long time. Since we're clearing the air, I may as well put it out there. Do you remember the time I ran to Stewart's to meet you after your shift? It was the day it was pouring down rain and I was nearly run over by a truck. I couldn't put into words what happened that day but ... now here's where it gets strange, Tyler was the one that pushed me off that road. I'm sure of it. I know, I know. Tyler couldn't have, because he's gone, but believe me, he had his hand in it. Take time to mull that information over.

I'm sending this letter to your parents' house in hopes that it'll make its way to your hands. Really I just want to say thank you for apologizing. We were both to blame, and yes, we were so young. Please write back when you can. I'd love to keep in touch. Say hi to your family for me. If you ever find yourself in St. Louis, look me up.

I guess that's it from here. It seems like the lines of communication are intact again, so I'm going to sign off by saying:

Bye for now,

Callie

Feeling satisfied with this letter, I place it in an envelope, address it to his old address, and put it in the mailbox to be sent out tomorrow. Now I wait. How long will it take for a reply? Maybe a week or two? Feeling exhaustion set in, I move the wash over to the dryer and go to bed.

CHAPTER 49
Jimmy

September 2012

"Daddy, what if she doesn't like me?" Prue innocently asks Jimmy.

"Oh, baby, what's there not to like about you? Of course your teacher will like you. She'll love you!"

"Do you know Mrs. Canfield?"

"I've met her before a long, long time ago. Her son Charlie and I have been friends since college."

"Really? So she must be really old." Jimmy has to laugh at that one.

"She's not that old, but everything is relative, honey," he says, tousling her hair. "You should make sure to have a good breakfast. It's hard to learn on an empty stomach."

Prue finishes her breakfast, brushes her teeth and grabs her lunch box. She and Jimmy walk to the end of the driveway where her bus stop is. What luck it was to find a home in Newtown after all these years. He was so fortunate to get a transfer with his job back to this town. They have great neighbors who are kind and compassionate in this quaint, quiet town. Feeling his daughter's anxiety build, Jimmy says, "Hey, what if I drive you this one time. It is your first day of first grade. That only happens once, right?" Prue smiles broadly.

"Okay!"

So off they go to the school in Jimmy's car. He walks up to the front of the building and presses the buzzer for admittance.

"Good morning. Can I help you?"

"Hi. Good morning. I'm Jimmy Lamply here to drop off my daughter, Prue, at Mrs. Canfield's room." The buzzer releases the locked door, and they enter the building. Walking through the hall, he notices all the cute decorative ways the teachers have made the school enticing to learn. It has a warm, feeling and he is happy he chose Sandy Hook Elementary for his only child.

"Well, hello there, Jimmy!" Mrs. Canfield exclaims with a bear hug. "It's been years since I have seen you. You're all grown up." She speaks maternally. "And this must be Prudence. It's a pleasure to meet you." She and Prue shake hands. Mrs. Canfield walks Prue to her desk, and as Prue puts her supplies away, Mrs. Canfield walks over to Jimmy and says, "I'll take it from here, Dad."

"Oh. Okay. Bye babe ... I mean, Prue. Have a great day!" Upon hearing her father, she runs to him quickly and hastily gives him a hug.

"It's okay, Daddy. I like her," Prue whispers into Jimmy's ear. "See you when I get home." As she releases him, and returns to her desk, Jimmy feels a nostalgic pang in his chest.

During his hectic workday, he receives several texts from Riley, asking how Prue did getting on the bus today. She is curious if Prue has asked about her and asks him to please tell Prue that Mama's thinking of her. Jimmy deletes the message. Riley still hasn't gotten her life back on track. Since the divorce and birth of their child years ago, Riley has been in and out of rehab, but nothing seems to work. Unfortunately for Riley, this means there will be no visits with Prue any time soon.

The front door bursts open. "Daddy! You're never going to believe what kind of day I had! I have a new friend named Libby, I love my teacher, we have a hamster in the class named Squishy, which seems like a weird name, but it's funny and I like it." She rambles on with such enthusiasm that Jimmy can't help but smile. He loves his daughter's excitement. Oh, to be six again. Pardon me, six and a half.

Laughing, Jimmy scoops his daughter up and says, "This is big news! I think it deserves a celebratory ice cream!"

"Yessssss!" Prue pumps her fist in the air.

They drive to the Ice Cream Shoppe in Newtown and enjoy a delicious treat. All the while, Prue talks nonstop about her day and how she can't wait to go back tomorrow. This is great news. Jimmy thinks back on his first day of school. Always feeling uncomfortable with a bellyache. Each first week of school, he would ask the teacher to go to the nurse's office day after day, until one day, the nurse called home to speak to Jimmy's mom. His mom took him for ice cream, and they had a little talk. Once he was able to describe his feelings, he seemed to feel better and was able to make it through one day without going to the nurse. That day turned into two, and before he knew it, he had made it a whole month. He's grateful that his daughter is such a charismatic child. She never meets a stranger. God, how he loves her. Watching Prue's expressions and her zest for life brings a tear to his eye.

Prue stops talking and reaches out for Jimmy's hand.

"Daddy, are you okay?"

Wiping his eye, he says with a self-deprecating laugh, "Ha, yes, sweetheart. These are called happy tears."

She smiles and then continues on her one-way conversation without missing a beat.

A text message comes through while they walk hand-in-hand back to the car. It is Riley.

Can I please talk to Prue. It's been weeks since I've heard her voice.

He doesn't really want to open this can of worms, but maybe she's sober. Maybe she really is interested in her daughter. He texts her back.

I'll have her call you in a minute.

Thank you

"Sweety, Mom wants to talk to you. It's been a long time, and she just wants to hear how your day went." The look on her face speaks volumes. "Just for a minute." He dials the number as they sit in the car.

"Hi, sweetheart! How was your first day?" Jimmy hears as he hands Prue the phone.

"Fine. I have a pet in school named Squishy..." she continues telling her mother about the day's events. It seems she has talked all the excitement out of the day with Jimmy, leaving few emotions to describe the day to Riley. "Bye, Mom." Prue hands the phone back to her dad.

"She sounds weird."

"Mom was probably nervous after not talking for so long," he manages, trying to make up something on the fly. It appears that Riley has been drinking again.

"When will I get to see her again?"

"When Miss Swaller says she can. Do you remember that nice lady that sits with you and Mom when you two visit?" Prue nods her head. "She helps Mom make good choices. If she makes good choices and Miss Swaller sees this, then you and Mom can visit on your own again.

Prue mulls this information over. "So like if she stops drinking that smelly stuff, she can see me?"

"Yes. In the meantime you're stuck with me, kiddo."

"That's okay, Dad. I have more fun when I'm with you anyway."

Jimmy smiles at Prue, but inside, he feels something pull at his heartstrings. Someday he knows Prue is going to need her mother. He just prays that she will get her act together before that time comes.

CHAPTER 50
Callie

The holidays come and go without much fanfare. I see Duncan a few times but only to listen to him play his gigs. He is always preoccupied with some girl, a different one at each show. I can't compete with that so I don't try. By the first of the year, I receive a letter from Rhode Island and briefly can't place the address. Then it clicks. My heart starts beating quickly and my hands began to perspire. It's like I'm a teenager again. Quickly setting the groceries on the counter, I put everything aside. The groceries can wait. I flop on to the couch and carefully open the letter.

Dear Callie,

I truly wasn't expecting a letter in response to my note. Don't get me wrong; I am thrilled to hear from you, just not expecting it. My mom gave it to me on Christmas Eve when Mary Jane and I went to their house for the holidays. Imagine the surprise on Mary Jane's face when she saw the name on the return address.

I had no idea you were an art therapist in Missouri. Good for you! What an accomplishment. Your folks must be so proud. I told my pop about that. He was very impressed. Speaking of my parents, they're doing well. The holidays were especially difficult for my mom, which in turn makes my dad anxious, but we got through it. Samantha and Brian were over with Tyler. What a great kid he is turning out to be. He's full of piss and vinegar just like his Uncle Tyler used to be. I'm a little worried about Tyler, though I wouldn't say anything to my parents or Samantha. He keeps complaining about severe headaches. Doesn't it seem weird that a seven year old would have migraines?

So let me get this straight … you hear from Tyler? As in my dead brother? Have you lost your mind? This sounds like something we need to discuss in person someday. I don't even know what to ask or say about that topic, so I'll move on.

It's been fun reminiscing with you. I feel like I'm on the lake back in the day. Boy, does that make me sound old.

I agree, I think we should stay in touch. Write when you can.

Bye for now,

-W

It is exciting to hear from him again. Strange that even after all this time he can still make my heart skip a beat. Not wanting to seem too excited, I decide to wait a few days to write him back.

"So he just left a note under your pillow after the funeral?" Tasha asks inquisitively.

"Yep. It came out of left field. I was not expecting that at all," I grin.

"By the look on your face, I'd say you're pretty happy about this turn of events."

"I am, but it's not going to turn into anything. I'm dating people out here and he's in Rhode Island with his girlfriend."

"Uh huh. You just keep telling yourself that." Before I can make a witty comeback, we're walking through the door to the art room.

Arianna sits at the table with her pink tutu on over her black dress, painting. Looking up at me as I enter the room, she says, "I'm painting today. Look at my art!"

"Whoa, that's so pretty! What a great job you're doing," I say, crouching down next to her. She is giggling today. Something I haven't heard from her in a quite some time.

"Mama's painting, too." Arianna points to a painting her mother is working on. It is a sea of circles covering the paper in all different sizes and colors.

"I'm calling this one *Running in Circles*." She laughs.

"That's very clever," I say.

"My picture is going to be perfect!" Arianna yells. "Can I see your picture, Mama? You have a better picture. It's cool," She says, smiling at her mom.

Arianna looks down again at her own artwork, which is a smattering of paint splotches on the page. She giggles and claps her hands in delight. She holds the painting up for another child to see. "This green is a lake, this brown is an island, and the white is a boat. That's me waving." To the unprofessional eye, it looks like a green circle, a brown square and a white blob with a stick figure waving. Listening to her description, I can't help but think of Lake Carmi. Pointing at the other child, she says, "Look at my picture!"

"His name is Andrew," Arianna's mom says.

Andrew looks up at the painting and says, "It's so pretty." Andrew, 13, decides he wants to use clay now while his painting is drying. Upon seeing this, Arianna says, "I wanna do that."

"You want to do clay?" I ask.

"Of course." Switching to another activity is not uncommon for Arianna, and we don't mind accommodating her. Natasha and I have told her mom before that she can't control anything in her world right now, so for the time she's in art, she gets to dictate what takes place.

"I'm making meat. Callie, can you make peas?"

"Sure thing. What color should they be?"

"Green, of course, because peas are green." This comment makes me smile.

"When she's on chemo, she doesn't like to eat. We are begging her to eat." Arianna's mom says.

"Here are two more peas," I say, rolling them across the table to her.

"Thanks," Arianna says.

"You're so polite, Arianna." She smiles back at me.

Andrew's mom comes back into the room to check on him. The nurse, Tish, follows to check on Arianna's beeping IV bag. Replacing it with her last chemo bag for this treatment, her mom says, "It's almost time to go home!"

Andrew holds up his painting for his mom to see. "It's a dancing owl. It's a happy owl." Andrew has just finished his treatments and is doing very well. He has lived with cancer for three years, and now it appears he is cancer free. "Do you want to keep this one?" Andrew says, looking at me.

"Yes, please. Can you put your name on it so that I can put it up with the other artwork in the hall?" He does as I ask and hands me the painting, looking very proud of himself. "Would you like to go get a snack from the other room?" He exits, nodding. Andrew's mother starts speaking.

"He's doing so well. We've had quite the week. The news that his cancer is gone, we just found out the bid we put on a new house was accepted and my husband got a new job. That is a lot to take in in one week."

"Congratulations on everything. Where are you moving?" I ask.

"Burlington, Vermont."

"Really? I have family in Vermont." *And Wyatt.* "It's a beautiful state. I spent my summers growing up there."

"It really is beautiful. I'm so happy my husband's promotion came through with Energizer."

"It really is a small world. My brother works there, and my grandfather used to work there."

"To think I didn't expect to live to 30. It's a miracle that I'm still here and I have six beautiful babies in my home." Andrew's mom has told us before about feeling guilt about his cancer. She was diagnosed when she got engaged to her now-husband 14 years ago while she was in the middle of treatment. They had found a tumor in her lungs. Something people didn't usually survive. The chemo wiped out the tumor in her lungs, but then they found a tumor on her sacrum. Oddly enough, when they went in to biopsy the tumor, it had disappeared. She had informed us that usually when a parent has a sarcoma, there is a higher probability that a child of theirs could get cancer. As luck would have it, Andrew was the one to get it.

As Andrew went through treatment, he had a side effect from the chemo. It caused neuropathy. He was unable to use his hands for a while, which meant he was unable to do the art therapy that he loved. He would get frustrated and crumple the paper up and walk out of the room. Now that that has improved, he is back to doing the art he loves. Usually I encourage the child to work through a project when frustration sets in. Work through it to completion. But Andrew has so much anxiety that when he gets frustrated, I have him start over.

Andrew's mom leaves, thanking Natasha and me for our help today. Meanwhile, Arianna's mom says, "I hate chemo. I hate it so much," as she looks at the IV attached to her daughter.

"I bet."

"I was so mad when I found out she was diagnosed with cancer again. This time in her brain. I would just come here with her, and we would sit in a room by ourselves playing anything and everything she wanted to. I didn't want to talk to anyone. We'd come in, have treatment and leave."

"That's understandable. You knew what was in store for you this time around."

"Yes. I couldn't stay isolated for long. I just can't stay mad or be rude, so I came out and now we play in here."

Looking at Arianna, I ask, "Have you been feeling tired this week?"

"No … well, just a little bit tired."

I repeat to her, "Just a little bit tired?"

With a deep sigh, Arianna says sweetly, "I'm okay. This is really fun. Making sausage out of blue. I'm gonna make some really good soup." She continues playing with her clay.

"It's almost over. The gauge is at six. We'll do a countdown when it gets to five," Arianna's mom explains that sitting here for so long, so many times, she's started playing games with herself. "When you sit and watch the monitor, it goes so slow. I'm timing it from last time. We're about to go home!"

"Just stop," Arianna says, making her mom laugh. "I want to go home. I want to go home," Arianna chants as the numbers count down to one and the beeper goes off.

Arianna is about to embark on a really dark path. She is about to go into isolation for four to six weeks with really strong rounds of chemo to bring her immune system down to nothing. Then she will have a stem cell transplant using her own stem cells. It's a very long, tiring, painful process. There is a lot to worry about going forward, and I just hope Arianna and her family are ready.

CHAPTER 51
Callie

Dear Wyatt,

I'm concerned about Tyler (your nephew, not your dead brother, as you so eloquently wrote in your last letter). Most definitely, he should be checked out. I don't know if it's just the nature of my job or who I work with, but I think this is something you shouldn't ignore. That said, I'm sure it's nothing and he will be fine. Just to be on the safe side, I'd check it out.

This has been so much fun writing again! I'm worried I may have started an argument with you about your brother. It's just something that I've been keeping to myself. I feel like I can be honest with you. It's so much easier writing it down versus saying it out loud. Saying it out loud makes me sound a little loony tunes.

You asked about my boyfriend, Duncan. Well, truth-be-told, I wouldn't categorize him as a "boyfriend." He kind of has a wandering eye. I can laugh at this because I saw it a mile away but still went for it. We see each other occasionally, but believe me when I say it's nothing serious. He's a musician. Enough said.

If you're up visiting your folks anytime soon, please check in on Aunt Marilyn. Can you do that for me? She doesn't live far. She's a little out there, and I worry about her.

I guess this is bye for now. Write when you can.

-Callie

I wait several weeks for a return letter. It seemed to take longer than expected, but life sometimes gets in the way. I am not quite prepared for what he has to say.

Dear Callie,

I can't believe I'm writing these words. I took your advice and strongly suggested to Samantha and Brian that Tyler be looked at by a professional. At first they brushed me off, but then one afternoon Tyler had such a massive headache that he started vomiting and couldn't stop. Sam called an ambulance to take him to the hospital where they did a CT scan. Callie, Tyler has a brain tumor. Can you believe this? My family is just sick over it. I don't know what the future holds for Tyler, but I'm worried. He said something weird the other night. He said he had a dream that Uncle Tyler was in his room sitting at the edge of his bed. He said that Uncle Tyler told him not to be afraid, that he would help him get through this. I have to admit, I'm beginning to believe your story about Tyler.

Thank goodness Mary Jane understands that I need to spend time with my family. I was worried that she wouldn't get it. I've been going home a lot on weekends. Sometimes she comes with me, sometimes she doesn't. She said it's really hard for her to be around such sadness. She's pretty sensitive, and this seems to be affecting her.

I'll write when I can. Thank you for pushing me to say something to Samantha. I just hope we caught this thing early enough to make it go away.

-W

This is just terrible news. I need a sounding board.

"Hello?"

"Hey, Maddie, It's Callie. You busy?"

"Define busy. If by busy you mean I'm categorizing my baby outfits according to shades of blue and it's taken me forever to waddle to the phone, then yes."

"You're having a boy?" I ask excitedly.

"Yep. Can you believe that? A boy. I still can't picture another penis in this house."

"You're going to make a great boy-mom," I say with a laugh.

"I suppose. I really thought I would be looking at a lifetime of cheerleading and dance competitions, not baseball and hockey."

"There are a lot of good looking baseball and hockey players out there."

"That's disgusting. That's my little boy you're talking about," she teases. "So what did you want to talk to me about?"

"Have I told you that Wyatt and I have been writing letters again?"

"What? No! See, perfect example of being completely removed from your life lately?"

"You're a little busy growing a human being," I pause for effect before I continue. "Can you believe this? It's like I'm reliving the past."

"Are you? Like the time you spent a hot evening on that island up in Vermont? Or that time you did it in Gramp's camp? Eww, I think I'm getting queasy in the pants just thinking about it."

Laughing out loud, I respond, "How do you come up with this stuff, Mad?"

"Not for nothin', but it was pretty hot stuff."

"It's not like that. He left me a note at my aunt's house when I was in Vermont for my grandmother's funeral." I continue to tell her the story about the note. Then I bring her up to date with the latest news.

"Wyatt just sent me a letter about his nephew, Tyler. He has brain cancer."

"No shit? Aw, man, I'm sorry to hear that."

"Yeah, me, too."

"Do you plan on going up there to help him get through this?"

Not sure if she is referring to Tyler or Wyatt, I assume the latter.

"It's not like that this time around. He has someone to help him through it. Mary Jane."

"Mark my words, she won't be around for the long haul. I just have a feeling about this one."

"You and me both. I can tell she likes him and they've been together a long time, but she doesn't seem like one that can handle the heavy stuff."

"This is definitely heavy."

We continue talking about her pregnancy and how Zach is so excited for the new baby. She says that he's spoiling her rotten.

"Just yesterday he came home early from work and set up this very romantic scene in the living room with candles and music; the whole nine yards. It was sweet, but I looked at the distance between my belly and the floor and thought, there's no way in hell I'm getting down there. And if I did get to the floor, I would never be able to get back up again, so I said, 'Zach, this is sweet and all. I love you, but hell no.' I think I may have offended him."

"You think?" I laugh.

"We ended up doing it on the couch. My leg was up on the arm rest…"

Interrupting her, I yell, "Mad...Maddie...Madelyn!" stopping her before she can continue her description of her escapade. "I *really* don't need to hear about your sex life. I get it. You had a great night. End of conversation."

"You're just jealous," she snickers.

"You're absolutely right."

I feel lighter than I had when we started. Maybe everything will be all right with Tyler.

CHAPTER 52
Callie

Dear Callie,

Things are much worse than I thought when I wrote to you originally. I'm sick over watching Tyler suffering in the hospital. Poor kid. He's being so brave, so strong. He's just like my brother. I swear, sometimes things come out of Tyler's mouth and I'm speechless because it's something that my brother would have said under the same circumstances.

Tyler is quite the artist. I'm going to enclose a drawing he made for me. He really has a knack for using charcoals. With you being the art therapist, I thought you'd appreciate that. Hey, maybe you can interpret the drawing for me? I know there's meaning in it that I'm unaware of.

His cancer is called clear cell sarcoma, which causes tumors in the body. He has tumors in his lungs and in his brain. Neither is a good place. He's doing chemo to get rid of the tumors, but if the chemo doesn't work, then he'll have to try a more aggressive chemo and find a stem cell match. If he can't find one, then he'll have to use his own. I have to say, it's comforting to know that you understand what I'm talking about. Mary Jane is being as supportive as she can be, but it's difficult for her.

Through it all, I'm impressed with the way Sam and Brian have persevered. They certainly have staying power if they can make it through this.

Thanks for listening (or reading, as the case may be). I'll keep you posted.

-W

I've heard of this type of cancer before with one of my kids. It's a long hard road, but I don't want to discourage him.

Dear Wyatt,

I'm sorry to hear about Tyler's diagnosis. I've had a few kids come through my office with this very same thing. I'm going to be honest here; it's not going to be easy. There are going to be many bad days ahead, so cherish the good ones when they show up.

I'm glad to hear that he enjoys art. I hope he continues with it. I think it really helps kids take their minds off of what they are going through. Once they become deeply involved in their art, It's almost a transcendent experience. Even if it's for a short time. As for the drawing itself, yes, you're right, he's very talented. What stands out to me in the picture is the battle between one soldier and his enemy. This is very common for boys to draw. I can tell he's at the beginning of his treatment because he is fighting to defeat his foe. Let's hope he continues to draw himself winning the battle!

I continue my letter, catching him up on my life, which at the moment is pretty boring. Not much other than going to listen to Duncan play his music. This isn't happening very often, however, because he tends to have a lot of groupies hanging out at the side of the stage. Just waiting for him to finish his set so that they can fawn all over him. Of course, I don't tell Wyatt that part.

If you think it would help, I could see Tyler when I come up this summer to visit my aunt. Maybe having someone for Samantha to talk to about it all would make her feel better? I don't know.

Whatever you guys think. I'm planning on coming up around the end of June and staying through the 4th.

Talk to you soon.

Prayers for Tyler,

Callie

Placing the letter in the envelope, I wonder if I am overstepping the boundaries of our newfound friendship. I add the stamp, walk out to the mailbox, and put up the flag. Inhaling deeply, I notice a change in the air. It feels warmer than it has in weeks. The dampness of the air, ever so faint, conjures thoughts of spring.

Standing at Maddie and Zach's house a beat longer than necessary, Maddie finally opens the door looking frazzled. Without as much as a hello, she hands over her bundle of little boy.

"Here!" she says.

"Uh, okay," I say, taking the little boy into my arms. "What's going on? I thought we were going out for dinner? Where's Zach?"

"He's not home yet. He's running late. When he gets home I have to look like I know what the hell I'm doing. Like I know how to handle having an infant, clean a house, make a meal all at the same time."

I smile down at the cooing baby, play with his little fingers as they try to reach up and grab my hair. "Hey there, Dylan. Aren't you the cutest little boy in the world? Yes, you are. You are Aunt Callie's little snuggly wuggly bear, aren't you?" I continue with the gooey sentiments and notice that everything around me has gone quiet. Maddie shakes her head at me. "What?"

"I never would have guessed you would have turned into a pile of goo when I squirted this little peanut out of my vag."

Continuing in my singsong voice, "Don't you listen to your mama, Dylan. She's lost her mind." I smell something delicious emanating from the oven. "What is that deliciousness?" I ask, nodding my head in the direction of the oven.

"That, my friend, is Parmesan chicken, garlic knots, and apple crisp."

"Impressive," I add as I pat Dylan gently over my shoulder.

"Yeah, I'm freaking Betty Crockering the shit out of dinner!"

Laughing at this, I place Dylan in his bassinet. He seems to have grown sleepy with all the movement, though I don't know how he can sleep with all the noise Maddie's making in the kitchen.

"So should we just eat here with Dylan and Zach?"

"Are you shitting me? We're going out. I haven't had a damn drink in over a year, which is like fifteen in pregnant years."

"Okay, we'll wait for Zach and then we'll head out."

As if on cue, Zach opens the front door and says, "Honey, I'm home," swooping in on *me* with a hug and a kiss. This makes Maddie smile. "Hi, Cal."

"Hi, Zach."

Zach then waltzes up to Maddie and gives her a passionate kiss. Maddie blushes.

"Get a room," I tease.

"Zach, dinner is ready and Dylan is sleeping, so I would eat now while everything is hot and you have your hands free. I'm going out with Callie for a few hours. There are bottles for Dylan in the fridge. Just warm them up in some boiling water for about a minute. Make sure and test the temp before you give it to him."

"Maddie, I think I can handle it. Go. Have fun. We'll be just fine while you're out."

She gives him a peck on the cheek, and as she leaves the room he swats her behind, making her giggle. It's so nice to see them behaving this way.

"Give me one sec, Cal, and I'll be ready to go."

Within two minutes, we are out the door.

Driving to dinner gives us a few minutes to talk without the buzz of a restaurant.

"Mad, you seem so happy."

"I really am. Don't get me wrong, he bugs the shit out of me sometimes, but he's a really good guy."

"Dylan is adorable. Is he sleeping at all?"

"Are you kidding me? He's only a few weeks old. He doesn't know how to let Mommy and Daddy have sexy time yet."

"Are you ready for that already?"

"Not quite. We make do."

"Spare me the details. Please."

Pulling into the restaurant, I say, "I'm so glad he makes you happy. You deserve it."

We have a great meal and conversation. Maddie is animated and happy the whole evening. I can tell she is getting tired, though. She has had a whopping two glasses of wine and I think I'll have to carry her to the car.

"Man, am I out of practice."

"Well, you've been a little busy with a new husband and baby. It's understandable."

"I should, I think, get home," Maddie mumbles.

On the way back to the car, I say, "I'm going to Vermont for a few weeks to visit my aunt."

"That's cool."

"Yeah, I think I'm going to see Wyatt."

"Yeah! Get it!" she says, while humping the side of the car. *Oh boy.*

"I told him that I would go see Tyler at the hospital during one of his art therapy sessions during his treatment. It seems the first round of chemo isn't working. He's going to have to have a more aggressive chemo soon to get ready for his stem cell transplant," I explain while watching Maddie try, without success, to click her seat belt.

"They found a match?" Maddie asks as I reach over to help strap her in.

"No. He's using his own, which will be harvested in a month."

"That sucks," Maddie says as she rests her head against the side window.

"It does. I think it'll be good for Samantha to have someone to talk to. Someone who kind of understands what's going on. Give her a break if she needs one."

"Mmmm," exhaustion takes hold, and my Maddie falls asleep. I wake her only when we reach her house. She wakes briefly to walk inside and goes straight to bed. I let myself out, walking quietly past Dylan who is peacefully sleeping on his daddy's chest. Zach opens his left eye and smiles as I softly close the door.

CHAPTER 53
Callie

I feel a little anxious on the way to University of Vermont Medical Center. I try to keep in mind that I am here to see Tyler. How to explain my relation to his family is definitely a reason for anxiety.

"Hi, I'm here to see Tyler Doyle. I believe he's in with the art therapist right now."

After consulting the computer screen, the nurse at the desk says, "Yes, follow me."

Walking down the stark white hallway with the smell of antiseptic in the air, I notice a change in atmosphere as soon as I reach the door. Artwork lines the walls of the nurses' station leading to the art room. The walls are painted in blues and greens with soothing words of encouragement above and below the art. When I open the door, Samantha greets me. "Callie," she says with a warm hug. "Thank you for coming to visit us."

I step back and say, "It's my pleasure. So nice to see you again. How's Tyler doing?"

"He's been better. He'll be back in a minute. He had to use the restroom. With all the I.V. fluid they're giving him, he needs to go all the time."

The door I just entered opens and in walks the spitting image of Wyatt's brother.

"Hi, baby. All better?" Samantha asks Tyler. He nods, looking at me strangely. Following his gaze, she explains, "This is my friend, Callie. She's an art therapist in Missouri. She wanted to see how they do therapy up here in Vermont."

"Hi, Tyler. So nice to meet you," I say extending my hand, taking his fragile hand into mine.

"Hi," he says meekly, releasing my hand quickly and setting his eyes on his mother. "Is Uncle Erp still here?"

"No, sorry, honey, he had to go pick up Mary Jane from work. Her car is in the shop."

Looking dejected, he takes a seat at the round table with his half completed painting.

"Now what's that look for? He'll be back later on. You know how much he loves hanging out with you during your treatments." My stomach drops.

A middle-aged woman with a pleasant disposition walks through the door. "Well, there you are," she says to Tyler. "Next time I'm going to time you when you take a pee break." This produces a smile from Tyler. Turning to me, she says, "Hi, there. I'm Lisa. And you are?"

Samantha speaks up, "This is our family friend, Callie Lamply. She's an art therapist from Missouri."

"That's right. I'm here visiting my aunt and thought I'd come over and see what you guys do here in Vermont for art therapy."

"I see. Well, it's probably very similar, but welcome," she says, dismissing me. For the next two hours, she speaks directly to Tyler and Samantha and ignores the fact that I am in the room.

The door opens up and a beautiful redhead walks in. She does not look happy. Wyatt arrives mere seconds after her, nearly bumping into her as she stands just inside the door, staring at me. Apparently no one told her about my arrival.

"Well. What a surprise," Mary Jane says with disdain.

"Mary Jane, you remember Callie? My friend from years ago," Wyatt speaks.

"Mmmhmm," Mary Jane musters.

"Hi, Mary Jane. It's nice to see you again," I say as pleasantly as possible.

"Hey, big guy. What are you up to now? Did you get into any mischief while I was gone?"

Laughing, Tyler says, "No, Uncle Erp, I didn't have enough time. You got back too quick."

"There's always next time. So what's this drawing you're working on?" Wyatt asks as he picks up Tyler's drawing.

Tyler points at the large building in the center. "This is a castle and these are the good guys protecting the castle."

"What's happening over here?" Wyatt asks, pointing at the gruesome attack on some unsuspecting soldiers.

"Those guys are obviously the bad guys," Tyler says in mock disgust, rolling his eyes at his uncle.

"Yeah, I figured that much out, wise guy." Their playful banter is refreshing. It's obvious that Wyatt adores his nephew.

"The good guys are out for blood and will do anything to protect the castle."

As he speaks, I notice a soldier drawn on the castle, away from the carnage.

"Can I ask you something, Tyler?" I begin quietly. He nods, so I continue, "What's going on with this soldier up here in the castle?"

After a brief pause, Tyler explains, "That soldier is trying to figure out how to attack. He won't come out of the castle until he's ready to fight."

"I see. He looks very strong. I'm sure he'll know when the time is right to fight." He looks me in the eye and holds my gaze for a beat longer than expected.

"I guess he will, yeah."

Back at Aunt Marilyn's, I sit quietly in the kitchen as she prepares dinner.

"You're awfully quiet tonight, dear. Everything all right?"

"I'm not sure Tyler is willing to fight." I go on to explain what transpired at the hospital minus the description of Tyler's artwork. As I speak, she seems to take on that otherworldly look in her eyes. "I'll have to have a little talk with Travis."

"Who?"

"My Travis." Aunt Marilyn repeats matter-of-factly. She has said for years that her guardian angel is her deceased boyfriend.

"Be sure to let me know what he says," I say, tongue in cheek.

"Oh, I will," she says in all seriousness.

I leave the kitchen to change into something more comfortable before dinner. As I come down the stairs, I can hear Aunt Marilyn in an animated conversation with the pot of mashed potatoes.

"...Should I tell her that? Okay. If you think so."

"Let me guess. Travis?"

She winks at me. "You got it."

"So lay it on me. What'd he say?"

"The soldier inside the castle will come out and fight."

This statement floors me. I haven't told her about the drawing.

She continues, "It'll take a few days for him to realize that he's strong enough to overcome this. The transplant will be rough going for a while, but within a month, he'll make great progress and come out the other side."

Could she really be telling me the truth? I just stand there, unable to move, watching Aunt Marilyn with surprise. She says, "Fiddlesticks. I'm just standing here blathering on and on while you must be starvin' marvin.' Sit down and we'll eat."

One would think that I wouldn't be shocked by this revelation, but I haven't been around her quirky ways in a while and I am out of practice on how to handle this.

"Well, that's good news. Tell Travis thank you."

"You just did," she smiles.

Laughing I say, "Of course I did."

CHAPTER 54
Charlene

December 14, 2012
9:34 A.M.

"... under God, indivisible, with liberty and justice for all. Good morning, students and faculty. Here are your morning announcements for today. Those students in scouts, please remember to meet in the gymnasium after the final bell. Today's lunch menu is chicken patties on a bun, orange wedges, your choice at the salad bar and a milk or juice. Let's make it a great day today."

"Okay, kids. Take your seats, please." Walking to a little girl's desk, Mrs. Canfield hands her the daily attendance. "Libby, would you mind bringing the attendance to the office?"

Smiling, Libby looks at her best friend Prue with a twinkle in her eye. This job has always been a prized one in the classroom. "Sure, Mrs. Canfield." Practically skipping, she leaves the room. As the door closes, Mrs. Canfield says, "Let's take out our math textbooks and turn to page 324. Prue, will you read the directions on page 324, please." As she speaks, she notices the hum of the intercom still engaged.

"Help Jack by solving the problems below."

"Good, now please read the first problem." She is listening now to the voices coming through the intercom as Prue continues to read the problem in the textbook.

"Jack's hen lays six eggs on Monday, three eggs on Wednesday and seven eggs on Saturday. How many eggs did Jack's hen lay all together?"

"Very nice, thank you. Now, who would like to show us on the Smartboard how to solve this problem?"

Several hands shoot up as Mrs. Canfield surveys the group and decides on Kenny to come to the front to solve the problem. As Kenny walks to the front, Mrs. Canfield hears a popping sound as if someone has let off a firecracker somewhere in the building. Not about to let it disrupt her lesson, she continues, "Well done, Kenny. How do we know that we add all of the numbers together? What words tell you to do that?"

"All together?" Kenny ventures.

"Yes, excellent job." Pop, pop, pop. The unmistakable sound of gunfire blares through the intercom, then silence.

"Please continue on to page 325, working on problems one through five." Mrs. Canfield continues to teach as the fidgeting students hesitantly turn to page 325, the classroom now full of nervous energy. The tension in the room thickens as Mrs. Canfield slowly walks to her classroom door and pulls away a portion of the black construction paper that she placed on the window earlier in the week during a lockdown drill. Several students turn their heads, watching as she looks through the window into the hall. Across the way, a teacher mouths the word "shooter" with wild eyes. Quickly placing the construction paper back on the window, she speaks calmly to the children, choking back the panic rising like a tsunami inside her body. *Secure the children, yet keep them calm.*

"Boys and girls, I need you to put down what you are doing and go to the back of the room. Quickly please." Whispering now, she urges, "Quickly, and quietly. Everyone into the bathroom. Everything will be okay. Shhh. We have to be very, very quiet. Can you all do that for me?" With wild, dilated eyes, they each nod in silence.

"Mrs. Canfield, what about Libby?" Prue asks on the verge of tears.

"Sweetie, she'll be fine. I'm sure she's found a place to hide." Unsure if that is true, Mrs. Canfield tries to be as convincing as possible. She continues to whisper to the children. "Remember the intruder drill we had last week? Well, we're practicing again. I'm going to lock the door behind me. You need to stay very quiet until we hear the 'all clear' from Mr. Aldridge, okay? I'm going to make sure you all are safe. I'll be right outside the bathroom door."

The terrified children all nod their heads. Mrs. Canfield opens the bathroom door and locks them in from the outside. Hearing the commotion in the hallway, she realizes this 'practice' is life or death and the thought of these first graders getting hurt terrifies her. With a sense of urgency, she fumbles with the keys and drops them on the floor. The popping sounds are getting closer, and she hears screams. The front lobby is four classrooms away. How long is this intruder going to be in the building? She doesn't have time to formulate a plan, because the intruder is now in the hall outside her classroom screaming, "Look at me!" and "Come over here!" and "Look at them!" She can't process whom he is talking about as she hurriedly picks up the keys and runs to hide under her desk. The door bursts open, and she finds herself holding her breath. From under her desk, she can see his scuffed black leather boots and rifle dangling by his side. He walks in a few feet away from her desk at the front of the room. He stops, stands, surveys his surroundings, and begins to retreat through the door. There is a fraction of a second during which she feels relief that he is leaving and exhales. It is nearly an inaudible sound, but he turns around causing her heart to seize, making it difficult to breath. Trying to catch her breath and slow her racing pulse, the fear is paralyzing.

He marches toward the desk, pushes the chair away and pulls the trigger.

CHAPTER 55
Callie

I let a day pass before returning to the hospital to visit Tyler. I've been keeping in touch with Samantha, and she informs me that he will be in today from 9:30-12. I communicate to Samantha that I plan on being there around 10:30. Walking up to the hospital, I spot Samantha out front, smoking a cigarette. Upon seeing me, she immediately snuffs it out. She laughs as I approach and says, "Old habits are hard to break."

"It's understandable considering the stress you are under at the moment."

"I should really stop. Maybe when Tyler is better," she trails off.

I open the door to the hospital, and we walk together to the elevator. Samantha speaks up as we enter the elevator.

"Callie, I truly appreciate you coming over to visit Tyler. I know this can't be easy on you." Now she's gone and done it. Mentioning the elephant in the room.

Blushing, I respond, "Wyatt has always been my friend. I hope we continue being friends. He's a big part of my life in many ways, and hopefully, that won't change."

"Well, if it's worth anything, I was always pulling for you two. Between you and me I think Mary Jane is a little too needy."

"She seems very nice. I'm just happy Wyatt is happy." Saying this out loud brings on a sudden heaviness in my chest. As the elevator door opens, I walk through the art therapy room and turn my head toward a commotion in the cave. Wyatt turns and smiles at us. *Butterflies.*

"How's the patient today?" I ask sincerely.

"He's whooping me on video games right now."

"No drawing today?"

"He started drawing but set it aside for now. He needed a break."

"Come on, Uncle Erp, pay attention to the game!" Tyler barks from his seat on the couch in the game room.

"Well, that's important, also. Maybe I should come back another day?"

"Uh, no, you should stay." Wyatt says rather quickly, dropping his remote and standing. "That is, if you want to."

"I was just thinking if he's busy playing video games, he may not want to draw today while I'm here."

"You can play with us if you want. There's another controller here," Tyler offers, holding up said controller.

Smiling, I take the controller, "If you feel like losing," I tease as I take a seat on the couch next to Tyler, who sits between Wyatt and I.

ᵕ ᵕ ᵕ

"Ha! Gotcha!" I scream, feeling the thrill of victory.

"Ahh, not again." Tyler playfully tosses his controller on the couch.

"She's pretty good, isn't she?" Wyatt asks with that familiar twinkle in his eye.

"Well, isn't this fun," comes a voice from the door.

Oblivious to her defensive tone, Tyler says, "Hi, Mary Jane!"

"Hey, Tyler. What's going on?"

"My infusion is almost done, and I'm just playing a few games with Uncle Erp and Callie until I'm done."

"Huh, sounds like fun." I sense a coolness sweep over the room.

The beeping from Tyler's monitor causes the friendly nurse, to enter.

"All right, big guy. Time to switch out bags. One more to go."

"Ah, man. I thought that was it."

"Nope. You're not that lucky. You still have an hour. Let's move to the other room to start the last bag." Tyler and Lisa leave the room, and with them, all conversation ceases. It feels like an eternity until Tyler returns, sitting at the art table. *Oh, thank goodness,* I think to myself and walk to him.

For the remainder of the hour, Tyler, Lisa, and I work on some art. Lisa has finally warmed to me being in the room. Wyatt and Mary Jane stay in the video game room. I have a feeling they need privacy. Some time later Wyatt walks into the art room, minus Mary Jane. I sense something is wrong. He sits down at the table and starts working on a picture of his own. Tyler sits watching him work.

"What's that supposed to be, Uncle Erp?"

"Me."

"But it's a bunch of blotches."

"More like targets."

As we walk out of the hospital, I thank Tyler for letting me spend some time with him over the past few days. "You're really a very talented artist."

"Thanks," he says genuinely, and continues walking with his mother to the car.

"Bye, buddy. I'll catch up with you soon," Wyatt says warmly to his nephew.

"Bye, Uncle Erp. Catch you later," Tyler says warily. It seems the visit is beginning to take its toll on him.

Once Samantha and Tyler move out of earshot, Wyatt stops walking.

"Everything okay, Wyatt?" I ask, curious.

"Not exactly," he says, hesitant to continue.

"Did Mary Jane have some place to be?" I press him.

"No. She's a little upset with me right now. What else is new?"

"I'm sorry if I make her feel uncomfortable."

Turning towards me now with confusion on his face, he asks, "Did you come here to see me, Callie?" He runs his hand through his hair.

Well, this is unexpected. Not sure where to go with this I say, "You mean here to the hospital, or here in Vermont? If you're implying that I came here in an effort to win you over, you're mistaken. I'm here for Tyler. I'm here to see Samantha, and that's all."

Are you sure about that? A voice inside my head speaks up.

"Mary Jane seems to think…" he begins, blushing now in the hollows of his cheeks, "never mind. She's just reading something into this visit that clearly isn't happening."

"Do you want me to talk to her?"

"No. That would seriously make matters worse," he says with a nervous laugh. "Thanks, though."

"I think Tyler is doing really great, Wyatt. I have a good feeling about this transplant. Just remember things will get worse before they get better," I advise, pretending his comments never took place.

"I hope you're right. I'll keep you in the loop on his progress."

"You don't have to write if it's going to get you into trouble," I say with concern.

"I want to write you." *What's that in his eyes?*

Taking a chance, I say, "I look forward to hearing from you."

"Safe travels home," he says, not moving from his spot.

"Thanks, Wyatt. Take care of that nephew of yours," I say, leaning in for a hug. Gently, he takes me into his arms and squeezes, kissing my cheek, he lingers there. The warmth of his breath sweeps across my lips. Still standing inches away, he looks into my eyes, searching for something.

"Are you sure?" he whispers. For a moment I don't know what to say.

"No, I'm not sure." I speak, just above a whisper myself.

With each beat of my heart, he leans in closer until our lips touch. A spark ignites in my chest. He wraps his arms around me again and pulls me closer. He kisses me again with the weight of a feather, as I stand frozen.

Two short beeps come from Samantha's car. She passes us with a wave as Tyler presses his nose to the passenger side window, smiling ear to ear. We immediately separate, remembering where we are.

CHAPTER 56 🪰
Prue

December 14, 2012
9:41 A.M.

All fourteen children remain silent as they hear the footsteps echo in the classroom. They hear nothing but their shallow breathing between footsteps as they hold on to one another. The footsteps approach the bathroom door, and the children watch as the doorknob rotates but does not open. Turning once more, still it remains closed. The footsteps retreat, and soon the room is silent. Prue begins to think about her daddy and how he made smiley faces on her pancakes this morning. She is trying to think of happy thoughts so that she won't cry. *I fed Buttercup this morning. I love my kitty. She's so soft and warm. I made my bed, sang with daddy at the bus stop while we were waiting. He loves to make silly voices when he sings.* Thoughts of her best friend, Libby, come creeping in. *Where's Libby? I hope she's all right. What if she's with that bad man in the hallway?*

Prue hears a lot of muffled commotion through the door; many voices screaming. One voice sounds like Mr. Aldridge, yelling, "Shooter! Stay put!" *Shooter? Someone has a gun at school? I wish my daddy were here.*

"Help me! I don't want to be here!" A child's voice rings out.

"Well, you are here." Followed by a hammering sound.

How long do we have to be here? The classroom clock ticks slowly, deliberately.

Then, from the hallway, "Put the gun down!" More popping sounds. Sirens nearing in the distance. Placing her hands over her ears, Prue squeezes her eyes shut, wishing for this to be over.

Again from the hallway, "Let me in!" followed by loud banging. One last pop rings out, then silence. Deafening silence.

Footsteps echo through the classroom once more, and not knowing who is making them is torture. The steps approach quickly. The children once again watch as the doorknob rotates but does not open. As it turns once more, the children hear a man's voice that isn't Mr. Aldridge's. Knocking now, the man asks, "Kids, are you in there?"

Terrified, they look at one another and don't say a word. "Don't be afraid. I'm a Newtown Police Officer please open the door."

Two children begin to weep openly, not knowing what to do.

"Kids, if you can hear me, please knock on the door."

Prue knocks three times in response. "Okay, thank you. We're going to get you out of there real quick. Did you lock the door from the inside, or did your teacher lock it from the outside?"

Prue speaks up, "Outside."

"Okay, great, thank you. I need to get a janitor to get a key to open the door. Stay right where you are and don't worry. I'll be right back with the key. Everybody understand?"

In unison, they all reply "yes".

As the footsteps retreat, the children hear another set of footsteps, along with the sound of squeaky wheels. There is a lot of commotion, then the squeaky wheels leave the room.

"I'm back now. We have the key, so if you're leaning against the door, please move back. I wouldn't want anyone to fall through the door."

Opening the door, the police officer's heart breaks into fourteen pieces; a little bit for each of the terrified children looking back at him. He tries his best to smile, but this needs to be quick. He doesn't know if there are accomplices on the campus. "Quickly now, I'd like you all to stand up in a single file line and place both hands on the shoulders of the student in front of you. Can you do that for me?"

Again, a universal "yes".

With all fourteen students attached hands to shoulders, the officer moves them quickly out of the bathroom to the front of the room where one of the students notices Mrs. Canfield's shoe beside her desk.

"Where's Mrs. Canfield?"

"The ambulance came and took her to the hospital." He provides no further details.

Prue's body begins to tremble.

CHAPTER 57
Callie

"So you kissed. Big whoop." Maddie says, bouncing her bundle on her lap, inducing a burp.

"Mad, he's in a serious relationship with Mary Jane. This is bad."

"Sounds pretty good to me. Can't be that serious," she says, wiping Dylan's mouth with a burp cloth. "Just because she thinks it's serious doesn't mean Wyatt feels the same way. Look at Duncan, for example. Do you think he thinks you two are serious?"

"No."

"I rest my case."

"But that's different."

"Oh, really? Did you think you two were an item at the beginning? Don't answer that. You know you did. Then you saw him swapping spit with some groupie and figured it out. He's not your forever man. As much as I love Charlie, I don't think he's the one either. Only you know who's gonna rock your socks off; make your toes curl forever and ever, the end."

"No...I...he..."

"You're stammering, Cal. Only one person can do that to you. Think about it. You have a history. He's your first love."

A foul smell emanates from Dylan.

"Oh, gawwwd. He had a blow-out." Maddie stands, holding Dylan at arm's length. "This is going to take some time. You can wait, or we can discuss this at another time," Maddie says, scurrying to the bathroom with Dylan extended from her body.

"Yeah, I'll let you handle Dylan and see myself out," I holler at Maddie, who has already started the bath water.

One week later, a letter arrives, and with it a familiar fluttering inside my chest. With my hands shaking and my breath quickening, I briskly walk inside and sit on the couch. As I open the letter, a drawing falls out. It is a small drawing on a square of paper the size of a sticky note. It is a sketch of a couple that look like they belong in a fairytale. Tyler drew it in the car after seeing Wyatt and I leaving the hospital. Wyatt received it on his next visit with Tyler, according to the back of the note. Setting the picture aside, I read the letter.

Dear Callie,

Apparently, my young nephew saw us as he was leaving the hospital. I'll just leave it by saying that he likes you. In the drawing, I'm not sure who the male is, Tyler, or me, but I'd put money on the female being you.

I'm happy to report that his drawings have been much more interesting. There's always a woman in the drawings now, go figure. He's been putting up a good fight, but he's been really weak lately with his treatments coming to an end. You probably know this already, but prior to his transplant he's in isolation to start the really hardcore chemo. That's considered day -10. From there, we count down to day zero or transplant day. At this point he has no immune system left, poor kid. After transplanting the stem cells, he'll work up to day 28. About 4 weeks after transplant day. When all is said and done, he'll be down and out for about 6 weeks. He's going to be really sick for a while.

So, I guess if you're still reading you can see that I'm avoiding the topic that is on everyone's mind. I'm not going to apologize, Callie. I kissed you and I don't regret it. I told Mary Jane that I had some thinking to do. See, she's ready to get married and settle down. We've been together for years, and even though it seems like the natural thing to do, taking that next step, I just can't do it. Something is holding me back, and after seeing you again, the few brief encounters we've had, I realize what's holding me back. It's you. It's always been you. It's taken me several weeks to figure out a way to tell you. Several times I tried to mail this letter and even thought about calling you, but I just couldn't bring myself to do it. I guess I'm a little worried about what you'll say. The kicker is Mary Jane says she'll wait for me to make up my mind. She's willing to do that for me. Something I should have done many years ago for you. I can't ever take that back, but I'm hoping that maybe, just maybe, this is our time.

I'm going to end this letter at that. Please write when you get the chance or give me a call. I'm not sure what to do at this point. I'll just wait for your response.

-W

Setting the letter down, I let out my breath. I lean my head back on the couch and close my eyes. My mind is reeling.

The blare of the phone shakes me from my reverie, "Hello?"

"Hey, good lookin', what's cookin'?"

"Duncan. You have impeccable timing," I say sarcastically.

"That sounds interesting. Care to meet up so we can discuss further?"

"Where are you playing?" After jotting down the address, I take a quick shower and drive to his gig.

Inside, I notice the usual bar flies hovering. I sit in the back of the room, order a beer and listen to the familiar tunes. On the last song of the first set, he spots me and smiles. He certainly has a way with the ladies.

"I'm gonna take a quick break and be back for my second set shortly." he says setting down his guitar. Immediately, two ladies with copious cleavage take that as their queue. *The flies are attacking.*

Politely, he hugs each lady. Giving each a kiss on their cheek, he continues walking in my direction.

"Hey, beautiful," he says, pulling me up off my seat into a hug.

"Hi, Duncan."

He sits next to me and we talk about my visit to Vermont to see my aunt, Tyler, and Wyatt.

"Wow, some heavy stuff this weekend, huh?"

"Kinda."

"So this Wyatt guy is a friend of yours," he says while catching the eye of a cute redhead near the stage.

"Yeah, we've known each other for a long time. There's a lot of history there."

"Mmmhmm. And Tyler is your nephew?" he asks, redirecting his focus to me.

"No, not mine. Wyatt's. He has brain cancer and is going through a tough time with chemo."

His eye wandering again, he says, "Wyatt has brain cancer? That stinks. Sorry to hear that."

"Not Wyatt, Tyler." I look to the direction in which his eyes focus and see the redhead playing with her hair and toying with her skirt. "And my brother just created a submarine made from screen doors. It works really well."

"Really? That's cool."

"And my mom is really my sister. She has horns for ears."

"Horns? Sweet. Hey, it looks like my break is up. Wanna come home with me tonight?"

"That's such a sweet offer, but no. I think you should take the redhead home."

Finally listening, he says, "The redhead? You think?"

"I know," I say, chuckling to myself. "Get back up there, Romeo." He leans in and kisses me on the cheek. It feels like I'm being kissed by my brother. *At least I know where this is going. Nowhere.* Enjoying his last set, I begin to daydream of Wyatt. The way he kissed me was different. More mature. He's changed and I like it. Like I was kissing a new and improved Wyatt. I wonder how much more has improved?

CHAPTER 58
Prue

December 14, 2012
9:53 A.M.

With eyes closed and hands on the quaking shoulders of the child in front of her, Prue and her classmates follow the direction of the police officer. She hears the first responders coming to the aid of those who have fallen. Approaching the front lobby, she hears a familiar cry to her left, and with one eyelid open she looks toward the sound. "Libby!" the exclamation escapes her lips without a second thought. Eyes wide open now, she breaks free from the line of students and runs to the library door where her best friend sits on the opposite side of the glass, crying. There is a medic attending to the wound on her leg. Prue wants desperately to reach her friend to comfort her, but as quickly as she breaks free, the officer leading the students out the door scoops her up.

It appears Libby has been struck by a ricocheting bullet the gunman had discharged as she was walking the attendance slip to the office. As Prue is whisked away, she takes inventory of the school. There are bullet holes in the walls, windows have been shattered, and frightening splashes of red are all over the building. There is a fog with the scent of gunfire.

"I want my daddy," she moans as she is set down on the curb.

"We're going to do everything we can to make that happen. Can you be strong for me just a little bit longer?"

Nodding her tear streaked face, she complies, but thoughts of the carnage she has witnessed are fresh in her mind.

11:17 A.M.

Jimmy sits in the church waiting for word of his only child. He sits with his elbows on his knees and his hands in his hair. His head hangs low. He picks up his phone and calls his sister, Callie, who picks up on the first ring.

"Jimmy? Is Prue with you?"

"I'm waiting in our church to hear something. Can you believe this?" he says, and I can hear the hysteria in his voice rising. "Waiting is agony! What if she isn't coming back, Cal? I can't bear the thought of losing my little girl…" He stops speaking, and Callie hears his labored breath as he tries to remain in control. Through the receiver, I hear a squeaky door open and heavy footsteps enter the room Jimmy is in.

"I gotta go. The police just came in to talk to us," he says in a hushed voice.

"Okay, let me…" Jimmy impatiently ends the call.

The officer speaks to the distressed adults. "I'd like all the parents in this room to follow me to the firehouse, please. We have information there for everyone." Parents bombard the officer with questions, but he keeps repeating, like a broken record, "All questions will be answered when we get to the firehouse."

In the firehouse, chairs are lined up in rows for the parents. Everyone goes in and takes a seat. An officer calls out last names from a list in front of him and asks those people to follow him to the back room. He calls twenty names.

Through the thin wall, Jimmy can hear a familiar male voice speaking to the group. It's the Governor.

"Two children were taken to the hospital and expired."

Parents from within the room say, "We want to be with our kids."

The Governor says, "Nobody else was taken to the hospital."

There is a pause, then a father speaks up in an anguished voice, "So what you're telling us is they're all dead?"

"Yes."

CHAPTER 59
Callie

You are cordially invited to Central Connecticut State University's Class of 1988 reunion. The evening will be a great way for students to reconnect with one another. It will be held on campus at Kaiser Hall from 7-11 P.M. on Saturday, November 23rd. Please RSVP to...

"Schmaddie, did you get the invite to CCSU's reunion?" I say over the phone, tapping the invitation on the couch cushion.

"Cal, I didn't graduate with you, remember? I had a few issues back in the day. I graduated a year after."

"Oh, right. Damn."

"Are you going?" Maddie asks inquisitively.

"Thinking about it."

"Will Liz and Charlie be there?"

"No idea."

"Schmal, you should go."

"It would be fun to see everyone from the dorm again. Do you think you could come with me?" I ask hesitantly.

"Let me check with Zach and see if he can live without me for a weekend. I'd love to see everyone, too. You know we'll regret not going if we don't go."

"True. Check with Zach and let me know."

"I'm on it."

Staying with Maddie at her parents' home is a real trip. I had envisioned what it would be like living in what Maddie always refers to as a prison. In reality, her parent's home is lovely. They are kind and warm and extremely happy to have Maddie home again.

"Ma, what'd you do to my room?" Maddie asks, standing in the doorway of her childhood bedroom.

"I needed a sewing room."

"Oh *marone*! Since when do you sew?" Maddie asks, rolling her eyes.

"Since you left." Maddie's mom smiles as she walks into the kitchen.

This conversation makes me laugh out loud, rendering Maddie speechless. I can see that Maddie gets her sense of humor from her mother.

The kitchen begins to smell delicious as her mom makes "gravy" for the lasagna. I had no idea what she meant by gravy. The only gravy I know is the gravy that goes on top of mashed potatoes. This, however, is a delicious tomato based sauce that will eventually cover the lasagna. *Too bad we're eating at the reunion.*

"Mad, you ready to go?" I ask, feeling my anxiety build.

"Yeah, I'll meet you outside in a sec. Gotta hit the little girl's room."

Waiting in the rental car, my mind begins to wander with thoughts of this evening. *I wonder if Charlie and Liz will be there.*

As she climbs into the passenger side door, Maddie says, "Hey, I wonder if Charlie and Liz will be there tonight."

"You read my mind. I guess we'll see in 15 minutes."

While we drive to the school, I feel as though I never left. Kaiser Hall brings back memories of snowball fights in the quad and the first time Charlie and I went sledding right through the center of campus, in trash bags.

"Well, here we are…I have to say, being here kinda gives me the shits," Maddie admits with a slight shiver.

"I know what you mean."

We walk in together and immediately see our old R.A., Deidra. It has been years since we have seen each other, and it is great to see a friendly face in the crowd.

"Callie! Maddie!" Deidra exclaims, pulling us into a forceful hug.

"Man, is it good to see you guys!"

"Hi, Deidra. It's so great to see you too." I say with complete honesty.

"Hey, Deidra. You look great!" Maddie says.

We sit at a nearby table and share how our lives have turned out. Maddie glosses over her past experiences with Frankie. Deidra doesn't press for details.

"Let's just say it ended badly."

"That's an understatement," I say under my breath.

"I'm sorry you had a rough go of it, Maddie. Good news is it's in the past now and you have an awesome future ahead of you!" praises Deidra, ever the optimist.

Walking to the buffet line, Maddie and I laugh at how Deidra is always so positive. We continue talking throughout the line, not noticing that Charlie and Liz have entered the room. A ruckus erupts, causing us all to turn our heads. People have gathered around someone.

"Who's that?" I ask Maddie.

"Not sure. Can you see who it is yet?"

We walk back to the table where Deidra is and set our food down.

"Aw, look! Charlie and Liz are here!" Deidra sings.

My stomach drops. I sit with my plate of food as everyone around us walks to Charlie and Liz. Crazy, kooky Charlie. The life of the party. The Toddle King. We heard many people saying things like, "Remember when you"…"You got in so much trouble when you…" followed by a lot of laughter. Finally, the crowd breaks up, which allows Charlie and Liz to enter the room. I am not quite ready to say hello yet. My nerves have gotten the best of me. As the evening progresses, I'm able to avoid contact until, "Hey, Callie. It's so great to see you!"

"Hi, Charlie. It's great to see you, too!" I stand and we hug briefly.

"Hi, Liz. Congratulations on the whole wedding and having babies. That's really great," I say, emotionless.

"Thanks, Callie. We've got another one on the way. Can you believe it?" Liz says, placing her hands on her protruding belly.

"Oh, my gosh. Congratulations! When are you due?" Maddie asks, giving her friend a hug.

"In about seven weeks," Liz says, grabbing a chair and sitting down. We all follow suit, sit around, and talk like we haven't missed a beat in the past several years. The only thing different is that Liz is living the life I thought I would have. Married with three kids. *I bet they have a dog, too.*

As the evening comes to a close, Charlie says, "Who wants to Toddle?" Of course, his sense of adventure is infectious, and we all follow Charlie to Toddle House. We settle quickly into a familiar pace of conversation and laughter. It feels like old times. The longer we sit and talk to one another, the more I realize I am genuinely happy for Charlie and Liz. Looking around the table at the faces of my close college friends, I stop when I reach Charlie. Fine lines have creased around his eyes. His mahogany hair has turned darker through the years, and *what's that? Is that gray hair?* That twinkle in his eye is just as bright as it was in college. I begin to feel melancholy as I search for the signs of my college friend, Charlie. He's still fun loving but with fatherhood came wisdom. It is written all over his face.

"Cal?" The voice surprises me, and I jump in my seat.

"Huh?"

"What's going on in here?" Charlie asks with concern, tapping his forehead as everyone else is preoccupied with conversation. Liz is in full mom-mode, showing people pictures of the ultrasound of their unborn child. Charlie's worried, soft brown eyes make me well up unexpectedly.

"Me? Oh, yeah. I'm fine. Just going down memory lane all by myself," I admit, pointing to my own head. "You know me. It's a party up here." I try to laugh off the uncomfortable stare.

"It really is great to see you," Charlie says sweetly.

"And it's great to see you, too. You've gone and grow'd up on me, Charles. How did that happen?"

Laughing, he says, "No idea."

"How you doing in Missouri? Everything good? Your parents good?"

"Yep. They're great. They say hi, by the way."

"Hi back at them."

"You're gonna be a dad again. Are you nervous?"

"Nah, been there, done that. It's old hat now. Should be easy this time."

"Liz seems like a natural." I look over at her animated conversation with Deidra. They look at the ultrasound pictures, trying to figure out if this baby is going to be a girl or a boy.

"You know I forgive you."

Come again?

"I know you didn't mean to end it so abruptly between us. It wasn't entirely your fault."

Beginning to feel uncomfortable with the turn in our conversation, I search for Maddie for help.

"Uh. I don't know how to respond to that," I say at a loss for words.

"You don't have to say anything. I just wanted to let you know, that's all."

Maddie gets up to use the restroom, and I jump up to follow suit. Relaying the conversation to Maddie on the way.

"Oh, *fangul!*" she says, gesturing with her hands and closes the bathroom stall door. I've grown accustomed to this swearing in Italian. "Don't listen to him. You have nothing to say sorry for. He has issues."

"I'm so glad you're here with me, Mad. What a weird night."

"I'm ready to make like babies and head out if you are," Maddie jokes.

"I'm ready."

We walk back to the group and say goodbye to everyone. We linger for a moment, not wanting the night to end yet knowing that it is time.

CHAPTER 60
Jimmy

December 14, 2012
11:22 A.M.

Jimmy is rattled to the core. What does that mean? There is a commotion outside the firehouse. The door opens and in rushes a group of children running to their parents. Some laughing, some crying, but reunited just the same. These reunited families with arms wrapped around each other leave the firehouse for the safety of their own homes. Their nightmare is over. *Where's Prue?*

Jimmy looks around at the remaining parents, waiting anxiously for reunions of their own. Listening to the agonizing howls of parents in the adjoining room, Jimmy waits. Each tick of the second hand on the wall strikes a nerve. He feels as if he can't take one more torturous second. Then the door creaks open, making him jump. The last of the surviving children rush in. "Daddy!" Prue screams as she runs, and jumps, into his welcoming arms.

"Oh, my God. Thank God. My baby. Oh, God." Tears stream down his cheeks. As he sets her on the floor, he drops to his knees and cups her frightened, tear-streaked face, "It's okay, baby, Daddy's here," he kisses her sweet, innocent face.

Once more the doors open, and Charlie rushes in. In the moment, Jimmy can't figure out why Charlie is here.

"Charlie?"

"Jimmy, have you seen my mom?" Charlie turns to Prue, "Sweety, have you seen Mrs. Canfield? Is she okay? Is she with you?" he says, breathless.

Turning from her daddy's shoulder, she looks at Charlie, "Mrs. Canfield was shot," she says bluntly.

Charlie's knees buckle, torture twisting his face. "I just talked to her last night. She was fine. She was excited to listen to the holiday concert. She was excited to hear you sing," he says to Prue.

"Have you asked the police if she's in the hospital?"

"I haven't spoken to anyone. I got a call that anyone with EMS training needed to get to Sandy Hook Elementary School immediately."

"Let's not jump to any conclusions. Let's ask someone." Jimmy walks, carrying his precious cargo to a police officer that is consoling a parent.

"Can you please help us? Do you know if Mrs. Canfield, Charlene Canfield, first grade teacher, is alive? This is her son, Charlie."

He looks through a list and speaks directly to Charlie, "Son, your mother was shot multiple times and is at Hartford Hospital."

Panic strikes. "Is she ... alive?"

Tapping his finger on her name, he says, "Yes, she's alive."

Without responding, Charlie runs from the firehouse.

CHAPTER 61
Tyler

"Uncle Erp, I'm tired," Tyler says on the phone to Wyatt.

"Okay, buddy. I'll put the bookmark on this page and we'll pick up with this chapter another time. Get your rest now. Love you, Ty."

"Love you, too, Uncle E," Tyler weakly responds into the phone. Samantha picks up the line.

She whispers, "He looks like the shell of himself." Her voice quivers.

"Sam, you have to stay strong for Tyler. He really, really needs you right now."

"I know. I'm trying. Brian can't even come to the hospital. He's a mess."

"And that's okay. Everyone deals with this stuff differently."

"Thanks for reading to him a few nights a week. He really looks forward to it. He idolizes you, you know. Don't let that go to your head," she snickers.

"I love that kid. I'll call again in a few days. Same time. Love ya', sis. Stay strong."

"Thanks, Wyatt. Love you too, E," using the childhood nickname she gave him many years ago.

With the end of their conversation, Samantha goes to her son's bed and pulls the sheets up, checks his temperature by placing her lips on his forehead. Even through her respirator mask, she can tell he is burning up. She presses the nurse's button, and quickly a nurse enters the room with a mask, donning gloves.

"How's Tyler?"

"I think he has a temperature."

"Let's check him out."

Tyler is on the cusp of unconsciousness as the nurse checks his vitals. Right as he is falling into a deep sleep, he begins to relax. His body is moving, and as he looks down, he sees that he's walking barefoot on wet grass in an expansive field in his hospital gown. Pure joy fills his being. He's happy and healthier than he's been in months. Turning his head to look at his surroundings, it appears to be hazy, almost foggy. Light splinters through the haze in shafts.

Wings flutter somewhere, invisible. Looking down at his arm, Tyler notices an insect has landed there—a beautiful silver-winged dragonfly. Its body shimmers with colors that have no earthly description. It's vibrant and warm like the summer sun on his skin. He raises his arm and blows on it, causing it to fly away. As he watches it ascend, he notices other dragonflies flying about. He continues to walk as the wispy grass brushes against his bare legs. He's drawn to the sound of rushing water ahead. He wants to see it. Scratch that: he *needs* to see it. As he approaches the water's edge, he sits beneath a weeping willow tree watching the babbling brook ripple along the smooth river rock in front of him. A young girl with auburn hair and the most unique auburn eyes appears beside him and reaches for his hand.

The silver on the wings of the dragonflies illuminates the hazy sky as together they walk through the tall grass.

He feels the sensation of someone watching him and lifts his eyes to reveal a man on the other side of the brook. The man smiles. Tyler isn't afraid. In fact, just the opposite: he feels as happy as the first day of summer vacation. The man looks familiar, though he isn't sure who it is. Tyler turns to the young girl, unsure of what to do. Without a word, she releases his hand, and with a nod in the direction of the man, she walks back to the tree, disappearing in the mist. He turns back to watch with curiosity as the man bends to roll up his pant legs. Removing his shoes, the man crosses the brook. Now the man stands in front of Tyler, looking familiar. That face, like an older version of himself.

Without saying a word, Tyler knows who it is. He has heard stories since he was a little boy about his uncle, his namesake. Young Tyler stands and is enveloped in his uncle's warm and welcoming embrace.

ACKNOWLEGMENTS

Thank you, Natasha Wood, for allowing me to shadow you. The knowledge I gained through you proved instrumental in Pheonix's storyline. She was a beacon in the dark when formulating this story. I hope I do her justice. Thank you for all the conversation involving your "kids," life beyond death, and art therapy. It's been an amazing journey.

Sharisse Coulter, thank you for your friendship and confidence. It's so awesome having you in my corner. I'll be ready for our next writing adventure soon.

Denise Cronin, Cindy Eckenrode, Bobbi Lampman and Natasha Wood, thank you for being my beta readers. Your input is invaluable!

Keltin Barney, you still get me. I have had fun picking your brain and discussing character development. This has been such a wild ride, and I truly hope you hang on a while longer. I have other books floating around my head that will need your expert editing; especially the final installment of this trilogy.

Katie Mullaly, you have added just enough enchantment to this book to make it appeal to the eye. Thank you.

Stacy Dymalski, thank you for continuing to support me and providing me with feedback whether I want to hear it or not. At times, it may not seem like I appreciate it, but truly I do.

Ivan Terzic, you did it again. I'd love to peek inside your mind and see how it ticks. Each time I describe what I'm looking for in a cover, you manage to formulate an image that surpasses my wildest expectations. Thank you.

Mom and Dad, thank you for your never-ending support and love. Your excitement makes it so fun to share my ideas with the world!

John, Jack, Ian, and Michael, thank you for your patience and understanding. I love that you are all mine. Ian, I hope you like this story as much as the first one. Thank you for reading it and getting the word out to your friends. I certainly hope the rest of my fellas will read this series.

ABOUT THE AUTHOR

Cindy Lynch lived in many states growing up, but still considers Newtown, Connecticut home. Living in Sandy Hook throughout her high school and college years brought her many great memories; many of which occurred up at "Gramp's Camp." She always wanted to write a fictionalized memoir of her time on the lake, but never found the time. The Sandy Hook shootings both devastated and resonated with Cindy in a way she couldn't ignore, and the time to bring forward the stored memories of her youth felt more important than ever. These images of her past were woven into a fictional story that became the fabric for the "Bye For Now" trilogy.

After meeting her husband, John, at Central Connecticut State University they moved to Missouri to be closer to Cindy's family. They live in Chesterfield, Missouri with their three growing boys, Jack, Ian and Michael. When she's not writing, editing or otherwise engaged in writing activities she's coming up with plot line and character development while running, biking, swimming and spending time with her family.